Woman in the Waves

A Driftwood Mystery

William J. Cook

ISBN-13: 9781724070326

Cover designed and created by Roslyn McFarland.

Books by William J. Cook:

Songs for the Journey Home, a novel of spiritual discovery
The Pieta in Ordinary Time and Other Stories
Catch of the Day, short stories
The Driftwood Mysteries:
Seal of Secrets, a novel
Eye of Newt, a short story
Woman in the Waves, a novel

Table of Contents

For my wife, Sharon, and our children: Jason, Julie, Matthew, Kimberly, Amy, and April. And, of course, our grandchildren: Indira, Kalila, Ciana, Cecelia, Kaiden, Kamryn, Capella, Paul, Courtney, Jacob, Kendall, Parker, Owen, Savannah, and Dakota

"I am in so far in blood that sin will pluck on sin."

- King Richard, *Richard III*, William Shakespeare

"Lie down, you stupid brute! Don't you know the devil when he's got a great-coat on?"

- Bill Sykes, *Oliver Twist*, Charles Dickens

"I have done a thousand dreadful things as willingly as one would kill a fly; and nothing grieves me heartily indeed, but that I cannot do ten thousand more."

- Aaron, *Titus Andronicus*, William Shakespeare

1. The Bride on the Beach

SUNDAY, JANUARY 21, 2018. Clouds the color of Navy gunboats were deploying along the southwestern horizon, preparing to lay siege to the January sun.

"Rain before noon," he said. Peter Bristol was out on the beach, enjoying the last rays of sunshine before a week of rain descended like a pall over the small coastal town. Far to the north, Cascadia Head reached into the ocean like a giant fist at the end of a muscular arm. To the south, the shoreline curved in a lazy arc, interrupted by outcroppings of mussel-covered rocks. Here the surf was big and loud, urged on by the storm still far at sea. The sound of the crashing waves was the perfect background for meditation or a mindless walk along the shore.

Peter quickened his pace, anxious to return to the gravel bar he had found last Sunday a half mile up the beach. At the bar, stones of various sizes would roll in the swiftly moving currents and converse with each other in a language of rattles and clicks. He smiled at the recollection as he inhaled a deep breath of briny air.

Since the beginning of the New Year, he had been hunting agates, gem-like stones buffed by the sea and left as gifts on the sand for eager beachcombers. The best ones were closest to where the waves broke, out of sight of the ordinary passerby out for an easy stroll. They required following a wave as it withdrew, hastily scouting areas where rocks that ranged in size from marbles to golf balls were common, then running back up the beach to keep from getting wet by the next incoming wave. It added an element of sport to the simple gathering of stones.

"There!" he said aloud. He laughed as he ran toward the retreating water. Like a heron grasping its prey, he struck with his right hand and grabbed a promising stone. Then he hurried back up the beach. The rock in his hand was apricot-yellow, streaked with white. He compared it with the cherry-red one he pulled from his pocket and held them up to the sun. Both were translucent, allowing sunlight to reveal their inner beauty. "You'll be spectacular when I finish polishing you," he said, still talking to himself. He had purchased a rock tumbler on *craigslist* to polish his finds but was dismayed at the irritating noise it made. He finally banished it to his garage to keep the weeks-long chatter of stones and abrasive sand away from his living space.

Before he ran after the next wave, Peter looked westward toward the horizon. A regular pattern of waves was rolling toward the beach. He knew how deceptive that could be. As a local, he kept a watchful eye out for *sneaker waves*. The Oregon coast was notorious for these occasional waves, much larger than their companions, surging much farther up the shore than the waves that preceded them. Sneaker waves could pounce like predators, sweeping an unwary beachcomber from his feet and dragging him out to sea. Every year they claimed victims, usually visiting tourists unfamiliar with the casual violence of the Pacific Ocean.

He scurried down the sand and caught two more stones before the water returned. When he discovered they were not agates, he threw them back into the surf and continued on his way along the shore. Although the sun was still warm on his back, he felt the temperature beginning to drop as the storm approached. A light breeze from the south was rising, and it bore the smell of the coming rain. He zipped up his windbreaker and re-positioned his black baseball cap over hair that was the color of the sand he walked upon.

As the breeze became stronger, he saw seagulls take flight and hover over the beach, deftly using the air currents to keep themselves aloft without having to flap their wings. "God's kites" his daughter Mira had called them all those years ago. She had been four years old and danced ahead of him along the beach. He sometimes found it difficult to understand where the time had gone, now that she was such a beautiful and independent young woman. Einstein be damned—he had his own theory of relativity: time passed more quickly the older you got. Period.

He turned again to the southwestern sky and saw that the clouds had almost reached the sun. "Storm is moving faster than I thought," he muttered. He smiled again and nodded. His colleagues on the campus were always teasing him for the way he carried on conversations with himself. "The house is pretty quiet without Helen in it," he'd respond, and they'd remind him that she had been gone three years already. What had begun as a way of coping with the emptiness of his house had now become a habit that drew chuckles from students and teachers alike. It confirmed his reputation as an eccentric Psychology professor.

His footsteps stretched back along the way he had come, the most recent attached as securely to his feet as his shadow. "When the tide comes in they'll be gone," he whispered. "It'll be like I was never here." He frowned. "But Helen was here. I remember." He turned and resumed walking.

"I'd like to get a couple more agates before the rain catches me." He increased his pace, sure that the real treasures lay ahead. When at last he reached the gravel bar, he swooped down the sand and grasped several stones with each hand. "No good. No good," he ticked off as he discarded ordinary rocks. "There's a keeper. Not that one." He pocketed one of five stones. Already it was a good day. He wished he could spend more time on the beach, but Sunday was his only free day.

He shook his head and frowned. He was a creature of habit, living by a schedule. He awoke every morning at 5:30, donned his sweats, and drove to Driftwood Athletics, where he worked out for forty-five minutes. Upon returning home, he prepared breakfast—a single egg over easy, perched on a slice of sourdough toast, with a cup of french roast coffee and eight ounces of orange juice. Once all the dirty dishes were rinsed and stowed in the dishwasher, he showered, shaved, dressed, and made the bed. The drive to Pacific Crest University took only five minutes, up to the top of Cascadia Head. Upon arrival, he picked up his mail, phone messages, and the roster of student appointments. Preparation of classes for the next day was his final act before leaving the school in the late afternoon. Evening was governed by routines similar to the morning. Saturday was the day ordained for cleaning house, doing laundry, and shopping for the next week's groceries. Occasionally, he would host a dinner party for his faculty friends, giving him an opportunity to indulge his neglected hobby of cooking. Sunday was his only relatively unscheduled day.

He knew his actions were more than habit. His obsessive-compulsive behaviors had worsened when he was coping with Helen's terminal illness. After her death, they became proof that he could survive alone. His rigidity was a small price to pay for being able to manage his day, feed himself, take care of the household. More than that, his patterns comforted him—eased his anxiety and soothed his stress. They were a map for the uncharted wilderness of life without Helen.

Peter wondered if he would ever return to church. Christian faith had been a foundational part of his life for as long as he could recall—from the Baltimore Catechism answers he had memorized as a boy, to his flirtation with atheism as a late adolescent, and finally to his embrace of a non-denominational church as an adult. But faith and pain are a volatile mix, and watching his wife suffer had soured him to the notion of a loving God. The age-old conundrum of how God could be both all-powerful and all-loving at the same time was more to him than a problem in Philosophy 201. He shook his head at the remembrance of all the Ingmar Bergman films he had been forced to watch for his undergraduate Art of Film class decades ago. *God as Spider. Was that in "Winter's Light?"*

But why hadn't he started dating? Didn't he need a woman in his life? He could spend all of his working days teaching the theories and therapies of psychology, but he refused to turn the lens of that study upon himself. His own motivations remained opaque to him. He eschewed any grief support group, refrained from engaging in any individual counseling. Against all he knew to be wise, he determined to go it by himself.

"You need to get yourself a dog," his best friend and colleague David had insisted.

"But I don't like dogs. They're dirty. They smell. They're like babies that never grow up. You have to take care of them 24-7."

"Bingo. You took care of Helen for two years through her terrible decline. Taking care of a dog would be good for your soul because the dog will take care of you in return. Unconditional love. Constant companionship." He could see David raising his eyebrows, lips tight across his teeth. *Probably searching for more arguments to convince him.* "I can only imagine how alone your house feels when you drive home after school."

He shuddered as he came back from his brief reverie. *Alone.* It was a word he tried to expunge from his vocabulary, afraid that uttering it would be a spell conjuring up the emptiness that stalked his days.

"No. I'm not getting a damn dog and that's final."

He returned to his agate-hunting. As a wave slid out, he spied what he hoped would be a trophy as big as a golf ball. He lunged for it, but missed, and it rolled toward the water. He tried again, snatched it, but the delay was a microsecond too long. A new wave washed over his gym shoes and sent a thrill of cold though his body. "Guess it comes with the territory," he laughed. "One of the hazards of playing."

He held the stone up to examine it more closely. It looked like a cloudy ice cube, rounded on the edges, with dark inclusions inside. "What a beauty! You've made my day."

The wind was blowing briskly now. He turned westward to examine the growing surf. The waves were beautiful things, towering masses of moving water, transparent blue-gray near their crest, where their foamy white edges curled forward like shark's teeth. He admired their power and grace, and he scooted up the beach to give them a wider berth.

When he turned back to the north, his jaw dropped. There on the beach, about 500 yards ahead of him, stood a woman dressed in a flowing white gown. A veil covered her face and streamed in the wind behind her like the tail of a comet.

"Helen?" The name escaped his lips without his bidding. The vision couldn't be real. "Dear God, now I'm hallucinating."

As he stood transfixed, the phantom began walking toward the water. Her pace was slow and deliberate, as though walking in her sleep. He closed his eyes and slapped himself in the face. When he opened them, the woman in white was still there, closer to where the waves broke on the shore.

And then he saw it—a wave that didn't look so much taller than the waves that went before, but one that carried with it a far more massive amount of water. It surged over the rocks and up the beach straight toward the woman.

"Stop!" he yelled. "Get back! Get back!" His cries were lost in the wind and the surf. He began wildly gesticulating with his arms to get the woman's attention. No response. While keeping to the higher ground, he ran in the direction of the mysterious figure. The soft sand sucked at his feet. It was like running in gelatin.

The sneaker wave charged headlong up the beach. The woman stopped.

"Run away!" Peter hollered. "Helen, no!" He couldn't help himself. It was his grief-stricken cry to his wife on her deathbed —the long wail of agony, trying in vain to persuade her soul to stay. It had been the most selfish thing he had ever done, attempting to keep her in her body of pain.

His throat felt dry. His heart pounded in his chest. His legs ached from the exertion of running in the soft sand. The woman never turned but looked mesmerized by the onrush of water. To his horror, she opened her arms as if to embrace her doom.

With an animal roar, the enormous wave surged over the sand. The swirling currents wrapped the woman like tentacles, yanking her off her feet and hurling her up the beach. Then it dragged her back, kicking and flailing, into its gaping maw and withdrew to its lair in the sea. The monster had fed.

He ran out onto the wet sand, chasing the retreating wave. His shoes slapped in the shallow rivulets rushing down the slope. Shreds of foam like torn cotton littered the sand and were blown away by the wind. Not a footprint. Not a trace there had ever been a life in the balance there. The beach was swept clean. Tears streamed down his face.

He doubled over, hands on his knees, gasping for breath.

He raised his head, but he could see no sign of the woman in the churning waters. Had he imagined the whole thing? Was she only a product of his unresolved grief? He couldn't risk it. With trembling fingers, he took the cell phone from his pocket and dialed 911.

"What is the nature of your emergency?" came the voice.

"A woman...swept out to sea..." He was still struggling to catch his breath. "In Driftwood...about a half-mile north of the Sailboat Inn."

"Please stay there, sir. Help is on the way."

He squinted at the too-bright sea, until spots danced before his eyes. A regular pattern of smaller waves had resumed, feigning innocence. The water rolled up the beach and back down. He saw no thrashing limbs, no white train of lace from her gown, no gossamer veil. It was as if the woman had never existed. *Or had been swallowed*, he thought, remembering the childhood story of Jonah and the whale from Bible school. He cried for her, and he cried for himself, bereft again.

Less than ten minutes later, he could barely make out the wail of a police siren above the roll of the surf and the gusts of the wind. He saw two policemen climb down the stairs at the nearest beach access and come running toward him. Then the buzzing roar of rotor blades as the bright orange and white Coast Guard helicopter from Newport approached like a huge insect. As the policemen waved to it, the crew began a methodical search back and forth above the water, parallel to the shore.

"I'm Officer Antonio Esperanza." The bigger of the policemen extended his hand and shouted to be heard above the boom of the rising surf and the thunder of the patrolling helicopter. His face was hard and angular. His head looked as though it were attached directly to his broad shoulders without any intervening neck. His strong grip was just short of painful. "This is my partner, Officer Charles Whitehorse."

"I'm Peter Bristol." He relinquished Esperanza's hand and grasped that of the Native American. "Glad you got here so quickly." He saw a pattern of old scars on the man's bronze face.

16

A fighter?

"Can you tell us what happened?" Whitehorse said.

"This woman. I'm sure she saw the wave coming. She had to." He was shaking his head back and forth. "She didn't run away. Big waves like that are scary, but she didn't flinch. Just stood there."

"Then what happened?"

"It took her. Just like that. She was there one minute and gone the next. I've been staring at the water ever since, but I haven't seen a sign of her."

"The boys in the chopper will help, but if the wind gets worse they'll have to call it quits."

"I understand. The storm is almost here."

"What did she look like?" Esperanza asked.

Peter hesitated. *I can't tell them she reminded me of my wife.* "She was dressed in a long white gown."

Esperanza's eyebrows shot up. "Like a wedding dress?"

"She even had a veil over her face."

"Not your standard beach attire then." Whitehorse pursed his lips.

"Somebody in town would have to have seen that," his partner said. "She couldn't have walked down here from a beach access off the sidewalk or from a hotel without attracting a lot of attention, don't you think?"

"Unless she carried it in a bag or a box and changed down here." Whitehorse looked toward the bluff that bordered the beach on the east.

Esperanza radioed the helicopter with the new information about the long white gown the victim was wearing. He jotted down some notes while Whitehorse walked away toward some large boulders at the base of the cliff. Beautiful homes with commanding views of the ocean were garrisoned along the summit.

"Anything else?" he asked Peter.

He shook his head. *This was real, wasn't it?*

A few moments later, Whitehorse came back. "Nothing.

The beach is empty. You OK, Mr. Bristol?"

"I'm just feeling a little crazy talking about a woman in a wedding dress out here. And now no trace of her."

"We'll check all the missing persons reports." Whitehorse looked toward the houses on the bluff. "Maybe I'll do a little door-to-door and check if anybody saw anything. You need a lift?"

"No thanks. My car is up in that little lot at the next beach access farther down."

Esperanza pulled out his pad again. "Would you give us your address and phone number in case we think of anything else to ask you?"

"Sure. I live in Chinook River Estates at the base of Cascadia Head. Just below the university." He rattled off his cell phone number.

Whitehorse whistled. "Definitely the nice end of town. How long have you lived there?"

"It's been about fifteen years now. Makes for a real convenient commute to school."

"School?"

"Pacific Crest University. I teach Psychology there." He saw Whitehorse stiffen. "Your *alma mater*, Officer?"

"Afraid not. Never had that kind of money. Didn't you lose a dean up there almost a year ago?"

"Yeah. Dean Wasserman in the Biology Department. Helluva nice guy. Heart attack." Peter saw Esperanza watching Whitehorse. "Know him?"

"No. Never had the pleasure." Whitehorse turned toward his partner as Esperanza put a calming hand on his shoulder.

"We should get back and check missing persons," Esperanza said.

Whitehorse shook Peter's hand. "Storm's about to break. Might want to get inside."

2. Coronado Cab

The two policemen got into their vehicle. The temperature had dropped ten degrees and the first big drops of rain smacked the windshield.

"Let it go, Charley. It's just a coincidence the guy works there."

"How can I let it go? That sonofabitch Friese is still up there, laughing at me."

"You can't let yourself get all riled up whenever you hear *Pacific Crest University*, for Chrissakes. It's not professional."

"C'mon, Tony. We both know Friese poisoned Wasserman to make sure Wasserman couldn't screw him out of tenure."

"We can't prove that. The family cremated the body. Hell, you got their lawyers, the mayor, even the damn governor breathing down our backs. Don't mess with the high rollers, and PCU is the highest roller in town, next to the casino."

"It's not right."

"Never said it was. It just is. Let's get back to the station."

"You go. I'm gonna knock on some doors. Find out if anybody saw anything."

"Jesus, man. You're gonna get soaked. The goddamn sky is falling."

"I'll be OK. I threw my coat in the back. I want to talk to people while things are still fresh—before they start forgetting stuff. Besides, the rain'll cool me down."

"Whatever you say, Chief. Call me when you want me to pick you up."

Whitehorse winced. "Chief? You turning racist on me, Wetback?"

"Ouch! Sorry, Charley. Won't happen again. Truce?"

"Yeah. Truce, Tony." He offered his hand. "I guess I'm a little uptight." He reached over the seat to get his coat and got out of the car. Rain was pouring off his hat before Esperanza pulled away.

He still smarted from the fiasco at Pacific Crest a year

ago. Dr. Sterling Friese had committed murder and had gotten away with it. End of story. There was nothing Whitehorse could do about it, and it rankled him like a thorn he couldn't remove from his flesh.

Since he and his friend had just climbed up the beach access nearest to where the woman had disappeared, Whitehorse thought he would confine himself to the houses on either side of it. He doubted the woman would have walked far on the beach in her outfit. The Sailboat Inn was another possibility, but the half-mile distance made it unlikely she would have come from there.

As the rain beat on his shoulders, he smiled. He liked Driftwood in winter. Although it occasionally got a dusting of snow, precipitation was usually in liquid form, from a gentle spritz to a howler like today, when the rain gushed from skies the color of buffed steel. The only tourists were the storm-chasers, eager for a front row seat in a seaside hotel when Mother Nature battered the beach. Traffic was at a minimum. The restaurants that were still open always had seating available. In January and February, you knew who your friends were.

He showed his badge at the first door that opened to him. "I'm Officer Whitehorse."

"Why, Officer, you'll catch your death out on a day like this," said a gray-haired lady with a face as wrinkled as a walnut. "Come in out of the weather."

"I can't, Ma'am. But thank you. I just wanted to ask you if you saw anything unusual this morning. Maybe a woman in a white dress going down the stairs to the beach?"

"Can't say as I have. 'Course I wasn't looking out the windows. My church shows are on TV on a Sunday and I have to listen to 'em pretty loud on account of I lost my hearing aids last week."

He tipped his hat. "Thank you very much. I won't trouble you further."

"Oh, it's no trouble. Can I interest you in a cup of tea?"

"Thanks anyway." He turned and walked to the next house. This was a much larger structure, with a three-car garage and a circular drive. He imagined the west wall facing the sea would be all glass. He rang the bell.

"Yes, sir, what can I do for you?" It was a man in his mid-forties, with a black apron strapped to his waist and a large spoon in his right hand. The apron said *Taco Bill's Grill* in garish yellow letters. "Just about to stir the beef stew," he said. "Great comfort food for a day like today, don't you think?"

"You bet. Makes my mouth water smelling it from here. Just wanted to ask if you've seen anything unusual out front or on the beach today. I'm guessing you've got great views of the shore."

"Indeed we do, but I've pretty much been keeping to the kitchen." He called over his shoulder. "Hey, honey, there's a policeman here wanting to know if we've seen anything unusual on the beach today."

"Like what?" A blonde woman came up behind the man. Her purple exercise outfit looked as though it had been spray-painted onto her skin.

"Maybe a woman in a long white dress?"

"Nope. Nobody on the sidewalk. But I don't look at the beach all that much. Isn't that the way of it? You visit the coast, and you can't take your eyes off the water. You buy a place here, and you never see the beach again. Go figure."

"Well, sorry to interrupt you. Thanks for your time."

Whitehorse made nine more inquiries with the same result. "She's a ghost lady," he muttered. "Our very own phantom."

He ducked under an awning to use his phone.

"Are you wet enough yet?" came Esperanza's voice.

"Any more and I'll need a snorkel."

"I'm on my way."

Below him, the surf roared in protest against the storm that lashed it to a frenzy. The howling wind had increased to the point that it was raining sideways. He turned his back into it and felt the drops pummel him like pellets from a paintball gun. It would feel good to be dry again. Soon the lights of the police cruiser emerged from the torrents of rain like a submarine surfacing.

"Need mouth-to-mouth?" Esperanza quipped, as Whitehorse opened the door and jumped in, showering him with water.

"I'm only half-drowned."

"Well, you look whole-drowned to me. Why don't I swing by your place so you can get a dry uniform?"

"Great idea. I'll only be a minute. Our gal show up on missing persons?"

"Not a peep. Probably too soon. Nobody knows she's gone yet."

Whitehorse began shivering.

"Jesus, man. Don't you go getting sick on me now."

"I'll be OK once I warm up. Dry clothes will be the ticket." He became thoughtful. "Knocked on a lot of doors. Nobody saw anybody walking the street or the beach."

"Suppose our guy is a crank? Made it all up?"

Whitehorse shook his head. "I don't think so. But I do think there's something he's not telling us. Anyway, I still can't figure how she got to the beach."

"Simple." Even with the windshield wipers on their fastest setting, Esperanza was squinting to see the road ahead. "Somebody drove her right to the stairs."

"What friend is going to drive somebody to the beach in a wedding gown ahead of a storm like this?"

"No friend. Anonymous. A taxi."

Whitehorse arched his brows. "Damn! I guess you use your head for something more than a hat rack."

"That's what my mommy told me."

Forty-five minutes later, they were back at the station. Windows in the old building rattled their complaints under the onslaught of wind and rain.

"Crap! That spot on the roof is leaking again." Esperanza hastened to set a big pot at the southwestern corner of the offices, where a steady drip of water had created a large puddle on the floor.

Whitehorse grabbed a mop and bucket from their supply closet. "Thank God it's not on our computers or printers. Squeezing another dime out of this town for office equipment is about as likely as snow in August." He thrust the wet mop into the bucket to wring it out. "I thought we had the roof fixed last summer."

"We did. Let's not use Driftwood Remodel again."

Whitehorse dumped the bucket and returned it to closet, careful to hang the mop to dry. Then he set the coffee pot on to brew. "Want to join me in a cup?"

"How many times we have to go through this, Charley? The coffee you make takes the silver plate off spoons. Navy ships have been known to use it to degrease their engines, for Chrissakes."

"It's not that bad." His lips protruded in a pout.

"We could probably put a dent in the cocaine business if we marketed it as Cop's Caffeine Coup."

Whitehorse harrumphed and logged on to the computer on his desk. "Looks like nobody's missing yet. So what about taxis?"

"Well, Uber hasn't really penetrated our little burg yet. Coronado Cab has the business all sewed up."

"I think I read about that a while back in the *Beachtown News*. That's the guy up from California, right?"

"That's him. Ex-Navy SEAL. Can't remember his name. Couldn't afford to live in California on his pension, so he moved up here. The taxi is just supplemental income now. And he's big on serving the community. Gives senior discounts, coupons to kids at the college, transports pregnant ladies to the hospital for free. Quite a guy. They interviewed him on Channel 6 last spring."

Whitehorse strummed his fingers on the desk. "Suppose our knight is shining armor gave our mysterious lady a lift? What are the odds?"

"I'd say they're pretty good."

"Then I think I need to call a cab."

3. Pan Fried Oysters

Peter hastened down the beach but knew it was a hopeless cause. There was no way he could outrun the storm. He hadn't gone a hundred yards before the first big drops of rain struck his head and shoulders. Soon the heavens ruptured, and torrents gushed from the sky, converting his clothing into a soaked second skin. He shivered as the rising wind drove the rain into his face and glasses, distorting his vision in swirls of refracted light. He slowed his pace. He could get no wetter than he already was.

When he reached the 12-year-old Bimmer, he cranked up the heater as far as it would go. He sat and trembled for several minutes while the car warmed, blowing into his cupped hands and rubbing them together to stimulate their circulation. Then he blasted the defroster to clear the windshield. As the fog dissipated, he put the car into gear.

"Thank God, I don't have far to go."

Driving north on 101, he negotiated the flooded intersections slowly, grateful there were so few cars on the road. His wipers could not keep pace with the deluge, and visibility was barely a car's-length ahead. Rain drummed a deafening tattoo on the roof.

Several turns and twenty minutes later, he approached the entrance to his gated community. He pushed the button on his mirror and watched as the black steel barrier swung open. Two blocks down, he pulled into his garage. A sigh of relief escaped his lips as he closed the wide door behind him.

It was a fine house, unpretentious, but grand in its own way. The kitchen was the focal point, and it had been Helen's idea, of course. It was made for entertaining, with its double ovens and six-burner stove, its large refrigerator-freezer, and its beautiful center island. Counters were black granite with sparkling flakes that made them look like a night sky in summer. Twin skylights overhead gave the room an ambiance of elegance. Without Helen his gourmet to guide him, he did far less cooking now, though he was getting back into it with his monthly dinners for faculty friends.

"This is a fine mess," he said, as he trailed water onto the tile floors. He put his agates on the table along with his phone and set his wallet on the floor by a heat vent to dry. He stripped down where he stood and threw his clothes into the washing machine in the nearby laundry room. With a hand towel, he dried his feet so he wouldn't leave any more wet footprints in the house. Then he walked down the hall to the master bath.

The cold had settled into his bones and lowered his core temperature. "A shower is what I need." He turned on the water and watched the steam fog the mirror. As he stepped into the spray, a gasp of pure pleasure echoed in the marble stall. He stood motionless in the stream, letting it massage the chill from his body. Fifteen minutes later, fully restored, he pulled on some comfy sweats and a soft pair of slippers and ambled into the kitchen to put on a pot of coffee.

With the sounds of the brewing coffee punctuating the silence, he thought again about the apparition—the woman in white. "You have to be real," he said, as if to reassure himself. "I couldn't have made you up. But why did you let that wave take you?"

He imagined what a horrible death it had to have been, assaulted so violently by the sea, thrown about like a cat's toy, unable to take a breath when your lungs were screaming for air. The image of Helen came unbidden to mind. Helen trying so desperately to breathe while the disease choked the life out of her. Helen pleading to him with her eyes to let her go.

"I'm sorry, my love. I failed you when you needed me to be strong."

The coffee pot sounded the tone that it was done. From the right hand cupboard, he withdrew his favorite cup, the one with the missive, *Roses are Red/Violets are Blue/I'm schizophrenic/And so am I*. After filling it just shy of the rim, he walked into the den, where he sat in his favorite leather recliner, cradling the warm cup in his hands. The knowledge that just as things seen cannot be unseen, so some actions cannot be undone, was a bitter pill he had been trying to swallow for three years. It was the sliver in his mind, the regret that haunted his every waking moment. It was easier when he could rail against God, blame him for every death, every hungry child, every natural disaster that left chaos in its wake. So much harder now without him.

"When I finish my coffee, I'll call Mira. She'll cheer me up." Though she was a thousand miles away, she had a knack for sweetening his bitter brew. She could pull him out of a funk in five minutes. "That's what I need—a little San Diego sunshine."

Five minutes later, she was trilling in his ear. "Your granddaughter rolled over for the first time today. She's getting so strong. She'll be crawling before you know it."

"I can't wait to see her, darling." He still wished he had flown to California during Christmas break. But it was a difficult time to travel, and by the time he had decided, there were no good seats available. "Can she say my name yet?"

Mira laughed. "Oh, sure. Helena calls you professor. Says, 'When's Grandpa Professor coming to see me?'"

Peter chuckled. "She sure has a pretty name. And I've got a ticket to come and see her during spring break. Before she's all grown up." He smiled and sighed in satisfaction. "When's Mommy going back to work?"

"We're stretching it as long as we can. I'll start substitute teaching in the spring one day a week, and then go back four days next fall. K through 5." She was silent for a moment. "So how are you doing, Dad?"

Peter hesitated briefly, but then told her about the woman on the beach.

"That's awful! Not a trace?"

"None. It's like she was an hallucination." He took a breath. "I called her by your mother's name."

"Oh, Dad. I miss Mom, too, but you can't be doing this to yourself. There's gotta be some therapist you respect enough to work with."

"You haven't told me how Will is doing in his new job." He heard her exhale through her teeth.

"He's doing fine, Padre. Hospital staff like him. And did I tell you he's doing stand-up one night a week at that new club in town? Says he practices it on the nurses before he brings it to the stage."

"You married well, sweetie. I love that guy."

"He loves you, too. He misses those guys' nights when the two of you would rent a movie and drink whiskey."

"Seems to me I do recall some shoot-'em-ups we'd watch with the surround sound blasting and the subwoofer shaking the walls like an earthquake. Your mother would barricade herself in the bedroom. With earplugs, I think." He laughed despite himself. "As much as it drove her crazy, she never interfered with our getting together. She was a real trouper."

"It gave us a chance for girl talk. She'd be on the phone with me for most of that time."

"I didn't know that."

"There was a lot you didn't know. That's what made it fun."

He felt his eyes mist over. "I sure miss you, darling. It was hard when you moved away."

"You know the drill, Dad. Where did you do your psychology internship? Rhode Island, for goodness sake?"

"The Grace Pendleton Children's Center on Narragansett Bay. When I thought I wanted to be a therapist."

"Well, Will's gonna be a great surgeon. Already is. But he has to pay his dues."

"I know. It doesn't make it any easier."

They chatted for another fifteen minutes. Peter felt the knot in his gut untying itself. He would be good for another week.

When they concluded the call, he drained his cup. He put it on the table, made himself comfortable, and soon dozed off.

It wouldn't be accurate to say the sun had set. It was more a fade to black, as if on a movie set. When he awoke, he knew he was in for a week of twilight—no sunrise and no sunset, only shades of gray punctuated by darkness. So be it. Good weather for what he called *the interior life*. Reading books, watching movies, writing. Praying was significant for its absence.

"Is it happy hour yet?" he called to the empty house. "I believe so." He turned on several light switches to dispel the dusk. Then he turned on the gas fireplace. To sustain the improved mood his daughter had summoned, he decided to treat himself to a dinner of pan fried oysters. It had been a favorite of Helen's. He still chuckled whenever he recalled her oft-repeated comment to him: "You cook a mean oyster, mister."

"And I shall again." He took a chilled bottle of Sauvignon Blanc from the refrigerator and uncorked it with the skill of a sommelier. Filling a long-stemmed glass, he raised it to the picture of Helen that graced the far corner of the kitchen counter.

"To you, darling."

4. Mommy/Daughter Time

Chloe sat waiting in the correctional facility's visiting room. It was a bland space filled with small tables and chairs— an anonymous room with nothing to identify the unique individuals unfortunate enough to be living there. She had never mastered the creepy feeling she got every time she walked into the prison, but she relished her weekend visits with her daughter. Working at Coastal Information Technologies had precluded visits during the week, so she tried to see Kaitlynn every Saturday or Sunday, weather-permitting. She didn't like crossing the Coast Range in snow or freezing rain. Because of the warnings of a storm arriving this afternoon, she had come to the morning visiting hours, hoping she could make it back to Driftwood before the tempest broke.

It had been two years since Kaitlynn's misadventures with Raven, the man who had almost thrown her from the Yaquina Bay Bridge in Newport. Kaitlynn's quick thinking and Krav Maga training had saved her life—that and three shots from Chloe's gun. Chloe was surprised that she felt no compunction for having killed him. But she was a mother bear protecting her cub, and that man was a monster who had drawn Kaitlynn into his dark web.

It hadn't taken Chloe long to get used to the prison's rules —no skimpy or form-fitting clothing. No skirts shorter than two inches above the knee. Only a brief kiss and embrace at the beginning and end of each visit. No physical contact during the visit, with the exception of hand-holding across the table.

She stood as a scowling guard escorted Kaitlynn into the room.

"Hi, Mom."

"Hi, darling." She hugged her for a heartbeat and sat down. She grasped her daughter's hand. "Your hair looks different. I like it."

"One of my friends is learning to be a stylist. She plans on opening her own salon when she gets out. I let her practice on me. She's good." Kaitlynn smiled and ran her fingers through her reddish brown hair. "Completed another course. I bet I'll have enough for an Associates Degree before I'm done here." She saw the concerned expression on her mother's face and looked over her shoulder at the guard standing rigidly by the wall. "Officer Wiley doesn't smile very much, but he's really a good guy. You don't have to worry about him."

Chloe exhaled a sigh of relief. "I'm so proud of you, honey. You'll continue school when you get out?"

"I'm gonna try for a scholarship at PCU. I kind of like this IT stuff." She smiled at her mother. "So how's Charley? Has he asked you yet?"

The question surprised her. "Asked me what?"

"To marry him, of course."

"You could always see right through me." Chloe shook her head and squinted at Kaitlynn, a hint of a smile turning up the corners of her lips. "No, he hasn't asked me yet, but I think he will. Maybe we both need to talk about our past screw-ups a little more first. Make sure we're not getting into the same mistakes again."

"He's the best man you've ever dated, Mom. Totally."

"What makes you the expert in relationships?"

"C'mon, Mom!"

"I didn't mean that the way it sounded. I was actually referring to the way we were both snowed by Jack Wallace."

"He wanted to be good, I think. If you hadn't shot Raven, Jack would've taken him out. But Jack had way too much baggage. I'm glad you didn't get into him any deeper before we found out."

"It doesn't matter to you that I'm in love with the man responsible for sending you to prison?"

"We both know that's not true." Chloe could hear a note of frustration in her daughter's voice. "It was Raven's fault. He got me doing things I never would have done otherwise. And anyway, my good behavior here is paying off. I might get out early."

"Oh, honey, that would be wonderful."

"And living with a policeman for a stepfather will keep

me on the straight and narrow!" A big grin spread over her face. "Seriously, he's polite, kind, considerate. Bring him in with you sometime."

"I will."

"And bring Indie. I think your friend is chill."

"Do you need anything, honey? Anything I can get for you?"

"I'd love to see Tessa. I write her letters every week, but her mother is being a real hard ass. 'As long as you're living under my roof, there's no way you're going into that jail, and that's final!'"

"Is Tessa planning on moving out?"

"Once she finishes her two years at the community college. For now, she's saving her money. I hope I'm outta here by the time she's ready to leave. Then maybe we can rent a place together."

"That would be nice. She's your BFF, right?"

Kaitlynn laughed. "Nobody says that anymore, Mom. Except maybe little kids."

She chuckled. "I guess I just can't keep up, sweetie."

They chatted for two more hours, the kind of conversation Chloe imagined having with her daughter over coffee in the kitchen at their home—Mommy/daughter time—funny stories, sad stories, gossip, who of Kaitlynn's friends from high school had married, who was pregnant.

When visiting hours concluded, Chloe hugged her daughter goodbye and watched while the correctional officer led her away. As she left the facility and got to her car, her initial thought was *how normal that seemed.*

She sat in the car, debating whether to turn on the radio. Tears came to her eyes. *Normal that my almost twenty-year-old daughter is an inmate at a penitentiary? Dear Lord.*

The damp air had taken what she called the "lazy curl" out of her blonde, shoulder-length hair. *Maybe that's what I need, too —a new "do." But what I want now is a hot shower to warm this body up. Then maybe some Charley time.* She dialed his number.

"Hey, I got a little more than an hour and a half drive ahead of me. You busy? Want to get together? Maybe share a take-and-bake pizza later if the storm isn't too bad?"

"Unless I get any emergency calls, my day is wide open. And pizza is my language, hon. I got a Zin that should work with it. One with everything?"

"Yeah, the works. I'll call you when I get home. Love you."

She started the car and left the parking lot. The drive to Driftwood would give her plenty of time to think.

Charley had been so skittish at first, afraid of complications with Kaitlynn that never materialized. And Chloe had doubts about her own "relationship radar" after her disastrous marriage to Bruce. It wasn't physical abuse so much as Bruce's constant criticism that wore her down—that opened the wounds left by her father. Then after the divorce—miracle of miracles—Bruce had become a far better father than he had ever been when they were together. Kaitlynn told her he visited the prison every Thursday and Friday, his typical days off from the call center in Salem where he worked. She shook her head in disbelief.

Kaitlynn was right. Charley was the best man she had ever dated. He was everything Kaitlynn said and much more. Charley listened to what she had to say and took it seriously, never belittling her. He complimented her for her intelligence and insight. Gave her space but liked to be close to her. The respect he showed her was so refreshing, and so different from what she had been accustomed to from men. *Yes*, she thought. *I could marry you, Charley, if you ever get around to asking me.*

She was glad to be making the trip in daylight. She often came to the penitentiary's afternoon visiting hours, and in the shorter days of December and January, it would be dark before she was half way home. The Van Duzer Forest Corridor in the Coast Range was a winding black tunnel on a starless winter night.

Static from the radio alerted her that she was losing the signal from Portland. She turned it off and thought more about

Pacific Crest University. She hadn't said anything to Kaitlynn—didn't want to spoil her dream of going to school there—but she was privy to information that gave her pause. A predatory professor stalked those halls. A year ago, on the night that she and Charley had confirmed their wish to date each other—to become a "thing" as Kaitlynn might say—she had provided Charley with a clue that had helped him solve the murder of Dean Wasserman. But it had been too late. The body had been cremated, the evidence sealed. Ever since, it was exquisite torture for her to see the man she loved tormented by the fact that he could do nothing to bring the murderer, Sterling Friese, to justice.

"Stay focused, Charley," she said aloud to the empty car. "Don't let Friese distract you from what you have to do."

She gripped the steering wheel tighter and let out a deep breath. "Stay good, Charley. Just stay good." She lifted him up in prayer as the sky above her continued to darken.

5. Cabby

The Stones were belting out *Satisfaction,* as the man under the shop awning lit another cigarette. He had never smoked when he was on active duty, but it seemed to come naturally to him during his retirement, something to occupy his hands and curb his appetite. Something to pass the time while waiting for his next fare. *Caught it from those damn SoCal cabbies*, he thought. *Doc says it'll kill me, but I guess something has to.* He refrained from smoking inside the cab because so many people objected to the smell.

At six-four and 230 pounds, he knew he was overweight, despite his best efforts. He had shed the first 20 pounds easily, but now this plateau was frustrating him. *Too much time sitting on my fat ass. Wish I could lose weight like I'm losin' my hair.* He hated the horseshoe of hair that surrounded his balding pate. *Crunch time is coming, boyo. Shave it all off and go completely bald? Shave my beard off, too?* He was proud of his three-button beard, but as it turned increasingly white, he had his doubts. *Shit, I'll be Santa Claus by this time next year. But I swear I'll be back in shape. Back at the gym startin' tomorrow. Back with the weights.*

Chris Harper, erstwhile Navy SEAL and part-time cab driver, was parked at the mall, trying to stay dry while he smoked. He liked watching the rain. Rainy days were good for business, but this heavy storm would keep people inside. Very few were out shopping today. Fifteen more minutes and he'd turn the horse toward the stable.

A gust of wind spattered rain over his back. It was like being ten-years-old again, when his best friend Frankie sprayed him with the garden hose on that warm July day. Only it wasn't July, and it was anything but warm. He shivered and flicked the butt onto the streaming pavement. *This is nuts. I'm outta here.*

He jumped into the cab as another gust of wind and rain caught him in the face. *Toto, I've a feelin' we're not in California anymore,* he thought, as he put the car in gear and headed out. The windshield wipers could barely keep up with the deluge. *Shoulda*

34

brought my boat.

The DJ on the classic rock station commiserated with his audience. "For all you crazy people who have to be out in this mess, here's The Doors and *Riders on the Storm*." Harper laughed. Three blocks later he pulled into the parking lot of the State-run liquor store.

"Hey, Chris," said the cheerful proprietor. "You're my first customer all afternoon. Everybody else is smarter and staying dry. Can I help you find anything?"

"Thanks, but I know what I want, Reggie. Treatin' myself." He walked to the back of an aisle on the left and returned with a bottle of Macallan 12.

"That's a treat all right. Special occasion?"

"Eight year anniversary of bein' out of the Navy and five year anniversary of movin' up here to your lovely little town."

"Do you miss San Diego?"

"On days like this, but not usually. I like Oregon fine."

"Well, congratulations, man. We love having you here in town. Best damn taxi we ever had. But just between you and me, isn't that Prius cab a little wimpy for you? I kinda picture you in a muscle car. Or maybe a Hummer."

"Hey, it's damn good on gas."

"And you pass the savings on to your customers. You were a lifesaver getting my Cassie to the hospital that time I was out of town. She damn near delivered in your back seat—a whole month early. And you never charged her a dime."

"Least I can do." A shadow passed over his face but lifted as he handed the proprietor his credit card.

"Just curious. How do you take it? Neat? A splash of water?"

"Over a single ice cube. Opens it up real nice."

Reggie handed him the bottle in a brown paper sack. "Well, here you go. Keep your powder dry."

"See you around."

Harper was greeted with a slap of rain in the face when he opened the door to leave. "Gotta love the Oregon coast," he muttered, as he slid into the car. Ten minutes later found him pulling his taxi into the driveway of his little bungalow on the south side of town. He had no view of the ocean, but he loved the Douglas fir forest behind his house. Black-tailed deer were common visitors to his small yard, eager to sample the smorgasbord of flowers he planted every spring. *It's not a flower bed, it's a salad bar,* he had told Reggie. Once a herd of cow elk ventured to the edge of the woods. A black bear and a bobcat were on his wish list, but hadn't made their appearances as yet.

He hurried inside out of the weather. Although a gas furnace heated the house, he still preferred the wood-burning stove he'd had installed when he moved in, and he busied himself with getting a blaze going. A glass of Scotch by the stove would be just the ticket for a night like this.

With the fire crackling, he retrieved an ice cube from the freezer, opened the Macallan, and poured himself a generous glass. Then the boots came off, and he propped his feet on a stool close to the fire.

When the phone rang, he was relieved to see it was his ex-wife and not someone wanting a ride.

"Hi, Tonya. What's up?"

"Catch you at a bad time?"

"No. Just relaxin' at home. Pourin' cats and dogs outside."

"Well, I wanted to be the one to tell you..." The voice paused.

"Is Joe OK?" Alarms were going off in his brain.

"Yeah. Yeah. He's fine. Got a tech job for a little outfit down here. Loves it."

"So what is it you wanted to tell me?" He could hear her deep intake of breath.

"I'm getting married next week. I didn't want you to hear it from our son before you heard it from me."

He pursed his lips and sighed. A new chapter. So be it. "Kind of sudden, isn't it?"

"We've been dating for a year."

"He good to you? Not like that other schmuck? The one

with the earring?"

"He's very kind and loving."

"Joe never told me about him."

"Can you blame him after that last fiasco?"

"I'm sorry, Tonya. I didn't mean to make such a scene. But the thought of that scumbag slappin' you around fried a circuit breaker in me. Never did that again, did he?"

"Never." He could hear the smile in her voice. "I think he's still running. You always were my knight in shining armor."

"Yeah, well. It wasn't enough, was it?"

"His name is Robert. Joe likes him, too. He's a P.A."

"What's that?"

"A Physician's Assistant. Kinda like a doctor. Sees patients. Prescribes medicines."

"So you're comin' up in the world?"

"He's a good man. You'd like him."

Harper took another sip of Scotch. He nodded his head. "Congratulations, Tonya. I'm happy for you. And thanks for tellin' me."

"You're welcome. I gotta go. Fixing supper."

"Hey, take it easy. Tell Joe hi if you see him."

He tapped the screen of the phone and set it down beside him. He wasn't sure how he felt. He had loved Tonya. She had stood by him during the hard times in the SEALs, when he thought he was going to get killed or court-martialed. But retirement was the kiss of death. All that time together made them both realize they had grown into people very different from the couple who had walked down the aisle at St. Paul's. There was no bitterness, no fighting, just that slow, inexorable slide into what he called *strangerhood*. They no longer knew each other. It was beyond being on different pages—they were in different books. Divorce was the best option, before the last embers of friendship burned out, and they morphed into enemies.

Anythin' that makes her happy is good for Joe. And that makes me happy.

He put down his glass and walked into the kitchen to

decide on what to have for supper. Never much of a cook, he pulled a can of chili out of the cupboard and called it good. Ten minutes later, he was back in his spot by the fire, feet up, bowl of chili perched in his lap. "Life is good," he said to the empty house. He turned on the Channel 6 news.

A reporter in a hooded raincoat was huddled against the wind and rain. The brilliant spotlight upon him made the rain look like a display of fireworks from a Fourth of July sparkler. "And the weather isn't the only story on this blustery day, Kent and Angela." He turned and motioned with his arm. "Behind me is the beach at Driftwood, where a woman was swept out to sea earlier today. The Coast Guard from Newport was unsuccessful in its rescue attempt, and finally had to call off its helicopter search as the storm intensified. No word yet on the identity of the woman. We'll keep you updated as more information becomes available. Back to you, Kent and Angela."

Harper whistled between his teeth. *My one and only fare of the day? Is it possible? Shit! I've got to call it in.*

He took another drink and picked up his phone.

"Officer Whitehorse here. How may I help you?"

"I'm Chris Harper, the cab driver in town. I may have some information about that woman on the beach."

"Mr. Harper, you must be psychic. I was just about to call you. What have you got?"

"I think she's a student from Pacific Crest University."

Whitehorse exhaled.

"What?" It was Esperanza's voice behind him.

Whitehorse put his hand over the mouthpiece. "Guy thinks our victim is from PCU."

"Christ!"

Into the phone, he said, "Would it be too inconvenient if I came over to your place right now? It'd be easier than over the phone."

"If you want to go out in this mess, be my guest. Forty-Two Furlong. I'll put the light on out front. Can't miss it."

6. Church of Trees

Whitehorse was thankful the light was on. Furlong was a dark little road without any streetlights once he turned off 101. Harper's small cottage looked like it was about to be swallowed by the forest behind it, an effect made worse by the rain and wind pummeling it. Harper opened at his first knock.

"You must be the cop I spoke with," he said, offering his hand. "I'm Chris Harper."

"Charles Whitehorse."

"Come in where it's warm."

Whitehorse shook the rain from his slicker, and Harper hung it on a hook by the door.

"Can I offer you a drink? I've been samplin' some myself."

"No, thanks. Not while I'm on duty."

"Coffee then? Take the chill off? I always keep a pot goin'."

"That'd be nice."

Harper poured him a cup and the two sat by the stove. Whitehorse wrapped his hands around the mug, like an acolyte embracing a holy relic. He drew its warmth into his body. "Instead of asking you a bunch of questions, why don't you just tell me your story."

"You bet, Officer." Harper drained the Macallan, set the glass on an end table, and began.

*****

I get the call about ten o'clock, before the storm breaks. Girl's voice. Sounds like she's been cryin'. You know—that hitch in her breathin'? Wants a ride from the college down to the beach.

"Sure," I say. "But are you ready for the weather? It's gonna hammer us before long. Did you hear the reports?"

"I'm not worried about the weather," she says.

Her voice is...I don't know. Like a kid defyin' a parent?

But also somehow scared?

"Are you gonna want me to wait for you to bring you back?"

"No. I'll be all right."

Never said she'll give me a call when she wants a ride home. Never volunteers if a friend might be pickin' her up. Just wants me to drop her off at the beach.

"OK. I'll be there in about twenty or twenty-five minutes."

I can't shake this bad feelin' I have. Like somethin' is wrong, but I don't know what. But, hey, it's a fare. The only call so far that day. So I saddle up and head out.

I love the drive up Cascadia Head. The way it winds through those big stands of Doug fir. It gets quiet as a cathedral up there, except for the wind in the crowns of the trees. Reminds me to pray, which I don't do enough of. And you gotta love that campus. All glass and wood, and lookin' somehow like it just grew there right out of the forest. What a place.

Anyway, I pull up to the Columbia River Dorm, where she said she'd be, and in a minute she comes runnin' out. Has this long dark coat on, all the way down to her ankles. As she gets in, I can see she's got some kind of fancy white dress underneath.

"You don't look dressed for the beach," I say, tryin' to break the ice. She turns her head, and I can see where the tears ran through her makeup. That kind of stuff brings out the father in me. Know what I mean? "Are you all right, honey?"

"Just drive, please. OK?"

"Sure thing. Which beach access do you want me to take you to? The one down from Heron Drive? Sandpiper Lane? 45Th Street?"

"I don't care." Like she doesn't have enough energy to make a decision.

"How about 45th? It's got a nice little parkin' lot I can turn around in. The stairs down to the sand are good."

"Fine."

I turn around and look over the seat at her. Pretty blonde hair, all done up nice. Makeup job she must've spent a lot of time on before she ruined it with her tears. Expensive-lookin' black coat. She's like...like every father's beautiful daughter, all grown up and away at college. It makes me sad to see her that way.

"Wanna talk about it?" I say as I pull away from the school.

"Talk about what?"

"What made you cry?" And wouldn't you know it, that makes her start all over again, cryin' her heart out in my back seat.

"Here's some tissues, honey," I say, handin' her the box I keep in front.

"Why do you care?" she says as she dabs her eyes, her breath still catchin' in her throat.

I nod. "Good question. Maybe because I've done a lotta bad things in my life. Guess drivin' a friendly cab is my way of makin' amends." I take a deep breath and shake my head back and forth. "I don't want my gravestone to say, 'Here Lies Stupid. He Never Figured It Out.'"

She's quiet now, maybe decidin' whether she wants to talk to me or not.

"I don't think you're stupid." Her voice is quiet, sincere.

I pull the car over and roll down the windows. "Hear that?"

"I don't hear anything. Just a little wind."

"That's what I mean. This is the Church of Trees. You have to whisper when you walk under them. They're a lot older than you and me. That one there?" I point out the window. "Probably two hundred years old if it's a day. Gotta respect an old man like that. The things he's seen."

I put the car in gear and roll up the windows. "Gives you perspective, don't it? How small we are?"

We ride silently after that. I angle my rear view mirror so I can see her in the back seat. She draws her knees up and wraps her arms around them.

"Why couldn't I have taken a taxi two months ago?" she says, lookin' in the mirror at my face.

"Well, you're takin' one now. Never too late to for a cab, I always say. I'm Chris, by the way."

There's a moment's hesitation. You know, a little blip, like when you pick up the phone and the computerized telemarketer doesn't kick in right away? Anyway, I figure she's makin' up a name.

"I'm Mary."

It's regret I hear. Too much regret for someone so young and so pretty.

"Pleased to meet you, Mary." I reach for the radio. "Want a little music? Country? Pop? Alternative?"

"No, thanks."

I keep glancin' up at the mirror. There's a look in her eyes I can't describe. Far away? "May I ask why you want to go to the beach on a day like today dressed like that?"

"It's where I'll meet him." Her voice sounds different. Slower, like she's having trouble makin' the words. Her eyelids are droopin'.

"Who?"

"My groom."

"Your groom? What's he like?"

Then she mumbles somethin' weird that I can't quite make out. It sounds like *cow-chez spay-fud*. But she's slurrin' her words and it's gettin' me worried.

"I don't know what you're sayin', Mary. Do you need medical help? Should I bring you to the hospital?"

"The beach!" she shrieks, eyes wide open now. "Hurry!"

"OK, OK. We're almost there."

In a few blocks, I turn into the parkin' lot. There's a couple other cars there, probably people tryin' to get in a beach walk before the storm. She hands me a ten dollar bill over the seat and opens the back door.

"I don't see your groom. Is one of those cars his?"

"No."

"Want to wait here in the cab for him?"

She doesn't answer. Just gets out of the car. I see her stagger toward the stairs that go down to the beach. I roll down the window and call to her. She turns and mumbles more weird shit. A foreign language? Sounds like *car-do-ellis*-somethin' and *ix-oh-ray-us*-somethin'. I don't know.

Then she turns away from me and makes it to the stairs. She grips the railin' and goes down one slow step at a time. Never turns back around. Never says goodbye.

I've done a lot of things in my life I'm not proud of. I gotta lotta regrets. But that's right there near the top of the list. I let that poor girl walk down to the beach all by herself. Why didn't I stop her? What the hell was I thinkin'?

I gave her to the storm. It's my fault.

*****

Whitehorse took a breath and tucked the notes he had taken into his front shirt pocket. He looked at the man before him, cheeks wet with tears, now crumpled in his chair. The room had grown uncomfortably warm after the last time the man had stoked the fire. Outside, it was night. The slashing of the rain against the windows made it sound like the darkness was trying to get inside. The police officer shuddered despite the heat.

"You couldn't have known, Mr. Harper."

"Tryin' to pardon the crime?"

"You gave her a ride is all."

"But I knew somethin' was wrong. She was actin' drunk or high toward the end. Sayin' stuff I couldn't figure out. I had no business leavin' her there alone."

Whitehorse sighed. "I have to go. Mr. Harper. If you think of anything else, please call me at this number." He handed the man a card.

"She's somebody's daughter, Officer." He pulled a handkerchief from his pocket and wiped his nose.

"Yes, she is. I'll find out whose and contact them."

"I don't envy you that job. That's the worst news a mother or father can hear."

"It sounds like you're talking from experience." When the

man didn't answer, Whitehorse said, "I'll show myself out."

7. School Days

*T*he surf was thunder drowning all other sound. His bride was approaching over the water, the train of her gown sea foam on the sand, the veil a cloud blowing in the wind. Just as he opened his arms to embrace her, the wave engulfed them both. Her hand slipped from his grasp as he tumbled headlong in the frigid sea. Water filled his nose and mouth as he struggled to breathe. He dug his fingers into the abrasive sand, fighting the undertow, clawing his way up the beach, only to find himself in the cemetery, prostrate before Helen's stone. He laid his head on the cool grass, gasping for breath. Without warning, a skeletal hand reached up through the moist earth and twined its bony fingers around his throat.

Peter sat up in bed, heart pounding. "Shit!" he managed between ragged gasps for air. The sheets were wet with perspiration.

The green digital display on the clock face said 2:30. He turned on the bedside light and rubbed his eyes. After relieving himself in the bathroom, he pulled on a robe and went into the kitchen.

"What's going on, Helen?" he said to the picture. "Sending me a ghost to scare me into therapy?" He took a deep breath. "Well, it's working. These weekends off are getting harder and harder." He resolved to ask his friend Sterling if he could recommend a good therapist in town. He had to do something.

He shivered at the sound of the wind still howling outside. The rain had abated somewhat, if only temporarily. He filled a teapot and put it on to boil. "Chamomile might help."

A few minutes later, as he sipped the soothing elixir, he was reminded of Helen's love for all things *tea*—decorative china pots for steeping, delicate designer cups, infusers, canisters for aromatic loose teas, silk tea bags.

Then he saw her in the hospital bed Hospice had installed in their living room. Too weak to raise her arm. Struggling to smile at him whenever he entered the room. During those last several months, it seemed as though her body were evaporating before his eyes. He hated the image of his vacuum-sealing meat for the freezer, watching the plastic bag hug the food tighter and tighter as the machine withdrew air from the sack. Her skin had been like that, adhering closer and closer to her bones with every passing day, as her life was sucked from her body by the engine of her illness.

He shook his head to dislodge the dreadful thought. He willed himself to remember Sundays with Helen and Mira. They began with a breakfast of bacon and eggs and toast and coffee. Then they went off to church, where Mira would go to her Sunday school and he and Helen would be spiritually fed by a pastor on fire for the Gospel. Brunch at their favorite seaside restaurant would be followed by leisurely beachcombing. He saw Helen running and dancing with little Mira along the shore, picking up shells, fragments of sand dollars. Their laughter was the sweetest music he had ever heard, their unselfconscious pleasure, the purest joy he had ever known. Even now it brought a smile to his lips.

Calmed by the memory, he finished his tea and put the cup in the sink. He hoped a few more hours of sleep awaited him.

He was surprised when the alarm sounded. He had indeed fallen back to sleep. In moments, he was in his sweats and off to the gym. The rain was only a light mist, and the wind had lessened to a breeze. The streets were littered with debris from the tall fir trees, and he had to steer around the bigger branches. Driftwood Athletics, a new addition to the north end of town, was only a ten-minute drive from his house. He pulled into the small lot, locked his car, and bounded up the stairs to the front door.

"Hi, Peter." Mike was folding towels behind the counter.

"Good morning, Mike." He waved his key card at the check-in kiosk. The beep sounded, and he proceeded downstairs to find a locker. Once he had stowed his valuables, he secured them with a combination padlock and walked to the rows of machines. His routine was to do a half-hour upper body workout, then go upstairs for a half-hour on one of the many treadmills, lined up like worshipers before the row of flat-screen TVs mounted above them.

He adjusted the resistance on the first machine and began rhythmically thrusting his arms out and upward. A thud from across the way drew his attention to the free weights area, where a large bearded man was doing a clean and jerk with a barbell that made Peter gasp.

"Hey, ZZ Top," he whispered, staring at the man's huge biceps and thighs. "I couldn't lift a quarter of that. Wouldn't want to meet you in a dark alley." The more he looked at the man, the more he was certain he had seen him somewhere before.

Without giving it further thought, he continued his circuit of the machines. He could feel his muscles waking up, burning with the stress upon them. Soon he was back at his locker to retrieve his headphones. He conquered the boredom of the treadmill by watching and listening to CNN.

Once upstairs, he became engrossed in the latest Washington debacle, losing all track of time. Thirty minutes passed and the treadmill slowed for the five minutes of cool down. When the machine stopped, he returned to the locker, grabbed his jacket and valuables, and hurried to his car, half-expecting to see the woman in white, dripping water and seaweed, come walking out of the pre-dawn darkness. Relieved that she did not, he pushed the START button, put the car in gear, and drove off.

The rain had begun again in earnest. The wind remained calm. He adjusted the wipers and turned on the radio. A group out of Portland called Portugal.The Man was advising "Let's live in the moment."

"I want to, Helen. I'll get help."

Shower and breakfast were perfunctory. He was off to PCU in an hour.

"Good morning, Dr. Bristol." The red-haired office manager in the Administration Wing greeted every professor with her beatific smile.

"Good morning, Amelia."

"I've printed out your schedule and put it in your mailbox. Busy day. Your first class is in McCall at 9:00."

"Thank you."

He liked the Tom McCall Lecture Hall. The stadium seating gave him a good view of all the students—the ones sleeping or on their cell phones, and the ones taking notes. The acoustics were excellent, so he didn't have to shout or use the PA system.

He picked up his mail. Magazine subscription offers and other advertising he dropped into the green recycle bin located to the left of the mailboxes. Late student papers and faculty announcements he stuffed into his briefcase for perusal later.

It was a short trip across the center courtyard to his office in Rainier Hall. Helen had decorated it fifteen years ago, when he had accepted the position in the Psychology Department, and he had never updated it. He liked its comforting familiarity. Framed pictures of Sigmund Freud, Carl Jung, Erik Erikson, Ivan Pavlov, B.F. Skinner, Jean Piaget, and Abraham Maslow occupied one wall—what he called his Rogues' Gallery. Another wall featured abstract expressionist paintings by Helen and several of her artist friends—his Rorschach Collection. The third wall was made up of oak bookcases filled with tomes he hadn't cracked open in years. The final wall was glass, affording a beautiful view of the tree-studded campus.

In the decade and a half that he had been there, Pacific Crest had become a premiere university, attracting world-class faculty. And the ever-increasing tuition reflected that prestige. He winced. He would never have been able to afford to send Mira here unless her tuition had been part of his benefit package. "Thank God for large favors."

A look at his watch assured him that he had plenty of time before his class began. He decided another cup of coffee was in order and headed out to the Faculty Lounge.

"Hello, Peter!" came the cheerful voice as he entered. Sterling Friese had moved up from L.A. seven years before and had attained tenure a year ago, a scant few days after Dean

48

Wasserman's untimely death. At 42, with his blue eyes, auburn hair, and muscular build, he was considered the most eligible bachelor on the faculty. People wondered why he had not remarried after his divorce, but he was notoriously secretive about his love life. Peter had begun as Sterling's mentor, welcoming the younger man to the faculty. They had become friends afterward, but since Helen's death, they had not gotten together as frequently as they used to.

"Good morning, Sterling. Just the man I wanted to see. Let me pour myself some coffee and I'll come and pick your brains."

Cup in hand, he joined the younger professor at the small table.

"I'm embarrassed to admit that I don't know the mental health resources in our town. I mean, I teach Psychology and I don't know who the good therapists are. No excuse for that. Can you help me out?"

"Do you need to make a referral? One of your students?"

"No." He took a sip of his coffee and put the cup on the table. "It's for me." He took a deep breath and exhaled. "I think I'm finally ready to face my grief about Helen. I mean, I have to do something. Weekends are beginning to drive me crazy. And I think the death of that girl on the beach yesterday has tipped me over the edge. I was the one who reported it."

"Yesterday? Jesus! I haven't listened to the news. What happened?"

"It was all so fast. This young woman walking on the beach. In a wedding gown, no less! She just kept walking down toward the water and this sneaker wave comes and grabs her. The undertow sucked her right out. I never saw her again."

"Shit." Sterling stiffened briefly, then relaxed. "Any idea who it was?"

"None. Never saw her face clearly through the veil she was wearing."

"Good God. Freak you out?"

Peter nodded. "I'll say. Nightmares. Anxiety during the

day."

Sterling raised his head and looked toward the ceiling. "Let me think a minute." He stroked his chin. "I've heard good things about two therapists in town. Carrie Ellison, over on 3rd, I think. And Troy Hamel. Not sure where his office is, but you can look him up. Those are all that come to mind."

"Thanks. I'll check them out. How's your day shaping up?"

"Light day. Only one class. But a bunch of student appointments. I think I'll spend some time putting together the next exam for 303. And I want to talk to Brady about teaching in the post-grad program. You?"

"Four classes. And I have to get together with a couple doctoral candidates. They need some hand-holding."

"Aren't you generous. Well, duty calls." He took his last sip of coffee and brought the cup back to the sink. "Good luck," he called over his shoulder.

Peter finished his coffee and left the lounge. He went back to his office for his briefcase and then walked to McCall.

"I love the swirl of sounds at the beginning," he muttered, as students were filing in, finding seats, finishing discussions begun outside. It reminded him of the opening seconds of *Sgt. Pepper's*, with orchestra and audience sounds mingling in quiet chaos until the crashing chords of the first few bars. *It was twenty years ago today...*

"Good morning, ladies and gentlemen. Today we start our exploration of the Exner Scoring System for the Rorschach inkblot test. You all may feel a little crazy by the end of class, but that's to be expected."

He was greeted by a quiet murmur of laughter.

8. Pea Plants and Ph.D's

Sterling walked back to his office to finish preparations for his 10:30 class and to think about how he wanted to approach Chancellor Brady about teaching doctoral candidates. He was eager to get a leg up with Brady while the search for a new dean of the department was still underway. The school was quite conservative about assigning professors to the rarefied atmosphere of the Ph.D programs, jealous to maintain its reputation as the preeminent university of the Pacific Northwest, and one of the foremost in the country. Besides, having a cadre of doctoral students to correct your exams and teach some of your classes was a plum that had to be earned. He would have to be persuasive.

He unlocked the door and stepped into the modest space he claimed for his own on the campus. He had decorated the walls just as he had done at his home, with original wildlife paintings by a former student of his. Each was carefully labeled with its scientific name—the binomial name in Latin—and its common name. Every six months he would swap some of them out to refresh his vision at school and at home. Currently, his favorite was hanging behind his desk. *Taricha granulosa*—the Rough-skinned newt—had a special place in his heart. Salamanders, toads, birds, cats—he owned a collection of original watercolors that was the envy of the faculty members in his department. The artist, an attractive young woman in his class, had perished in a tragic snowboarding accident on Mount Hood two years before.

His degrees were especially important to him and occupied a prominent place on the wall opposite the door. They were large, elegantly framed trophies for all to see when they entered his domain.

The pride he felt at having been awarded tenure had not worn off. His long-term career goals were coming to fruition, and he was eager to repay the school with the kind of expert performance that came naturally to him. He would make a name for himself and enhance the university's stature at the same time.

As he sat down at his desk, he opened the file drawer on the right and withdrew the most recent of his articles: "Neo-Darwinism in the 21st Century—A Critical Review of Origins and Directions." *The Journal of Evolutionary Biology* had already received dozens of letters in response to its publication of the article two months ago, and Richard Waterbury, one of the leading scientists in the field, had contacted him directly to negotiate rights to include it in his forthcoming book, *From Fringe to Foundation: The Journey of Neo-Darwinian Thought.* Sterling pursed his lips. *This will bring Brady around.*

He put the article in his briefcase and perused his class notes—a history lesson for today about Gregor Mendel, recognized decades after his death as the founder of the modern science of genetics. He had to smile. *An Augustinian friar experimenting with pea plants in the mid-1800's discovers the rules of heredity. And he couldn't pass the oral exams to become a certified high school teacher! If God wrote screenplays, he'd be writing for the Coen brothers.*

A knock on the door interrupted his thoughts. His first appointment, Franklin Wise, was anything but. His future at Pacific Crest was hanging by a thread.

"Come in, Franklin. Have a seat." The greeting was cool and formal. Sterling always frowned when he saw the boy's pierced eyebrows, the line of silver rings reminding him of the post-surgical staples on his mother's side following her cancer surgery.

"Er...thank you, Professor." His long black hair fell over his collar in a lazy roll, *de rigeur* for the alternative rock band he played in on the weekends. His dark eyes scanned the room. When he sat, his left leg bounced on the floor as if there were a spring under his heel.

Sterling opened a file he had pulled from his drawer. "Your last paper left a lot to be desired. What exactly happened?"

"I got so busy. We had a big Chemistry exam I spent weeks preparing for. Then *3 Day Fish*—that's my band—got four gigs at Club Chaos in two weeks. And..."

Sterling raised his hand. "I understand you're busy, Franklin. We all are. Why didn't you write me the kind of paper you're capable of? We both know this is crap." He tossed the paper across his desk to the hapless student. "If I had more energy, I'd look for the website you copied it from, but it's not worth my time." He leaned over his desk and drilled the boy with his eyes. "I was out shopping a few weeks ago and noticed you entering Sea and Sand Cannabis Dispensary on 101. Your subpar performance wouldn't have anything to do with the amount of weed you're smoking, would it? Or perhaps it's the other drugs? Let's see, what have I heard?" He looked at the ceiling and stroked his chin. "Franklin is the go-to guy on campus for anything you want. He has it all.' That sound about right? Why, you're a walking drug emporium, aren't you?" Now he turned the blade. "You are aware, I'm sure, of the university's zero tolerance policy for recreational drugs? I wonder what I might find if I searched your dorm room?"

The boy squirmed in his seat. Perspiration beaded his forehead. His hands began to tremble. He yanked at the collar of his T-shirt as if it were strangling him. His mouth tried to form words, but no sounds came out.

"I don't want to have you expelled, Franklin." He sat back in his chair. "But I demand respect from my students—far greater respect than you have thus far displayed, with your missed classes, napping during my lectures, forged papers." He narrowed his eyes. "Why don't you prepare another report—one reflecting your native intellect—and submit it to me in one week's time? Then we can sweep this unpleasantness under the rug. Shall we?"

"Y-yes, Professor Friese. Thank you. Thank you. I'll have it for you in a week." He leaped from his chair as though it were suddenly on fire. "And I won't skip anymore classes. I promise."

"Good. Good." Sterling stood and extended his hand to the youth. "And who knows? Someday I may ask a favor of you, my boy. I'm sure you'll be ready if that time ever comes."

The boy nodded and ran from the room.

Sterling sat back down and smiled. *Have to keep the*

young ones on a short leash. He looked at his schedule and saw the name Grace Kaiser. Barely squeaking by with a C+, which would cripple her chances for a good graduate school. And sitting in the front row in her short skirt did not seem accidental to him. He would have to have a long talk with her.

He resumed his study of his class notes until a very faint knock sounded on the door.

"Come in."

A slim, blonde-haired girl with a face as smooth as a Michelangelo marble entered.

"Good morning, Grace. Please sit." He shook his head. "Your knock is as tentative as your class participation."

"Good morning, Professor Friese." She curled her red lips into a pouty smile. "What do you mean about my participation?" She crossed her legs and tugged at her skirt.

"I want you to engage more. Ask and respond to questions. Convince me you're learning the material. I hate to be giving you a C+ when I'm sure you can achieve more."

"Is there anything else I can do to raise my grade?" She crossed her legs again, exposing more of her shapely thighs.

Sterling considered. It was his Achilles' heel. He had never found the inner strength to resist the coquetry of a pretty girl. *She's not a minor,* he argued with himself. *She's responsible for her own behavior. It's consensual.* He found himself staring at her legs. *I'm still young. I'm handsome and intelligent. I have needs. She has needs. It's a win-win situation. After all, I'm relinquishing my power and sharing it with her. She should be grateful.*

"Perhaps we can work something out."

9. The Bearer of Bad Tidings

Whitehorse phoned Chloe just before she left for work. "Sorry about ditching you yesterday, honey. I'm sure you heard the news about the girl being swept away? I went knocking on doors to check if anyone might have seen something. Then we found out she took a cab to the beach. I had to interview the cabby right away. The sooner you talk to witnesses, the better."

"I figured something like that. I know it goes with the job. Was the cabby helpful?"

"Well, now we know she was a student at Pacific Crest. I'll go up there today and go over their rosters. See who's missing."

"What's that going to be like for you? What if you run into Friese?"

He could hear the note of alarm in her voice. "I'd like to punch that smug bastard in the nose, but I can't. I have to play nice. Maybe I'll audit another of his classes and see if I can make him sweat again. Make him think I've found something new." Just talking about the man made his blood boil.

"You know you can't do that, Charley. You can't let him distract you from what you're doing. You have to identify that girl so you can notify her parents." She sighed. "What an awful job."

"You're telling me." For a moment, his attention flagged as he recalled the times he'd had to tell parents their son or daughter had been killed in a car crash, a drowning, a drug overdose. Watching a mother or father collapse in grief made him physically ill. To claim, *I'm only the messenger,* was no solace.

"Where'd you go? You just got quiet all of a sudden."

"Just remembering the times I've been the bearer of bad tidings. Least favorite job."

"Sorry, hon. But you're strong, and it's part of what you do. And I love you for it."

"Thanks. I guess I better let you take off for work."

"Yep. Count Dracula will be walking by my cubicle soon, and I better be there to greet him with a smile. I need my paycheck. Catch up with you Friday night. OK? *Trattoria Italiana?*"

"Our favorite place. I'll pick you up at seven." He tapped the screen and put the phone in his pocket. He made a final sweep of his modest, outdated kitchen. The refrigerator was closed, the stove and lights were off, the back door was bolted. He poured the remainder of his coffee into a travel mug and locked the front door behind him.

The ten minutes it took him to get to the station were more than enough to get his adrenaline pumping again. He saw Friese with the chancellor, the school's security officer, and their lawyer shooing him off the university grounds, all clucking like self-satisfied mother hens. He had had the envelope of evidence right in his hands, and he couldn't open it—couldn't see what dirt Wasserman had dug up on Friese with the help of a private investigator. But then he smiled when he remembered nailing the sonofabitch in his own classroom, explaining aloud how the murder had been committed. Hypothetically, of course. The expression on Friese's face had been priceless. *I'll catch you yet, if it's the last thing I ever do.*

He left the mug in the car and entered the police station.

"Good morning, Tracker. Looks like the worst of the storm is over. How'd your interview with the cab driver go?" Esperanza was a morning person—always awake, even without coffee, by 5 A.M.

"It was her all right. He picked her up at PCU." He pulled out his pad and flipped through his notes. "She got weird at the end, like some drugs or alcohol had kicked in. Said some gibberish that's gnawing at me, like I know something that's on the tip of my tongue, just out of reach."

"Like what?"

"Something that sounded like 'cow chez spay fud,' for one. Then some other stuff. 'Car-do-ellis' and 'Ix-a-ray-us?' Something like that."

"Foreign language? Some kind of code?"

"Hell if I know."

"But you're gonna figure it out?"

Whitehorse smiled. "Somebody's gotta do it. Might as well be me."

"That's what I love about you, man. Never say die. Hey, want me to go to the school, what with your previous visit up there and all?"

"Nah. I can do it."

"And if you bump into Friese?"

"I'll say, very sweetly, 'Why, good morning, Professor. So nice to see you today.'"

Esperanza laughed. "Right. And you got a bridge to sell me?"

"I'll be OK. Really. I'll focus on the girl. Find out who she was."

"Better get a warrant to go through school records. I wouldn't put it past them to be real pricks about it."

"Good idea. I'll get hold of Judge Harowitz."

"Is he over that last debacle?"

"You mean when the governor reamed him a new one? Yeah. I talked with him a few months ago. He's OK. Good man."

"Well, you better get going. I'll hold down the fort. Light day, I hope."

"You again?" The smile on the judge's face belied his gruff tone. He removed his black robe and sat behind his desk for a much-needed break between cases. "Good to see you, Charley. Coffee?" He reached for the pot near his desk and poured himself a generous cup.

"No thanks, Judge."

"Well, what can I do for my favorite policeman? Got a pretty full docket, so make it quick."

"I need a warrant to go through school records at PCU—"

"Jesus, you're not still—"

"No, no, Judge. It's that girl that washed away on Sunday.

A cab driver picked her up at the university and took her to the beach. Must've been a student up there. I need to identify her so we can contact her parents."

"Hell, what a tragedy." He kept talking as he filled out the form and signed it. "So you think she's a college kid? Whole life ahead of her? Shit. Good luck telling her parents." He put the pen down. "Here you go." As he handed the paper to Whitehorse, he pursed his lips. "Just stay away from Friese. OK? I don't want my name associated with a..." He chose his words carefully. "Shall we say 'a known troublemaker?'"

Whitehorse smiled back at him. "Understood, Judge. Trust me."

The judge extended his hand. "Be safe, my friend."

Twenty minutes later, Whitehorse pulled into the visitors' parking lot at Pacific Crest University. The visually stunning wood and glass buildings were grouped in a large circle, like a modern Stonehenge. The enclosed courtyard was cut into wedges by sidewalks on the diameter, each passing through a large gazebo at the center. Even here, outside that charmed circle, he felt the weight of unfinished business, that thorn in his paw. His nemesis was here, the man who had gotten away with murder. A part of him hoped he wouldn't blunder into the professor today as he examined school records. Another part hoped he would.

He walked to the Administration Building and read the name tag on the receptionist's desk. "Good morning, Amelia. I'm Officer Whitehorse. I think we met last year around Dean Wasserman's death."

The woman sat bolt upright in her chair. "Y-yes, we did. I-I remember. You're not here to ask more questions?"

"No. No. I'm looking into the death of that young woman over the weekend. Did you hear about it on the news?"

"Terrible. But what brings you here?"

"That's the thing. We think she was a student here. I'd like to check your school records to see if anyone is missing. I have a warrant." He handed her the document.

"Let me call Chancellor Brady."

"Of course." As she made the call, he turned away and looked at the art work decorating the walls. Even the business office had been decorated with the eye of an interior designer.

A man in a blue blazer hurried in. "Officer Whitehorse?"

"Mr. Effling. We meet again." He extended his hand to the head of Campus Security. "I guess you've heard? We think that poor girl on the beach was one of yours. I'm here to find out."

"And how do you propose to do that?"

"I'd like to look through your records. See if anyone is missing."

Effling shook his head back and forth. "We have just under 3000 students registered here. Of those, we allow the Masters, Doctoral students, and Postdoctoral fellows to live off-campus in university apartments. Undergraduates live in the dorms."

Whitehorse felt like he was being lectured to.

"You must know college students are notorious for skipping classes, so even if they aren't present it doesn't mean they're missing."

Whitehorse clicked his tongue. "Guess I didn't really think this through. You have any ideas?"

"Students don't often miss exams without good reason. No one wants to flunk out of a school they or their parents are paying upwards of 50K a year to attend. Why don't I send an interoffice memo to all the faculty to report any student who fails to appear for an examination or any other classroom event where attendance is mandatory? Within a couple of weeks we should have a pretty good list for you."

"That sounds great, Mr. Effling."

"Philip."

"Thank you, Philip. And you can call me Charley." He pursed his lips. "I must admit, I didn't think you'd be so helpful after that..."

"Awkward mess in Wasserman's office? I think they were pretty rude to you—Brady and Friese and Fairweather. Hell, I'm an ex-cop myself. You were only doing your job."

"Thank you." This time he shook his hand more warmly. "I appreciate that." He turned toward the door, then turned back around. "Hope to hear from you soon."

"Count on it."

He was greeted by a sun break when he stepped outside to the inner courtyard. The clouds parted, if only temporarily, revealing a warm, late January sun that splashed a beautiful sheen over all the wet lawns and shrubbery. The purples and whites of flowering cabbages burst into brilliance on either side of the central walkways. He couldn't resist strolling out to the gazebo.

A deep sigh escaped his lips as he looked back toward McCall Lecture Hall. Was Friese in there now, wowing his class with his abstruse knowledge? What dirt had Wasserman dug up on him?

"I keep my promises," he whispered. "I will catch you."

10. Arm and Hammer

The week flew by. He had gone so far as to look up the addresses and phone numbers of Carrie Ellison and Troy Hamel, but the handwritten note sat neglected on his kitchen table. Peter hadn't brought himself to call either therapist.

Sunday dawned gray but dry. The heavens had emptied themselves all week and hovered flat and still above the little beach town today. Once the breakfast dishes were stowed in the dishwasher, he put on his sweats and a waterproof windbreaker, got into his car, and headed toward the parking lot at the bottom of Heron Drive.

In twenty-five minutes, he was on the sand, walking north. The wind was light, but the surf was roaring after a week of storms. Some of the swells were over twenty feet high, with foam-fringed crowns. Seagulls were busy along the beach, munching on the smorgasbord of mussels and crabs the waves had washed up. Judging from the footprints in the sand, only one previous beachcomber and his dog had ventured ahead of him, now out of sight in the mists toward Cascadia Head.

"It's a good day for walking, Helen. Not many people out. A little cool. Big surf. Air smells great." He picked up the pace to get warm, finally breaking into a jog.

He couldn't suppress a shudder when he loped past the strand where he had seen the woman swept away last week. "You don't forget those things. I don't anyway." With his circulation stimulated, he slowed to a brisk walk, still trying to put distance between himself and his memories.

Up ahead, he could make out a black shape cavorting on the beach. "Dog. But where's its owner?" As he got closer, the dog spotted him and came limping in his direction. "Oh, crap. Stay back, doggie. I'm not a dog person. No love here." He made shooing motions with his hands.

Instead, the dog tried harder to reach him. It whimpered as it did so, suspending its back right leg above the ground. Its paw was bloodied, its black fur, tangled and sandy.

"Don't jump up on me, you mangy mutt. You're all dirty. Where's your master?" No one else was visible within a half-mile. "How'd you get hurt like that?" As the dog bounced around, Peter heard its collar rattle. "OK, let's see if you've got some ID on you. E.T. phone home. Have somebody come and get you." He timidly extended his hand toward the collar, afraid the dog might bite him. The dog calmed and let him grasp the silver tag hanging there.

"'Hammer.' That's all it says. No phone number, no address. Just your name, I guess. Maybe you have a chip in you?"

The dog barked and turned away from the water. As it limped on three legs toward the escarpment that bordered the beach, Peter continued his walk north. The dog turned back and hurried as best it could to intercept him. It barked again and turned in the other direction.

"No, no. I'm out here for a walk. I'm not following you."

The dog's persistence began to bother him. It pushed against his legs as if to stop him from going forward. Its barks became louder and more insistent. "This way," it seemed to say.

"Look. Hammer. No offense, but I don't like dogs. I'm here for a little exercise is all." He resumed his pace and the dog finally relented. He hadn't gone more than thirty yards when the dog began to howl. It wasn't an excited "Come-with-me" bark, but a mournful cry that stopped Peter in his tracks. He turned to see the dog hovering around something in the sand, leaning over to sniff it, then leaping back. Again it wailed.

"OK. OK. You win. What the hell are you so upset about?" He walked toward Hammer, and the dog barked as if grateful for his change of heart. "I'm coming. I'm coming."

He wasn't prepared for what lay in the sand. He felt a wave of nausea wash over him. A rushing sound rose in his ears as though the surf had suddenly intensified. The dog barked wildly.

It was a human arm from below the elbow, fingers lifted as if in supplication, a wordless plea for help that was never answered. All along the arm were wounds that Peter guessed were bite marks from a shark. There were also little holes poked in the flesh that he thought might have been from seagulls before Hammer had scared them away.

Peter fell to his knees. "Oh, dear God. No." He couldn't tear his eyes from the macabre vision. Then he saw it. On the third finger. "Is that a ring? Is that a diamond ring?"

The dog had stopped barking. It nuzzled into his chest and Peter stroked its head, two strangers consoling themselves at a tragedy beyond their understanding. Peter regained his feet, but kept petting Hammer. "You did good, boy. Sorry I didn't listen to you right away."

He pulled out his phone and dialed 911. Not long after, Whitehorse came hurrying up the beach toward him. Hammer barked once and then was silent.

"Dr. Bristol? Professor?"

"Just Peter is fine."

"What are the odds? We meet again under the strangest circumstances." The policeman looked down into the sand. His face was grim. "Hmm." He exhaled and stooped down on one knee. "You haven't touched it?"

"No. I don't think the dog has either."

Whitehorse took note of the bird tracks around it. "Looks like the seagulls had a go of it until your friend here scattered them." He motioned to Hammer. "Your dog looks hurt."

"Not my dog. Dog found the arm and dragged me over here." He hesitated a moment. "I'm not sure if this is kosher, but may I ask if you've identified the girl yet?"

"I guess there's no harm in telling you. Cab driver picked her up in your bailiwick and brought her to the beach. I expect we'll know who she is by the end of the next week or so."

Peter whistled. "Pacific Crest? Like you said. What are the odds?"

The policeman returned to his investigation. "Not much decomposition, so it's pretty recent. Of course, it's been pretty cold, too." He withdrew a small camera from his utility belt and took pictures of the arm from every angle. "I don't see any other footprints leading up to it except yours. Pretty safe to say it washed up with the tide."

"Think a shark got her?"

"Her?"

"Well, I couldn't help but notice what looks like an engagement ring on her third finger, and there's remnants of polish on the nails."

Whitehorse nodded. "Very observant." Then Hammer wedged himself between the two men and stared at the arm. "Looks like he's conducting an inquiry of his own. I think your friend wants to be a police dog."

It struck Peter at that moment. Hammer had befriended him. The dog was no longer an *it*.

Whitehorse resumed examining the arm. "Does look like bite marks. Not too common around here, but every now and again a shark will harass those crazies who actually surf in this ice water." He stood up. "I suppose I could tape this place up and wait for forensics from Newport. But what would be the point? Make a circus out of it. I think I'll bag it and bring it to them." He withdrew a large plastic bag from a pouch in his coat and got the arm into it without touching it, the way a dog lover cleans up after his dog.

"Do you think it's..." Peter struggled to complete the sentence.

"Our bride? She's the only one on our missing persons list." He finished sealing the bag and regarded Peter. "I'd hate to think there's another body out there."

11. A New Best Friend

Peter was absently stroking Hammer's head and ears as he watched Whitehorse depart. "I've kind of lost my appetite for walking, Hammer. How about you?"

The dog barked in response.

"I'm still not sure about our...relationship. I have to see if I can find your owner." He frowned. "From the looks of you—the way your fur is all matted and dirty—I think you've been out here a while. I'll bet you stink, too. And we have to get your paw looked at." He shook his head back and forth. "I must be nuts. I have no room in my life for a dog. Maybe I should just bring you to the pound and let them take care of you."

Hammer looked up at him and cocked his head, as though he could understand what Peter meant. He made a low 'woof.'

"Don't like that idea, huh? What else can I do?" *Do older dogs get adopted? Or is it more likely he'd be euthanized? Crap.* "OK, boy. Let's take it real slow back to the car. Then we'll figure out what to do next."

The hardest part was negotiating the stairs up to the parking lot. Peter finally relented and picked Hammer up for the last dozen steps. "Geez, you're heavy. And you do stink! My coat is headed straight into the washing machine when I get home."

When they reached the car, Peter put Hammer down while he removed an old beach blanket from the trunk and covered the back seat with it. "In you go, big boy. I'll help."

With the dog safely stowed, Peter got behind the wheel and pulled out his phone. A Google search revealed **The Dog's Tail: Everything You Need for Your Best Friend. Obedience Training, Shampoo and Pedicure, Grrrroom and Board. Veterinarian on-call 24 hours. Open Seven Days a Week. 2200 Pelican Place, four blocks east of 101.**

"OK, Hammer. We've got you covered. Sit tight."

Fifteen minutes later, he pulled into the parking lot at The Dog's Tail. A computerized sign out front displayed six colorful tails wagging furiously. He helped Hammer out of the back seat and held his collar while they walked into the reception area.

A pretty, dark-haired adolescent sat behind the desk. "I'm Rhonda. Welcome to The Dog's Tail. How can we help you today?"

"This is Hammer. I don't know who his rightful owner is. I've heard they sometimes put chips in dogs, but I don't know anything about that. Maybe you could check for one? Or maybe there's been a report about a missing dog? Anyway, in the meantime, I'd like a vet to look at his hurt paw. And he really needs a bath."

"And you are?"

"Peter Bristol. And I've never had a dog before, so if we can't find out who he belongs to, I'll need directions to the nearest pound."

The girl frowned. "Do you know how many dogs they put to sleep every week? Is that really what you want for Hammer?"

"No, that's not what I want. I want to find his owner. I'm gone all day working. I can't take care of a dog."

"Older dogs that have been house-broken can go many hours without needing to go outside. They usually sleep till their master gets home."

"But I don't know how to take care of a dog. I don't know what they need."

"They need love, water, and food, in that order. The rest we can teach you while you wait. Hammer'll teach you, too."

Peter sighed. It was an argument he couldn't win.

"You're in the right place, Mr. Bristol. We'll take good care of Hammer. Our on-call Vet, Dr. Kim, is already here seeing another patient, so she'll be with you shortly. Can I ask you to fill out this registration form?" She handed him a clip board and a pen.

Peter took a seat, and Hammer lay on the floor beside him. "What have we gotten ourselves in for, Hammer?" He couldn't be sure, but he thought the dog smiled.

Two hours later, Dr. Kim was debriefing him. "Looks like he

might have stepped on something sharp on the beach. Cut his pad pretty good, but it should heal OK. He'll probably chew those bandages off. Maybe you could prevent him from doing that for the rest of today? Anyway, here's an antibiotic you can give him for the next ten days. Just mix it with some soft food." She handed him a small white bag. "And he's a little underweight. I'd guess he was on that beach for several days."

"Is there an ID chip? Any missing dogs reported?"

"I'm afraid not, Mr. Bristol." She scratched Hammer behind the ears. "He cleaned up really well, didn't he? Handsome dog. Sure seems to have taken a liking to you awfully fast." Hammer was rubbing his muzzle against Peter's pant leg.

Peter had spent the time waiting for Hammer by talking to Rhonda about the basics of dog care. She'd given him a handful of brochures and pamphlets. He felt marginally more comfortable, but still anxious. He had purchased a new leash, which he now attached to Hammer's collar. Two stainless steel bowls, a starter sack of recommended dry dog food, and several cans of wet food were in a large paper bag. Dr. Kim led them to the door.

"If you have any questions at all, please don't hesitate to call."

As they approached the car, Peter leaned toward Hammer. "OK, boy. This is us. For better or worse."

It reminded him of his wedding night.

12. Exercise Before Breakfast

The bearded man grunted as he curled the heavy barbell up to his chest and back down to his thighs. He repeated the exercise until his biceps were burning, then put the barbell down on the mat. He looked to his left at the man working out on the upper body machines. *Good for him. Must be a regular. Seen him every day.* He smiled. *Or maybe this is just a New Year's resolution and he'll quit in another week.*

The other man turned, and they made eye contact. He got up from the machine and walked over. "Hey, hope I'm not bothering you, but I've seen you over the last few days and you look really familiar. I'm Peter Bristol. Work up at Pacific Crest. Do I know you from somewhere?"

He extended a gloved hand. "Chris Harper. If you've taken a taxi in town you've met me. I run Coronado Cab. Decided I sit on my ass too much and I gotta get back in shape."

"Oh, shit." The color drained from Peter's face. "I've seen your cab up at the university. You offer discounts for students."

"And?"

"And you must be the guy who took that girl to the beach. The one the sneaker wave got."

"How would you know that?"

"I'm the guy who saw it happen. The guy who called it in. The police told me she took a cab to get there."

"Well, Sweet Mother Mary, what a world!" Chris offered his hand again. "You know, I can't get her out of my head. It's really messed me up."

"Me, too. If only I had seen her sooner. Or run faster."

"If only I had never let her get out of my cab."

The two men stood silently for a minute. Chris grimaced. "You want to go out for a beer later today? There's nobody I can talk to about it."

Peter hesitated. He nodded. "I'll be home today about 4:30. Gotta change clothes. Let the dog out and feed him. I could meet you somewhere around 5:15 or so."

68

"How about The Barnacle at 5:30? That's my supper break anyway."

"That's the place down on 101 just past 45th? I'll see you there."

Chris watched the man return to the machines. He picked up the barbell and resumed his curls. *What a freakin' planet this is.*

He was glad it was a busy day. That way he didn't have to think too much. No trips to the college, but one to the emergency room, multiple doctors' visits for residents at the Sandy Hill Retirement Community, and lots of happy shoppers to and from the White Sale at the mall.

When he deposited his last fare at Beach Strand Shoes, he parked and got out for a smoke. He squinted at the sky overhead, a flat aluminum gray. As the nicotine reached his bloodstream, he felt a slight kick in his alertness, the way that first cup of coffee in the morning made him feel. He looked at his watch. *Is Tonya married already? Will it be tomorrow?*

He wasn't angry. Jealous of her normalcy? Of her success? *It's a game-changer, for sure.*

He hadn't dated for several years. *Don't think I'm very good company. I'm a moody sonofabitch. That's what Tonya told me, and she should know. It finally got to be too much for her, like she was takin' care of another kid besides Joe.*

It was hard not to think about his last mission with the SEALs. Their bird had gone down and he was the only survivor. *Why me? Why not Larry with three little ones at home? Or Jack? Jack was Mr. Clean, probably the most decent of all of us. But it was scum-bucket me. The guy responsible for the deaths of those two civilians. Collateral damage, my ass.*

And now this. The girl he had brought to her own funeral. And his dream last night? His son Joe being swept off their fishing boat ten years ago, alive only because he had worn his life vest.

He finished his cigarette and ground it out on the

pavement.

What about this guy Peter? He's a stranger. Why did I ask him out for a beer? And what's his job at the school? Professor? Am I hobnobbin' with the big-shots now? Sometimes I should keep my big trap shut.

He got back in the cab and played with the radio dial until he found the tail end of *A Day in the Life*. His watch said 5:05. Half an hour till his meeting with Peter. Without thinking about it, he withdrew his phone and called his son, Joe.

"Hey, Dad. Just got out of work. Haven't heard from you in a while."

"Your mom called me last week. Told me about her weddin' plans."

Joe was silent for several breaths. "Yeah. I—"

"Don't sweat it. I know why you didn't tell me. I was a jerk last time. So tell me about yourself. How's the job?"

"Way cool. Good boss. Good benefits. I think it's gonna work out."

"What about your love life?"

Joe chuckled. "You tell me about yours first."

"Nothin' to tell. Haven't met anybody yet that's willin' to put up with my bullshit. You?"

"Might have a girlfriend. Cindi. Been out a few times. Kind of testing the waters. Know what I mean?"

"Sure. Good for you. Takin' it slow is a good thing."

"When we get off the phone, I'll send you a picture."

They chatted for a few more minutes until Joe said he had to go pick up Cindi for dinner. Two minutes later, Chris heard the sound of an incoming message on his phone and opened it to a picture of a pretty brunette. "Gotta hand it to you, son. You got good taste in women," he said to the empty car.

13. Shark Week

The Driftwood Police Department had come up with a brilliant plan to cut costs. They hired volunteers from the senior class work-study program at Driftwood High School to man the phones. The students got business credits toward their diploma, and the two-man force got their phones answered. Esperanza and Whitehorse shared on-call duties after hours. Just before five o'clock, the phone rang. Chiara, the purple-haired receptionist, gave Tony the "you're up" sign and put the call through.

"Officer Esperanza here."

"May I speak with Officer Whitehorse?"

"He's out right now. Can I help you?"

"This is Philip Effling, head of security at Pacific Crest. I think we may have identified the missing girl."

Esperanza sucked in a breath. "Great news. I'll have Officer Whitehorse call you as soon as he can."

In moments he was on the radio with his partner. "Got a match, Charley. Effling thinks he's ID'd the girl. I told him you'd call."

There was a nanosecond of silence on the other end. "Just finishing up a little fender bender over on Cruise Lane. I'll head right over there. OK with you?"

"Knock yourself out."

As he drove up to the university, he didn't know what to think. He felt a leaden heaviness around his heart. The two-week-long worry may be over, but now he would have to inform the girl's parents. If they were out-of-state, contact the closest police department and delegate the awful duty. If they were local, see them face-to-face. Tell them their darling daughter, the light of their lives, had drowned in a freak accident. Worse—her body had not been recovered and probably wouldn't be. There would be nothing to put in the casket. He'd have to watch their unbelief morph to shock as he assured them there had been no mistake. She was gone. Then stand there, dry-eyed, as all hope drained from their faces.

When he pulled into the parking lot, another thought struck him. What about the arm? What if it's their daughter's? Then the diamond ring belongs to them. And he'd have to tell them how it wound up in the possession of the Driftwood Police Department. He cursed under his breath and pounded on the steering wheel.

With his mini temper tantrum done, he left the car and walked to the Administration Wing. "Good afternoon, Amelia."

"Hello, Officer Whitehorse. I'll let Mr. Effling know you're here."

He heard the footsteps hurrying down the hall. "Hi, Philip."

"Charley. Why don't we use this empty conference room?" He closed the door behind them and motioned Whitehorse to a seat. "Here's her file. Missing since we spoke. Roommate hasn't seen or heard from her. Missed two important tests last Wednesday. Roommate's called her cell phone a hundred times. Just rings and rings. Left messages with no response. I think she's our girl."

Whitehorse opened the manila folder. The picture attached to the registration form was of a beautiful blonde girl. *Marisa Kennedy. Date of birth: 11/23/96. Major: Biology. Minor: German. Class of 2019. Full scholarship through the Gittman-Eldredge Foundation. Parents: Deceased. Emergency Contact: Pacific Crest University.*

"She has no contact people? No one to call in an emergency?"

"Nope."

"Do we at least have her parents' names and former address? Maybe track down some extended family?"

"When she registered three years ago, she insisted she had no one. Had been living on her own in a studio apartment in Longview-Kelso since her parents' death in an MVA in 2014. I think our Registrar went soft on her and allowed her to leave that stuff blank, with the idea of filling it in after she got further away from their deaths. Anyway, she gave up the studio when she started school here. Rents a room off-campus for the summers."

"So she's a cipher. We don't really know anything about her."

"Pretty much. I think she did some modeling as a kid down in L.A. If the agency is still open..." He leafed through the file. "Here it is. Dreams Come True. Maybe they could give you a lead."

Whitehorse sat back and looked at the ceiling. "Here I was, afraid I'd have to contact her parents, and now I wish I could. I hate unfinished business." He grew thoughtful. "Would you keep something under wraps for me?"

"Sure thing."

"We found an arm on the beach the other day."

"Jesus!"

"Probably shark. It'd be really helpful if I could get some kind of DNA sample from Kennedy's room to match against the arm. That would be a little bit of closure at least."

"Sure. Her room's over in the Columbia River Dorm."

Whitehorse took a picture of the front page of the file. Before closing it, he turned to the transcripts in the back. "An *A* student. Very impressive." Then he did a double take. Three of her six classes this semester were being taught by Dr. Sterling Friese. "Sonofabitch! Did you see this?"

Effling frowned. His voice sounded apologetic. "I didn't want to point it out to you. Didn't want to rub salt in an old wound."

"Well, thanks anyway." He took a breath and sighed. "I'm suspicious of coincidences. Don't really believe in them. Know what I mean?"

"Of course. We're cops."

"My partner calls me a paranoid sonofabitch."

"It's what keeps a cop alive. Let me take you to her room."

The men stepped out into the central courtyard and headed toward the dormitory. Ghostly tendrils of cold sea air were reaching through the Douglas firs that bounded the campus, and both men shivered.

"Can't wait for summer," the security officer said.

"At least we're not back east. Hear they got another eight inches of snow last night from D.C. up to Boston."

"I'm used to snow, but I hate it anyway. Grew up in Albany, New York. We didn't call it a snow storm unless it dumped at least twelve inches. Loved those no-school days. But I've shoveled enough for two lifetimes."

A voice called out from behind them. "Good afternoon, Mr. Effling. Officer Whitehorse. To what do I owe the pleasure?"

Whitehorse felt his stomach lurch, but he recovered quickly. "Professor Friese. Just the man I wanted to see. We think we may have identified the girl lost on the beach."

"Oh, dear. Someone from here?"

Whitehorse saw the twitch at the left corner of his mouth. "As a matter of fact, yes. One of your students. Marisa Kennedy."

"Marisa? She's got Zoology with me and two labs. What dreadful news!"

Whitehorse saw the man frown in sorrow. *But your eyes tell a different story, Professor. Is that fear I see?* "It's not ready for release yet until we prove it. But it looks like she's the one. Mr. Effling will let Chancellor Brady know."

"My, my. So young. What a tragedy." He cocked his head as though another thought had occurred to him, but offered no further conversation. Then, "Getting colder. I must take my leave. Do come by and audit another class, Officer Whitehorse."

"I just might do that, Professor Friese."

"Goodbye, gentlemen."

Whitehorse watched the man continue walking toward the parking lot, then returned his attention to Effling. "Let's find Marisa's room."

Once in the dorm, they checked in with the young woman doing homework on the desk in the small lobby. "I'm Whitney, one of the RA's for this dorm. Can I help you?"

"We're here to check in with one of the students. No big deal. We know how to find her." Effling signed the visitors' book for himself and his companion and noted the time. He looked toward Whitehorse. "Follow me." To Whitney he said, "Don't worry. No one's in trouble. Officer Whitehorse is a friend of mine."

Whitney followed the men to the elevator just beyond the reception desk and held a key card to the mechanism. The door opened to admit them, and Whitney went back to her desk.

"College wasn't like this when I was a kid." Whitehorse watched the door close as Effling hit the button for the second floor. "We could come and go as we pleased."

"Sign of the times. We've heightened security to prevent any trouble. There's an RA at that desk for day and swing shifts, and one of our own personnel for nights. Can't get on the elevator without a key card. Can't get into the dorms proper without one either, unless you're buzzed in by somebody inside. I keep a card in my wallet, but I like to see the RAs earn their keep."

The men got off in a small vestibule. To the left was an enormous oak door with a tall narrow window and a panel of buttons beside it. Each button was labeled with two names. A large impressionist painting hung on the wall opposite the elevator. Under it was a small table with a vase of fresh flowers. The effect was assured elegance.

"Like a classy apartment building."

"Yeah. And that glass is reinforced. Can't be too careful nowadays." The security officer leaned toward the panel, looking for the right number. "Marisa Kennedy was rooming with Alicia Farmington in 210. I'll let Alicia know we're coming." He pushed the button and spoke. "Alicia, this is Philip Effling from Security. We spoke earlier about Marisa. I just have to follow up on a couple things."

"Please give me a minute. I'll buzz you in when I'm ready."

Effling smiled at Whitehorse. "Prevents embarrassing moments." Soon they heard a soft buzz and the click of the lock disengaging. "Follow me."

They walked down a tiled corridor done in muted earth

tones and hung with an array of paintings between slim tables displaying sculptures in stone and metal. "Students from the School of Design compete to get their stuff here, where it'll stay for the duration of the year. It's considered quite an honor."

Effling knocked on 210. They heard a lock being turned. A slender young brunette in gray sweats opened the door and greeted them.

"Police?"

"I'm Officer Whitehorse, Alicia. We're treating this as a missing persons case. I just have a few questions."

"I told him everything I know." She nodded toward Effling.

"Well, I was hoping I might get some DNA samples so we could check more databases."

"Where would you get that?"

"Oh, hairbrush, tooth brush, maybe nail file."

"Well, we have separate sinks. I never touch any of her stuff. It's over here."

They entered the dimly lit room. Whitehorse noted the drawn blinds, the unmade bed with a quilt thrown over it, the dirty clothes peeking out from underneath. The other bed neatly made but covered with books and papers. He walked to the double sink. "Which side is Marisa's?"

"On the left."

The policeman pulled on a pair of latex gloves and withdrew a plastic bag from his pocket. He picked up the emery board lying on the counter and put it in the bag. A toothbrush was upright in an empty water glass and he put that in the bag as well. No hairbrush was visible.

"These drawers." He pointed to the cupboard between the sinks. "They yours or hers?"

"Top two are mine. Bottom two are hers."

He slid out the third drawer. "Bingo." He lifted out a hairbrush glistening with blonde hairs. "That'll do nicely." He opened the bottom drawer and withdrew a small spiral-bound notebook inscribed with the title *2017 13-Month Day Planner.*

Whitehorse leafed through the little notebook. "January to January. Looks like she's written down when papers are due and tests are scheduled. She also has little hearts and red x's on some of the days. Any idea what those are?"

"The hearts are her dates."

"So she was seeing somebody?" Effling asked.

"Like I told you before, she wouldn't talk to me about it. Very secretive. But she really had the hots for some guy. Took off every chance she got. Don't know how she ever got any homework done. But she did go to class."

"What about the red x's?"

"Those are for shark week."

"Shark week?"

"Yeah, I have an app on my phone for it, but Marisa was very old-school. Wrote it down."

Whitehorse looked at Effling, who shrugged. "I'm afraid we're lost. What's shark week?"

Alicia smiled. "It's her period. A red x for the day it starts and an x for every day of bleeding. Like I said, I use an app on my phone to track it."

Whitehorse chuckled. "I guess old farts like us are out of the loop on that one." He looked toward Effling and then back at the girl. "I'll take the planner and see if there's any other useful information in it to help us find her. Meanwhile, keep us posted." He sealed the bag, stripped off his gloves, and handed her his card. "Did she say anything about getting married?"

Alicia hung her head. "She made me swear not to tell. Guess it doesn't matter now. She said her secret lover"—she mimicked quotation marks with the index and middle fingers on each hand—"promised her a ring before spring break. She was all excited. I mean, Marisa can get like real buzzed sometimes. Know what I mean? Anyway, in one of her moods she went out and bought herself a wedding dress. Would you believe that? She stashed it in the back of her closet. Right here."

She walked across the room and opened a door. She pushed blouses and skirts and pants out of the way. "Well, WTF.

It's gone. Suppose she eloped?"

The men left the question unanswered and walked to the door. "Let me know if you hear from her," Effling said.

"Sure will."

They heard the door lock behind them and walked back down the hall toward the main entrance.

Effling reached for the door handle. "She didn't elope, did she?" It wasn't really a question.

"No, she didn't. And there was no shark week in November or December."

14. Reubens and Beer

Hey, Hammer. You look happy to see me. And where'd you get my slipper, you rascal?" Every part of the dog's body seemed to be in motion when Peter stepped through the door. He took the slipper and scratched behind the animal's ears in greeting. "Need to go out?" The dog raced to the back slider. "Gotcha covered, boy." He turned on the backyard light and opened the glass door. Hammer dashed out to the lawn. While the dog finished his business, Peter watched a fine mist drift like liquid dust motes in the bright spotlight. "Pretty cold out there, huh?" The dog bounded back into the house. Peter slid the door shut and locked it. "Your paw looks like it's healed pretty well. You're not favoring it anymore. And something tells me you're hungry." More wiggles and waggles from the eager animal. Peter refilled his water bowl and poured a mound of dry food into the bowl next to it. Hammer wasted no time in plunging his muzzle into his supper. Peter removed his coat and hat, then pulled up a kitchen chair to watch his new friend.

"You know I don't like dogs, right? Pets in general? So why am I beginning to like you?" Hammer continued to crunch away, heedless of his master's words. Peter sighed. "What do you think, Helen?" He looked toward her picture. "Yeah, it's nice to have someone to come home to."

Peter stood. "Gotta go put on a pair of jeans. Meeting someone for a beer." He shook his head. "Definitely outside of my comfort zone." When he returned to the kitchen a few minutes later, the dog was at the slider. "Back out? Your after supper dump?"

The dog was quick in the cold and, once back inside, he followed Peter into the living room.

"I've got a few minutes before I have to leave, Hammer. And I won't be gone too long." He sat on the couch and Hammer dropped down at his feet. Peter leaned over and stroked the animal, who rolled onto his back to get his belly rubbed.

"What are you doing to me, you crazy dog?" He exhaled

slowly. "I thought I didn't have any room left in my heart." He looked around at his living space. He had left everything the way it was when Helen passed.

"Well, I'd better go. Like I said, I shouldn't be too long."

He pulled on his waterproof windbreaker and his broad-rimmed black felt hat—what Mira described as "kinda like Indiana Jones but more upscale." It was good in the rain and the cold. "Keep the bad guys out, Hammer," he said as he entered the garage.

In about twenty minutes, he was driving into the small lot behind The Barnacle. The Coronado Cab was already there. Once inside, he shook the moisture from his hat and looked for Harper, who had taken a small table in a dimly lit back corner. Peter had never been inside The Barnacle before, and he was impressed by the décor. High around the room, brass and bronze maritime hardware—cleats, double blocks, mast bands, barrel bolts, boom jaws—hung like shiny Christmas ornaments. The wall opposite the gleaming oak bar held a large heavy-duty fish net, complete with glass and cork floats. A collection of nautical knots, including half hitches, figure-eights, bowlines, and reef knots graced the wall to the left of the shelves of whiskeys and rums. Other walls sported paintings of sailing ships in desperate seas. The crown of the collection, directly behind the cash register at the far end of the bar, was the owner's original oil of Shackleton's *Endurance* being crushed by Antarctic ice.

When Peter reached the table, he extended his hand. "Chris."

Chris stood and reciprocated. "Thanks for comin', Peter." He resumed his chair. "I eat here quite a bit. My favorite is the Reuben. It's to die for. Mack, the owner, and I go back to when I first got to Driftwood. He's also the main chef, and he knows his way around a grill."

"Sounds good to me." He slid off his coat and hung it on the back of his chair.

"And what do you like to drink? I'm kinda partial to IPAs myself."

"That'll be fine."

He held up two fingers toward the bartender. "Hey, Billy. Two of the regulars. With Reubens." The man nodded. "You won't regret it. Best in town."

In moments, Billy brought two draft beers and set them on cardboard coasters. "Drink up, gentlemen. Your sandwiches will be ready in a few minutes."

Chris raised his glass and took a long draft. "Oregon is Beervana for sure."

Peter nodded in agreement and took a drink.

"So tell me about yourself. You said you work at PCU?"

"Yeah, I teach Psychology there."

"So you're a doctor? Like in Ph.D.?"

"Mmhmm."

"Well, I guess this is above my pay grade. I barely squeaked by with a Bachelor's, and not sure how I got that. Never very much for the books. Former Navy SEAL. Well, I guess you're always a SEAL. I just don't work for 'em anymore."

"So you're the kind of guy who could kill me before I had time to raise my glass from the table?"

Chris chuckled. "Well, it might take me a half-second longer. But, yeah."

"Well, then, let's stay friends."

Their Reubens arrived with generous mounds of French fries. Chris squirted a pool of ketchup on his plate, while Peter hefted the thick sandwich. He hadn't realized how hungry he was, and the first bite convinced him that Chris was right.

"Hats off, man. This may be the best Reuben I've ever had."

"Glad you like it. I'm about ready for another round. You?"

When Peter nodded, Chris held up two fingers to Billy. The bartender filled two more glasses and brought them to the table.

They ate in silence after that. Peter felt the satisfaction of the sandwich and the warmth of the beer spread through him.

When both were sure they couldn't possibly eat another French fry, Billy removed their plates.

Chris looked across the table. His face grew solemn. "I haven't been able to stop thinkin' about her. It's got to where I'm dreadin' to get a call from somebody at the school. Like I don't wanna go back up there."

"I hear you. I've dreamt about her." He didn't know if he were emboldened by the alcohol, or by the fact that this man was a stranger he could walk away from and never see again, but he began to speak more openly than he had in months. "I called her by my wife's name." He saw the confusion on Chris's face. "My wife, Helen, died of cancer three years ago. Long, drawn out, excruciating." He paused, unsure if he should continue, then plunged ahead. "I couldn't let her go. She was in terrible pain, but I didn't want her to leave me. It's like I wanted her to stay and take care of me." He sighed. "There on the beach, for just a minute, I imagined her coming back."

He looked over at Chris, afraid he might see judgment in his eyes—a look that said, "Get me away from this psycho." Instead, he saw compassion.

"In dreams I see the water taking her away and leaving me alone again. I've even seen her in the cemetery." He harrumphed. "Now I look in my textbooks and try to diagnose what kind of whacko I'm turning into." He drained his glass and set it down. "I'm not much of a man."

Chris pursed his lips and shook his head back and forth. He pointed at the empty glass. "You want another one?"

"I can't usually do more than two, but tonight's an exception."

Chris motioned to Billy, who responded promptly.

"I got dreams of my own. My son fallin' off our fishin' boat years ago. So damn thankful I made him put on that life jacket before we shoved off." He took another drink. "And worse. My now ex-wife Tonya, the night she miscarried in our first pregnancy. Her water breaks when she's next to me in bed. We're both wet. She's screamin'. I'm callin' 911, but she's in hard labor already. It's like it all happens so fast. The blink of an eye. I see that small perfectly shaped baby boy just layin' there, wet and bloody. But not movin'. Like he's asleep...or drowned."

It was Peter's turn to stare at the man before him, unburdening himself, laying down baggage he had probably carried for years.

"And other shit. Like when my helicopter was shot down and I was thrown clear. In my dream, the smoke from the blast becomes like this huge wave that sweeps the bird away. All my friends gone. Nothin' left. So don't think for a minute you've cornered the market on *crazy*."

Peter wasn't sure what to say. He took a deep breath. "Thank you," he whispered at last. "Thank you for listening and thank you for sharing that."

Neither man spoke for the next several minutes. Peter drank slowly, trying to digest what he had heard and what he was feeling. His meeting with Chris had turned into something so unlike anything he had anticipated.

Chris broke the silence. "You believe in God?"

"Not anymore. Why do you ask?"

"Because I still do. And I don't think it was an accident that we bumped into each other at the gym."

Peter smiled. "I think there's a lot of accidents in the world. And a lot of them aren't very happy."

"Yeah, well. To each his own. You ever go to the movies?"

"It's been a long time. Used to have a guys' night with my son-in-law when they still lived around here. Rent a shoot-'em-up and drink whiskey."

"My kinda night. Anyway, that new Marvel flick is openin' if you're interested."

"I might be, but I'm a real creature of habit. Got a routine for everything. But give me a call just in case."

"May have to change out some of your routines, huh?"

The two men swapped phone numbers just as Billy brought the tab.

"This one's on me," Chris said, as he reached for the slip.

"You get the next one."

"Thanks." Peter arose and put on his coat and hat. He waited until Billy returned with Chris's credit card, and the two walked out to the parking lot together. The mist had congealed into a bone-chilling rain.

"Till next time," Chris said as he unlocked the cab.

Peter nodded. "Next time."

15. Don

Sterling Friese threw his briefcase into the back seat of his new Lexus and slammed the door. When he got behind the steering wheel, he pounded his right fist into the passenger seat beside him.

That arrogant little Indian! How many months has it been since he pulled that grandstand stunt in my lecture hall? Almost a year? He couldn't prove anything, but he had the gall to try to intimidate me in front of my students!

He started the car and put it into gear. *And now Marisa, sweet Marisa. Good in bed but emotionally, a basket case.* His liaison with her had been flirting with disaster, and he had known it from the beginning. Swept out to sea was the best possible resolution. *That act of God saved my ass.*

But that goddamn Indian! The last thing I need is someone like him snooping into my private affairs. I'll have to put a stop to that pronto.

The fifteen minute drive to his home in Neskowin, on a hill overlooking the sea, gave him time to calm down. He loved his new house—its modern flair, state-of-the-art appliances and furnishings, cathedral ceilings. The kitchen gave access to the den, creating a large open space facing the ocean through a wall of double-paned glass. Perfect for cocktails and hors-d'oeuvres and the late-night tryst. His deal with the devil had paid off.

He uncorked a bottle of Pinot Noir and poured himself a generous serving. With a sigh, he sank down into the plush couch and stared out at the night. A light rain was tapping on the skylight overhead. The wine began to relax him, its cherry and dark chocolate notes stimulating his appetite.

What to do about a nosy policeman? I'll think better with my favorite film. He placed his wine on the coffee table, walked to the entertainment center, and turned on the flat-screen. He inserted the disk into the player and listened as the trumpet began keening for Don Corleone, a sweet and melancholy charade that concealed the bloody violence of the Godfather's business. It was a silly affectation, but sometimes he imagined himself a latter-day Don, establishing his "family" at the university. For him, the thrill of power was an aphrodisiac.

He began to laugh. *Of course! Of course!* Soon his guffaws echoed through the house. He sat back down and withdrew his phone from his pocket. He tapped a number.

"Professor?" The boy was shouting. "Hey, I've got that paper all done. I'll bring it by your office tomorrow."

"Good, Franklin. What's all that noise in the background? Where are you?"

"Club Chaos. Me and my band—3 Day Fish—we're setting up for our gig tonight. Special party. There's a big crowd already, so it should be a good night. But like I said, your paper's all done."

"That's not why I called."

"Oh?"

Friese heard the note of dread in Franklin's voice. "There's been a policeman on campus asking a lot of questions about you." Friese made sure his tone was appropriately matter-of-fact. "Officer Charles Whitehorse from Driftwood. Asking if you had any drug connections. If anybody knew about any dealing going on at the university. Said he'd come back with a warrant to search your room. I think you'd better lay low for a long time." He heard no response for several breathing moments. Then a quiet voice.

"Thanks, Professor." It sounded as though the boy were forcing words from his mouth. "I guess I owe you."

"You take care, Franklin. And I'm anxious to read that paper of yours. I'm sure it's a good one."

He terminated the call and took another sip of wine. He wondered how far Franklin and the group he worked for would go in order to feel safe again in their trade. He supposed it depended on how lucrative their trade was. In a worst case scenario, it was small potatoes and his employers would simply withdraw from Franklin, leaving him high and dry. Franklin would lose some supplemental income, but no real harm would have been done, and he would have avoided some inevitable jail time. In a best case scenario, it was part of a big operation, and his employers would want Franklin to continue doing business. So they would consider Whitehorse a thorn in their side, a problem to be reckoned with. Scare him? Hurt him? Worse? To Friese, it seemed like a win-win situation. He had started the pieces in motion, given the snowball a shove down the hill. It would be entertaining to see how it all played out.

With the movie's glorious wedding on Long Island shimmering in the den, he walked into the kitchen and sat his glass on the counter. He took a bag of prawns from the freezer and quickly thawed them in running water. In moments they were peeled and in a bowl by the stove, awaiting their transformation into a delicate shrimp scampi. Asparagus and a green salad would be the final touches to a simple but romantic dinner for two.

Healed at last. His ex had thrown him off his game—gutted his savings, made him stumble in his last teaching appointment so the coveted tenure had eluded him until now, poisoned his relationship with his daughter, who wanted nothing to do with him after the divorce. But he was back with a vengeance. A new house, a new car, a preeminent position at the university. *I'm a success, Mother, despite your dire predictions.*

Just as he spread a white tablecloth and lit two slim candles for ambiance, the doorbell rang. He walked to the door and opened it.

"Why, Grace. So pleased you could make it."

The young woman stood there while the rain pattered like cats' feet on her pink umbrella. Her face wore an expression of fear and excitement.

"Where are my manners? Come in out of the rain. Let me take that." Friese shook the umbrella, closed it, and stood it in the corner. "Let me take your wrap. Any problem finding the place?"

"No, Professor, your directions were excellent."

"Call me Sterling. Please, my dear."

Her eyes went wide as she absorbed the opulence around her. "What a lovely house!"

"Why, thank you. I moved in here only four months ago. It

may take a woman's touch to get the interior design just right. Perhaps you could help me with that?"

"I'd be delighted," she said, her red lips curling in a flirtatious smile.

"Let me pour you some wine and show you the rest of the house."

16. 3 Day Fish

Franklin Wise was terrified. *Cops after me? Shit! What am I gonna do?* The first step was to tell his boss. He yelled at his fellow musicians over the pounding rhythms of the dance music. "Gotta talk to Abe! Back in a minute!" The bass player and keyboardist waved back at him. The drummer was too absorbed in setting up to even notice.

Beyond the stage, the dance floor was a mass of heaving bodies, swaying in time to music that was felt more than heard, silhouetted by flashing colored lights. Mini-skirted servers were picking their way through the crowds standing around the edge of the floor, targeting tables with their drink orders. Smells of sweat mingled with an occasional whiff of marijuana.

Franklin untangled himself from the nests of instrument cables and made his way to a door down a hallway off the back right of the stage. A large man with a *don't-make-me* expression on his face flanked the doorway.

"Hey, Joey, I gotta see Abe."

"Mr. Sokolov isn't expecting you."

"Something's come up. It's like urgent. Please ask him if I can see him for a minute."

The man pointed a beefy finger at him. "Stay." Then he knocked twice and entered the room behind him. He emerged moments later. "You got two minutes." He opened the door and allowed the boy to pass.

"Frankie. What brings you here?" The man behind the desk had the eyes of a raptor, dark and piercing. He ran his left hand over his short, neatly trimmed beard, turning gray at the chin. His brown hair, also shading to gray along the sides, was perfectly coiffed. The faint memory of a scar between his left lower eyelid and the corner of his mouth only added to the dangerous allure of his face. "I've got lots of work to do. These ledgers." He waved his arm over the books on his desk as a magician might before performing a trick. "I've got you here six nights next month. That's all I can do. And you know I won't have another shipment for two weeks."

Franklin felt his heart begin to pound and his throat go dry. "Abe—Mr. Sokolov—I think I'm in trouble. There's a policeman asking questions about me at school."

Sokolov leaned forward in his chair, his full attention on the trembling boy. Franklin felt like a rabbit who had just been spied by a hungry hawk.

"What kind of questions?"

"About drugs. If I have connections. Selling. I don't know." The boy wanted to be anywhere but here, talking to this man. His hands began to shake, and he stuffed them into his pockets. "M-maybe I should just lay low for a while. Skip the next few shipments. What do you think?"

Sokolov sat back in his chair and grimaced. His eyes drifted toward the ceiling. "But you're good for business, Frankie. Those rich kids love you. You have a lot of steady customers. I'd hate to have to retire you."

Franklin didn't like the sound of the word "retire." He felt as though the room were getting darker, the walls closing in. "W-what would you like me to do, Mr. Sokolov?"

"Do you know the name of the policeman?"

"Charles Whitehorse. Right here in Driftwood." He blurted out the words as though he were spitting something foul-tasting from his mouth.

"Of course. *Dermo!*" The man's smile lacked any trace of humor. He lowered his voice to a whisper, which Franklin found even more unnerving. "Just go about your job. Business as usual. Let me handle this...inconvenience." He made a dismissive gesture with his hand. "Go."

"Anything you say, Mr. Sokolov." He scurried out the door as his boss addressed the man standing there.

"Iosif. Come in here please. I must speak with you."

Franklin dashed across the stage and stood for a moment before his guitar, trying to catch his breath. He bowed forward, hands on his knees.

"You OK, man?" It was Mack, the bassist. "You look like

you're about to hurl."

"Yeah. Fine. Just let me check my tuning. Let's open with *Valkyrie's Dream*."

"You got it."

Franklin willed his body to stop trembling. He pulled the leather guitar strap over his head and settled the instrument comfortably in his hands. By the time he tuned the last strings, he was breathing more normally. He walked back to Larry, their drummer, who was also in charge of the pyrotechnics.

"We all set to go?"

Larry gave him a thumb's up sign and twirled his drumsticks.

Franklin did a final check that everyone was ready and raised a fist to the sound man in the rear of the club. The dance music stopped abruptly, and in that same instant the stage erupted in fountains of brilliant sparks and flames. The startled dancers began to cheer. Franklin slammed a fast riff of power chords, and the band exploded in a deafening crash of metallic fury. The crowd roared in approval as more flames burst from the stage. The members of 3 Day Fish were the rulers of the galaxy.

The smoke from the fireworks captured the spotlights now trained on the band. Their bodies bounced with the frenetic rhythms of the song like jungle tribesmen gyrating in religious ecstasy. Franklin felt his long hair become wet with perspiration as his shirt glued itself to his back. He no longer thought of Abe or drugs or policemen. He was possessed by the music.

Minutes later the song ended, and the audience screamed for more. The band tore into their next ear-splitting piece. The night belonged to them.

After forty-five minutes of auditory assault, Franklin yelled into his microphone that he and the band were taking a short break. Before the crowd could begin to express its displeasure, the sound man piped in the recorded dance music again, even louder than it had been before. Franklin, Larry, Mack, and Jorge, their keyboardist, fought their way to a small table reserved for them in the back. Glasses of ice water and cola awaited them.

"Good set, man." Jorge slapped Franklin on the back.

"We are definitely smokin' tonight," agreed Larry.

"This crowd loves us." Franklin looked around at his mates. "We feed off their energy."

"Damn straight," said Mack.

"But I'm thinking our pyrotechnics are a little lame. We need something bigger. Flashier." Larry scratched his head. "Let me ask my cousin. He's really good at blowing stuff up."

"I gotta take a piss." Franklin was up out of his chair and pushing his way toward the restrooms. Happy revelers patted him on the back as he passed them by. He was always surprised at how clean the men's room was despite the crowds the club entertained. There was no graffiti on the walls—no hastily scribbled pictures of men's or women's genitalia, no phone numbers "for a great blow job." It reminded him that Abe ran a tight ship. There was no room for error in his operations. No room for loose ends.

He shuddered as he wondered what Abe would do to a very unfortunate policeman.

17. Healing

The week galloped by, each day looking like the one before. The sky remained an eggshell white from dawn to dusk, without a blemish, and the streets and the beaches began to dry out. Temperatures climbed to the mid-fifties, and sheltered areas felt even warmer. A February thaw heralded the coming spring, a welcome respite from the cold and storms of January.

Peter and Hammer had gotten into a routine. Peter awoke a half-hour earlier every morning so he could take Hammer for a brief walk around the neighborhood before he went to the gym for his regular workout. Hammer didn't seem to mind the dark and eagerly sniffed every shrub and light pole along the way. Peter fed him breakfast after he got back from the gym so he would be there to let him out for his after-breakfast business.

This morning was no different. As soon as Peter reached for the leash, Hammer was bouncing with excitement. "Hammer, you're like a flea on a hot griddle. That's how my mother described us kids when she told us she'd take us out for ice cream." He pulled on his windbreaker, attached the leash to Hammer's collar, and they were off.

"Each day's a new adventure, huh, boy?" The fog in the air drew large white cones under each streetlight. They made their way across the wet pavement to the north sidewalk of the development, where the houses ended and the woods began. They heard a crash in the dark underbrush off to the right. Hammer tugged at his leash, ready to give chase.

"Hang on, boy. Let him go. It's only a deer. We like deer. Remember?"

Peter became thoughtful. "In fact, I've been liking a lot of things lately. Have you noticed?" The dog barked once as if he understood. "Something's happening to me, boy. Like some log jam inside me is breaking up. Know what I mean?" He picked up the pace. "I've even made a new friend. Do you know how hard it is for a guy my age to make a new friend? It's like, if I didn't grow up with you or go to school with you it's not gonna happen. But it's happening."

He began an easy jog, and the dog followed suit. The air was clean and redolent with the fragrances of forest—moist earth and mold and the faint citrus smell of Douglas firs. For the first time in three years, he felt happy.

"I haven't dreamt about her in almost a week, Hammer. The girl on the beach. The one in white. Did you see her, too? Were you there on the beach that day?" He slowed down and took several breaths. "Do you suppose that was her arm you found?"

He looked at his watch. "Time to turn around, boy. I gotta get to the gym. Probably see my new friend, Chris, there. I'll have to get him to the house so you can meet him, too."

Within a half-hour, Peter was negotiating a parking spot at Driftwood Athletics. He started his workout with the machines on the lower level. Ten minutes later, Chris arrived and moved right to the free weights.

"Hi, Chris," Peter called from the Triceps Press.

"Hey, man." Chris walked over to him and extended his hand.

"Another night without the dreams."

The bearded man gave him a thumbs-up sign. "I'm feelin' better, too. Glad we talked."

"You mentioned going to a movie sometime. Can't do it Saturday. That's my cleaning and shopping day. But I could do it Sunday afternoon, if that'd work for you."

"Got nothin' planned. Why don't we do a matinee and then go out for a bite afterwards?"

"I owe you a meal, as I recall."

"I was hopin' you'd say that." Chris smiled. "Now I gotta go whip this body into shape. Catch you later."

Sunday dawned with a sun break. The rays ignited every blade of grass, every shrub, bedecked with moisture from the mists of the previous evening. After breakfast, Peter looked directly at Hammer. "Wanna go to the beach?"

The dog burst into a frenzy of excitement, prompting Peter

once again to wonder just how much English his dog understood. They were in the car within moments and at the parking lot fifteen minutes later.

Once down the stairs, he let Hammer off his leash, and the dog began to gambol about on the sand.

"It's good to be here, isn't it?" The experience with the woman in white was finally fading, freeing the beach to be the refuge it had been before. "It's good for the soul, Hammer. Don't you think?"

The dog barked and charged ahead, running down the sand for his first real exercise in a week. "Damn! You're fast, dog," Peter called to the black streak hurtling down the shore. "I guess you needed this."

Hammer finally returned, winded, and walked beside his master, tongue hanging from his mouth.

"Looks like you love it here as much as I do."

The tide was wrong to look for agates, so he just kept walking toward Cascadia Head. The clouds opened into another sun break, and the light turned the ocean a deep azure. The swells were low and regular, and the surf was a calming hush across the sand. Man and dog walked two miles north and then turned around. Hammer met several other dogs along the way, but each encounter was friendly.

Back at the car, Peter took out a steel bowl and a bottle of water and gave Hammer a long drink before he climbed into the car. "Better?" he said as he stroked the dog's head. "OK. Now hop in."

Once home, he gave Hammer a rawhide treat and went to his room to shower. With that completed, he dressed in a sweater and jeans and returned to the kitchen, where Hammer was still busy gnawing on his gift.

"I'm gonna take off for a while this afternoon. I expect you to guard the fort. You OK with that?" Hammer put the rawhide bone down long enough for one quick bark, then returned to his attempt to demolish it within the hour.

Peter smiled as he entered the garage and got into his car.

As he did so, he looked into the next stall at Helen's black X-5. He had never sold it after her death, clinging to his memories of her behind the wheel. Several times he had been on the verge of putting it on *craigslist*, but each time something held him back. He had maintained the registration and insurance, faithfully started it several times a month, even driven it to Newport and back every few weeks. It didn't bring her back, of course, but it provided him a slim measure of comfort nonetheless. He nodded his head as the idea struck him. Hammer would be much more comfortable riding in the back of that SUV than being scrunched up in the back seat of his little 325i. "OK, Hammer. I guess you're family now. Time to switch to a family car."

He met Chris at the Driftwood Cinema 8. "So what do you know about this movie?"

"I've heard we should fasten our seat belts before it starts."

"I like the sound of that." As the clerk printed his ticket, Peter turned to Chris. "How about we try that Italian place afterwards? *Trattoria Italiana*? Been there?"

"Oh, yeah. I had their penne pasta and sausage a few weeks ago, and it's terrific."

Chris bought himself a popcorn, but Peter decided to save himself for a big lunch later. As advertised, the film was funny and action-packed, and both men enjoyed themselves immensely. Three hours later, they were being seated at a table with a beautiful ocean view.

"Split a bottle of wine?" Peter asked.

"I'm not much of a wine drinker. You'll have to show me how."

"Deal." He ordered a bottle of Primitivo and perused the menu. "You mentioned the penne and sausage, and that sounds good to me."

"I think I'll do the same. I should probably try something different, but that was pretty hard to beat."

They ate slowly as they became more and more comfortable with each other. Peter was surprised at how much he enjoyed the big man's company. *Safe* was the word that occurred to him. He felt safe around Chris.

"I don't think I told you before. The week after the woman disappeared, I found a severed arm on the beach. Or rather, my dog found it."

"You found what? Holy Christmas! An arm?"

"A woman's arm. Diamond engagement ring on her finger. Cops think maybe a shark attack victim. Kept it out of the papers. I'm guessing it belonged to the woman in white."

Chris shook his head back and forth. "That's just crazy. Nightmare city."

Peter nodded in agreement. "I've been thinking about it a lot. Kind of spooky." He raised his glass. "To change the subject, what do you think of the wine?"

"It's pretty good, actually. Goes real nice with our pasta."

Peter took another drink. "Did you like being a SEAL?" He reconsidered. "Don't answer that if you'd rather not. I don't mean to pry."

"You're not pryin'. I liked it OK for the first few years. But it wore on me. Some of the decisions I had to make. People died that didn't have to. Glad I'm out now. Too late to save my marriage though."

"You said last time you had a son?"

"Yeah. Stayed in California with his mom. Almost thirty now. Always worried about him. Had real trouble socializin' all through school. What do they call that? Asperger's? You probably know all about that. But he's got himself a new job, and it sounds like he's got a girlfriend to boot, so things are lookin' up."

"I've got a daughter. Mira. She's married to a surgeon. They're in California, too." He sighed. "I love that girl. She's so bright and smart and beautiful. Teaches elementary school." He raised his glass. "And I've got a new granddaughter I'm going to see over spring break."

"Good for you." Chris took another big forkful of sausage. He chuckled. "Let me know if you see any strings of cheese in my beard. Actually thinkin' about choppin' the thing off."

"Whoa! That could be traumatic. Looks like you've had it

a long time."

"Yeah. Haven't made up my mind yet. If I do, I won't know who I am when I look in the mirror."

"That's been my feeling for the past three years—ever since Helen died. Not knowing who I am. How I fit into a world without her in it. But that's changing."

Chris raised his glass and Peter joined him. "Here's to healin'. And new worlds."

18. Wrong Place, Wrong Time

Driving his little Honda announced that Whitehorse was off-duty, as did the sport shirt and slacks. Chloe was in the passenger seat.

"So where to, darling?" she said as she fastened her seat belt.

"What kind of food are you in the mood for?"

"Some kind of fresh fish."

"In that case, instead of going out, would you let me cook you a dinner? Stop at Hook, Line, and Sinker first and see what's come in?"

"Sounds like a plan. Let me run back inside quick and pick up that bottle of Chardonnay I got at that tasting yesterday." Within moments she was back in the car, wine in hand.

It was a quick drive to the fish store on 101. Paul ran a cash-only business, which could be difficult sometimes since Whitehorse never carried much cash. He checked his wallet and saw he had $25.

"Almost didn't recognize you out of uniform," the man behind the counter said. "What'll it be, Charley?"

"Hey, Paul. Anything special in today?"

"You bet. Just got some fresh razor clams down from Washington. That only happens about four times a year. Rest of the time all we get is frozen. They'll be all gone in another hour."

"Then by all means."

"They're in one-pound bags. Twenty bucks."

"Here you go." He handed the man a bill and took the clams.

"Need any ice to keep 'em cold?"

"Nope. They're going right into the frying pan, and I live only five minutes from here."

"Good deal, man. Enjoy."

In the car on the way back to his house, Chloe asked, "Got any veggies at home to go with this?"

"Got some asparagus to roast and a tomato we can slice

up."

"Perfect. We'll keep it simple."

They were eating within a half-hour.

"My compliments to the chef," Chloe said as she raised her glass.

"Thanks. That's about the limit of my culinary expertise." He took a sip of wine and looked at her. "What do you hear from Kaitlynn?"

"You know I try to visit her every weekend. She seems to be doing well. Did I tell you she finished her diploma a while ago, and now she's taking college courses? We're hoping they let her out early." She shook her head from side to side. "But I'm still not used to the idea of having a daughter in prison."

"I don't think you can ever get used to something like that." He took a breath. "What does she think of me? After all, Tony and I are the ones who arrested her."

"She doesn't hold anything against you. She understands. She was so relieved that she didn't get charged with murder for that poor man's death."

"He shot first. Her lawyer made a good case for self-defense. And the expert witnesses for Stockholm Syndrome really won the day."

She put her glass on the table. "I get a feeling there's something else, Charley. Something you're not asking me. Like, how does Kaitlynn feel about *us*? If that's what you're wondering, relax. She's glad we're dating." A sheepish grin spread over her face. "In fact, she thinks you're the best thing that's ever happened to me. She wants you to come with me and visit her sometime."

He breathed a sigh of relief. "I was really worried..."

"No need. She's a good girl. Now that she's out from under Raven's spell, she'll do just fine."

Both were silent for a moment. "Can I get you anything else, honey?"

"I'm stuffed. But I could use a little more wine."

He refilled her glass and his own.

Chloe pursed her lips. "OK. I gotta ask this. I hope I don't scare you away."

"You're not scary."

"Well, give me a minute." She cleared her throat. "Do you think you'll ever get married again?"

"Whew! Right for the jugular." He smiled. "I've actually been thinking about that myself lately. I guess if the right woman came along..."

"Charley!"

"Hey, that was a joke. You're the right woman. No question about that. My worry is the burden I'd be laying on you. Marrying a cop is no bed of roses. That's the main reason I haven't asked you."

"Well, mister. Now that Raven and Jack are gone, our drama quotient is way down. I think our little town can return to its sleepy old self."

Whitehorse frowned. "Not yet, I'm afraid. I haven't told you about the arm."

"The arm?"

He stroked the tablecloth with his fingers, then took a sip of wine. "The same guy that reported the woman who was swept away found a severed arm on the beach a week later."

Chloe's eyes went round. "What the—? An arm? Are you kidding?"

He raised his right hand. "Scout's honor. A woman's left arm. Complete with an engagement ring on the third finger."

Chloe sat back and exhaled noisily. "Jesus, Charley! I can't believe it. What's happening to our town?"

"Damned if I know."

She grimaced. "It's that girl's arm?"

"Has to be. Shark. Anyway, I should find out soon. I turned it over to Amy Cranston, the M.E. in Newport. She'll do a DNA check against some stuff I got from the girl's dorm room at PCU. I expect her to give me a call anytime."

"Does she have the ring?"

"I've got it at the station. It's a helluva rock. I'll bet it's worth a small fortune."

"Hmmm. You made it sound like the girl didn't try to protect herself from the wave. Like it was almost a suicide. Why would she have done that with a fortune on her finger?"

"Maybe found out her fiancé was cheating on her?"

Chloe nodded. "Maybe."

Whitehorse took a final sip of wine. "Hon, I've got a long day ahead of me tomorrow. Mind if I bring you home now?"

"Want some help with the dishes first?"

"Nope. I'll just throw them in the dishwasher."

"I did scare you, didn't I?"

"No, darling. Honest. I'm really beat. And I promise we'll talk more about...us next time."

"OK, but I'll hold you to it."

They walked outside and he helped her into the car. Their date ended with a kiss and he was back home twenty minutes later.

He was at the department by 7:00 A.M. the next day. He opened the shop and put on the coffee. Chiara, their purple-haired student secretary, wasn't due until 8:00, as was Esperanza. He busied himself with emails.

When the hour struck, Chiara burst in, ear glued to her cell phone, in the middle of a conversation. "Hey. I'm at work. I gotta go. Call you back later." She turned to Whitehorse. "My best friend Hayley says she has a better work-study than I do. No way. Being here with you guys is the best."

"What's she doing?"

"Working in a bank. Says the assistant manager is teaching her how to spot counterfeit money, phony checks. And something new is going down with ATMs. She'll tell me all about it tonight." She looked around the office. "Tony not here yet?"

"Probably still dropping his kid off at school. He'll call if he thinks he'll be running late."

"Did you see the note I left you? Strangest call."

"Yeah, I was just reading it."

"It's like this woman wanted to know the schedule here or

something. Who goes out for traffic calls. Who takes domestic calls. Do we have a system we follow. It was weird. Anyway, I told her you guys usually swap off a couple hours at a time unless things get really busy. Tony would be at the desk for the first couple of hours today and you'd be out responding. Then you'd trade. Not sure what she really wanted."

"OK. No harm done."

Just then the phone rang and Chiara picked it up. "Driftwood Police Department. How may I direct your call? Yes, ma'am. Are there any firearms in the house? And what's your address? So you're not at home?" She shifted her weight from one foot to the next. "The Blue Whale? We'll send an officer right away." She turned to Whitehorse as she completed the call. "Lady at the Blue Whale Motor Inn. Maybe the same one from yesterday. Said her husband just got back from the night shift. High or drunk. Yelling, breaking stuff. They're in the Blue Whale Motor Inn while the floors get refinished in their house. Sounded scared. I could hear him yelling in the background. No guns. Room one-eleven."

"Looks like I'm up." Whitehorse stood and adjusted his belt. "Man, do I hate domestic violence calls."

"Didn't you get shot once?"

"Yeah. Years ago. Minor injury, but it could have been a lot worse if it was two inches over."

The phone rang again. "It's Tony. Wants to talk to you."

Whitehorse picked up. "Hi, partner. Running a little late?"

"Just got my son's school project safely through the door. He's been working on it for three weeks and we couldn't take any chances. I'll see you in a few."

"Well, I'm heading out to the Blue Whale. Some guy in 111 threatening his wife."

"Hey, mind the store. The Blue Whale can't be more than two or three blocks from here. I'll handle it. Any guns?"

"No guns. But wait for me. I'll back you up. We'll do it together."

"C'mon. Just a little family squabble. I'll probably have it all wrapped up before you get here."

"Well, I'm on my way."

At the Blue Whale, the young woman in room 111 returned the phone to its cradle on the nightstand. Her brown hair was disheveled, and the eye shadow smudged under her eye looked like a big bruise. "How'd I sound, Joey?"

"You convinced me, baby. You shoulda been a movie star." The big man was smiling as he pounded a billy club into the palm of his left hand. "Your Beretta's under that pillow—in case he doesn't go down with the first love tap. If he gets his gun out, back me up."

"I'll keep you safe, Beefcakes," she said with a chuckle. "In a few minutes, Officer Charles Whitehorse will be walking through that door, and we'll teach him a little lesson he won't forget any time soon."

19. The Whale's Tale

Esperanza kissed his ten-year-old son Gavin on the forehead and waved to him as he left. His Leaning Tower of Pisa project was safely ensconced in the corner of Ms. Schreiner's classroom. He had been afraid it would collapse before he ever received a grade for it, so his father had helped him get it to school in one piece. The light rain had only complicated matters.

"Bye, Dad," he called to him. "Love you."

Whenever Esperanza heard him say that, it brought tears to his eyes, though he would admit that to no one. Gavin had been born three months premature and had required open heart surgery. The image of that precious baby with tubes and IV's sprouting out of him like malignant vines still caused him to shudder. *I'm one blessed sonofabitch*, he told himself several times a day. For his wife to have given birth when such medical treatments had become almost routine still made him feel profound gratitude.

"Time to get this day on the road," he muttered to himself. He had checked in with his partner and thought he could handle a little family squabble on the way to the department. Although he was wary of domestic disputes, he decided it would be safe because there were no guns involved, and it was in the semi-public space of a motel room—without a drawer of kitchen knives nearby.

He got into his cruiser and pulled out of the school parking lot. The rain had begun in earnest. He saw no point in turning on his siren for the short distance he had to go. There was no traffic except for the occasional empty school bus headed back to the station to await the after school pick-up.

A block along his route, he knew this was not the kind of neighborhood in which his colleague had been inquiring last month. Houses were a third the size, lawns were not manicured to perfection, and an occasional jalopy that would never drive the streets again would be parked to the side, rusting silently. To call them "starter homes" would be a misnomer. This is where you went when you lost your job and had to sell your house, when your wife clobbered you in the divorce, when your disability afforded you little else. It was far down the slippery slope of misfortune.

After all the mandatory training he had received, the policeman still struggled with profiling. He wanted to be better than that, to rise above the feelings engrained in him by years of living in Driftwood, but he had to admit to himself that he felt edgier in this neighborhood than he had along the bluff above the ocean. He knew wealthy people also committed crimes, but he still felt safer there than here.

As he pulled into the small parking lot, he shook his head. There were always vacancies at the Blue Whale Motor Inn. Locals called it "The Beached Whale," with good reason. Established in 1977, it had gone through a succession of owners who had not been kind to it. The neon sign announcing *A/C, Cable TV* had long since stopped working. The roof, home to raucous flocks of seagulls, was as white as the snows on Mount Hood. Worn out mattresses, peeling paint, and poor reviews on *Yelp* kept tourists away every season. Each year some energetic city councilman would try to get it closed and torn down, and each year it clung tenaciously to its small plot of ground one block from the shore. Rumors abounded that it was a front owned by Russians headquartered in Portland, but no proof was ever forthcoming. It remained a blot on the town's face, a blemish that embarrassed the Chamber of Commerce.

He stopped the car at the office and got out. A bell rang as he entered. The smells of stale cigarette smoke and burnt coffee assailed his nostrils. As he shook the rain from his shoulders, an old man with a scruffy gray beard looked up from the newspaper he was reading behind the counter. The man adjusted his glasses and looked the policeman up and down.

"Wet out there. Something I can do for you?"

"Yeah. My name is Officer Esperanza. I'm here to check out a complaint we received about the occupants in 111. Arguing. Fighting."

"I ain't heard nothin', but have at it. I always steer clear of that stuff. Live longer that way. Want a key?"

"Yeah. Just in case. But I expect they'll open up."

The man grabbed a key from the rack on the wall behind him. "Here you go."

"I'll bring it back when I'm done."

"Wasn't worried none."

Esperanza left the office and walked down the pavement. Rain pattered off the brim of his hat. The doors to the rooms looked old and battered. Here and there peeling mauve paint revealed a deep blue underneath. He stopped in front of room 111. *Who rents a room in Bed Bug Bungalow?* he thought. *I wouldn't stay here on a bet.*

He knocked three times. "Driftwood Police. Open the door please."

The door creaked inward. A short woman with a black eye squinted at him. Her white blouse was ripped at the collar and her brown hair was in disarray.

"Are you all right, ma'am? You called about trouble with your husband? Is he here?" He crossed the threshold.

"You're not the little Indian!"

"Ma'am?"

Just then a large man lunged from behind the door. Esperanza turned just as the man struck him with a club. It was a glancing blow, but still strong enough to stagger him. He toppled onto the woman, and both sprawled on the floor. The woman screamed in his ear. The man came at him again with the club. Esperanza rolled off the woman onto his back. With all the speed and strength he could muster, he thrust his foot up and into his attacker's crotch. The man doubled over in pain, and the woman leaped onto the bed. Esperanza scrambled to his feet. As he reached for his service weapon, he could see from the corner of his eye the woman snatching a pistol from under the pillow.

The muzzle flashed...

20. Officer Down

Whitehorse saw his partner's car at the office and pulled up next to it. Exiting his vehicle, he left the engine running and the wipers sweeping back and forth across the windshield, metronomes for the rhythm of the rain. He hurried inside.

"Another one?" the man behind the counter said. "Your buddy's down in 111."

"Have you heard anything?"

The man grimaced. "Like I told your friend, I don't mess where I don't belong." With trembling fingers, he drew a cigarette from a crumpled package in his shirt pocket. "I got another key if you want it."

"Thanks."

"Be careful." The man returned to his newspaper with a swift motion that led Whitehorse to believe he felt he had said too much.

He walked across the parking lot through the rain toward the door of 111, but stopped as he drew close. No voices came from the room. A premonition of dread swept through his body like a cold draft. The hair on his arms and the back of his neck stood up. He pulled his gun from its holster and stood to the side of the door as he knocked.

"Driftwood Police! Tony, you in there?" Nothing. He banged on the door again, louder this time. "Police! Open up!"

A flood of adrenaline pumped his body to high alert. He could hear his pulse pounding in his ears. A thought flashed through his mind. *Call Chiara and have her send back up from Newport.* But his partner was in there and he couldn't wait another second.

With his gun at the ready, he inserted the key and turned the knob. He pushed the door open and entered cautiously, scanning for an enemy hiding behind the door or the bed, waiting to burst out of the bathroom. Then he saw Esperanza on the floor at the foot of the bed. His head lay in a red halo on the rug.

"Tony! Tony!" He called it in. "Officer down, Chiara! Tony's been shot! Send an ambulance stat! And get Newport here now. One or more suspects, armed and dangerous." He heard her gasp, but hung up before she could say anything.

He got down on his knees and whispered in his friend's ear. "You're gonna be OK, man. You hear me? Just hang on. Help is coming." He got up and ran to the bathroom for a towel to stanch the bleeding. He rushed back to his fallen friend and gently wrapped his head, all the while whispering prayers. In minutes, he heard the ambulance siren. He ran to the door and ushered in the team of medics. With grim efficiency, they began attending the wounded policeman. As Whitehorse took a step away, he saw what looked to be a hastily scrawled note on the nightstand.

Back off Whitehorse if you know what's good for you and your friends

What the hell? Back off? From what? He mentally reviewed his open investigations, trying to find some clue or connection. Nothing rang a bell. Yet somehow he must have crossed the wrong person. He promised himself to review the list of new parolees when he got back to the department. For now, he pulled on a pair of the rubber gloves he always carried with him and put the note in a plastic bag. Then he saw the ballpoint pen behind the phone and bagged that as well.

By this time the medics had Esperanza on a gurney and wheeled him toward the door. "Officer Whitehorse," one called over his shoulder. "Initial examination looks good. As far as I can tell, the bullet didn't penetrate his skull, just scraped along the whole side of it. Took a fair amount of bone with it. Hopefully none of the fragments blew inside. We'll know more after an X-ray. I'm guessing he's got a helluva concussion."

As they crossed the threshold, Whitehorse leaned over and whispered in his partner's ear, "I'll get 'em, Tony. You have my word."

He walked outside as they hoisted the stretcher into the

ambulance. Rain mixed with his tears as the ambulance sped off, siren blaring, lights flashing. He stood there, mesmerized by the chatter of the rain on his hat and shoulders. The sky was an unrelenting gray, the perfect accompaniment to his mood.

Who was targeting him and his friends? And did friends extend as far as Chloe? Was she in danger? He pounded his right fist into the palm of his left hand. What the hell was going on? He stepped back under the canopy that ran the length of the motor court. He'd have to tell her. Better safe than sorry. But he hated to worry her.

Away from the rain, he pulled his phone from his pocket. "Hi, Chloe. Sorry to bother you at work, but Tony's been shot." He heard her sharp intake of breath.

"My God, Charley, is he OK?"

"He's alive but unconscious. We'll know more after they get him to the hospital."

"Are you all right?"

"It happened before I got here. Perps were gone before I arrived. But I've got to tell you something else." He grimaced and inhaled, wondering how to proceed.

"Spit it out, Charley."

"They left a note. Addressed to me. Told me to back off if I knew what was good for me and my friends."

"Back off? What did they mean?"

"Damned if I know. Can't think of any recent cases where I rubbed somebody that wrong. I'll check on new releases when I get back to the office."

"Do you think you're in danger?"

"Not sure. I've gotta figure out what they want me to keep my nose out of first. But I want you to be extra careful, OK?"

"Me?"

"Yeah. They said 'If you know what's good for you and your friends.'"

"I don't like the sound of that."

"Me neither. You're probably OK, but stay alert. It's dark by the time you get out of work, so don't walk out to your car in the parking lot by yourself. And leave the front light on at home so your doorway isn't dark."

Chloe was silent for a long time. "This is what you meant, isn't it?"

"What?"

"When you told me you were reluctant to ask me to marry you? The cop's life?"

"Yeah. Yeah. I guess you're right. This kind of stuff."

"Well, you can't scare me off, mister. I'm expecting a proposal in the not-too-distant future." She ended the call.

Whitehorse found himself smiling and shaking his head, in spite of himself. "Damn, I love you woman," he said aloud.

As he spoke, the cruisers from Newport streamed into the lot.

21. Spilled Coffee

It was 10:30 in the faculty lounge and both professors were between classes. Rain streamed down the windows in shallow waves, blurring the view of the Douglas firs beyond. It was perfect weather for a cup of hot coffee.

"Where've you been, Peter? Haven't seen you in a long time."

"I could be asking you the same thing, Sterling. We just haven't connected. What's your excuse?"

"Been after Brady to let me take on doctoral students. He's softening up. I should know for sure within another week, but I think it's a go. I really impressed him with that last article of mine."

"Congratulations. My mug to you." Peter raised his coffee cup and smiled at his friend.

Sterling joined him in the toast. "I've been meaning to ask. Did you ever check out either of those therapists?"

"No, I didn't. Would you believe I got a dog?"

"You? Dr. I'm-Never-Getting-A-Damn-Dog Bristol? No, I don't believe it."

"It's true." He took another sip of his coffee. "Actually, he got me. Found me on the beach. When he found the arm."

"What?"

"Oh, I forgot. I haven't had a chance to tell you. I found a woman's severed arm on the beach."

Sterling coughed and almost spilled his coffee. "No way. First you see a woman get swept out to sea and then you find an arm?"

"Crazy, isn't it? Some days I don't believe it myself. But it's true. I found a damn arm on the beach. I can talk about it now, but it really shook me. Just getting over it."

"You said it was a woman's arm?"

"Yep. Had a big diamond engagement ring on the third finger. What a rock!"

This time Sterling did spill his coffee. "Shit! I'm sorry.

Don't let it get on your pants. Let me get some napkins." He ran to the counter by the coffee pot and grabbed a wad of paper towels. "I'll get that. I'm not usually so clumsy." In moments he had cleaned up the mess. He took his cup to refill it as he disposed of the wet towels in the waste basket. When he returned to the table, he took a sip and paused. "You said there was a ring?" He lowered his voice to a conspiratorial whisper. "Just between you and me, did it find its way into your pocket?"

Peter laughed. "Purloin the diamond?" he said with a Shakespearean flair. "To embark upon a desperate life of crime? Methinks you jest." He raised his mug again and smiled. "Actually, I saw Officer Whitehorse bag the arm with the ring still on its finger."

Sterling sat back in his chair as though Peter had slapped him. He took a breath. "Sonofabitch," he muttered.

Peter looked confused at the soured expression on his friend's face. "What's the matter?"

"It seems I can't get away from that guy." The biologist frowned. "Did I tell you that last year he tried to illegally search Dean Wasserman's office? Without consulting the Dean's family? Or that he came unannounced into my classroom? I guess he was mad because I told Brady what he was doing and Brady got Effling from Security to put a stop to it. Anyway, the little bastard tried to embarrass me in front of my students. That guy's a real loose cannon."

"I had no idea." Peter knit his brows. "Thanks for the heads-up."

"Yeah. I'd stay far away from him if I were you." He stood up. "Well, I have to get back to my office. I'll catch up with you later." He tossed his remaining coffee in the sink, rinsed his cup, and waved as he left the lounge.

Peter finished his coffee but sat for a moment longer. He got none of the bad vibe from Whitehorse that Sterling had ranted about. In fact, he was surprised at the intensity of his friend's reaction. Still, why would a policeman search the office of a heart attack victim? That had to be illegal without a warrant, but why even seek a warrant? Was there some question about the Dean's death? And how could a policeman get away with harassing a college professor in the middle of a class?

Peter shook his head back and forth as he tried to make sense of the troubling encounter. And Sterling had spilled his coffee at the mention of the diamond ring. Was that just a coincidence, or did he know something about that ring?

Certainly he and Sterling had grown apart after Helen's death. No more dinners out, no more concerts or plays. "But that was my fault." He got up from the table and rinsed out his cup. It was only now with the advent of Hammer and Chris that he was beginning to appreciate how depressed he had been. Before Helen's illness, he had taken the younger professor under his wing, welcoming him to the campus, helping him negotiate all the hoops, supporting him as he adjusted to his divorce. Looking back now, he could see that Sterling had withdrawn also once he was fully engaged at the university. He never spoke about women or dating and changed the topic whenever Peter asked. Conversations became short and superficial—a book or movie review, comments about the weather. Did his discomfort at knowing Helen was dying make their relationship awkward, or was it something else altogether?

He left the lounge puzzled. Quick steps brought him back to his office in a few minutes, just long enough to help him decide to call Officer Whitehorse and ask him directly. Ostensibly, he'd be calling about the arm and the ring—just out of curiosity, of course. But maybe he could find out more about what had happened last year.

22. Poking the Hornets' Nest

He's in ICU. No visitors for now. We've put him into a medically-induced coma to prevent any further brain swelling." The surgeon spoke without emotion, relaying the facts as she knew them. Her white lab coat was unbuttoned, revealing the OR scrubs she wore underneath. Disposable booties still covered her shoes. "We got them all."

"The bone fragments?" Whitehorse struggled to keep his voice calm.

"Yes. Several chips of bone were pushed inward from the wound. They didn't penetrate too far, but we still had to do a fair amount of scraping around. The good news is that we expect your partner to make a complete recovery."

Whitehorse exhaled in relief. "When do you think he'll be awake?"

"Check with me late tomorrow. We should have a better idea by then."

Whitehorse thanked her and turned to leave. It seemed so surreal. Their quiet little town had erupted in violence. A woman lost, a severed arm, a gunshot partner, a written threat. And a whopping diamond ring. *Am I seeing patterns where there are none—imagining associations between unrelated events? Is it coincidence or connection?* Tony called him the "Tracker" as a joke, but there was a serious side to his moniker. He was relentless and obsessive in the pursuit of clues. But he was coming up dry this time. Meanwhile, he felt he had somehow poked a hornets' nest. That thought triggered a memory that shamed him deeply:

At six-years-old, neighbors began calling him "Geronimo" because of his frequent raids into their yards, stealing balls and bicycles and any other toys left unattended by their children. His father would discipline his wayward son the only way he knew how—beating him with a leather strap or willow switch. Those encounters left a residue of anger in the boy that sometimes exploded in fights and bullying. Other parents cautioned their children against playing with "the wild Indian." Today the extended family had come together to eat and drink and remember. He wasn't hungry and was prowling the perimeter with the small bow and arrow his grandfather had given him for his birthday. He had spotted the hornets' nest in the shrub yesterday and decided to show his cousins. As the little girls and boys gathered around the bush, he explained, "You have to lean in close to see it. Right there in the middle." Then he poked the nest with his bow and ran. He could hear the screams of his cousins behind him, fleeing in terror as the wasps stung them again and again. He laughed and hid in the woods.

The rain woke him from his unpleasant reverie. It still pained him to remember the harm he had done as a child. The hornets' nest was among the worst of his escapades. He hadn't been stung at all, but the children around him had been severely hurt. His cousin Rachel had to be hospitalized. She had never spoken to him again.

He closed his coat and adjusted his cap and collar to keep the rain from dripping down the back of his neck. He got into the cruiser and fastened his seat belt. Forensics from Newport would check the note and pen and telephone for fingerprints. They had found the shell casing as well. Still no word from Amy on whether or not there was a DNA match. The Medical Examiner had given him the ring for safe-keeping. "Don't want to lose that little trinket among the body parts in here," she had joked.

He started the car. The ring was locked up in the little evidence cabinet Tony and he maintained back at the station. He wondered what stories the ring would tell if it could.

He called Chiara. "Heading back. Anything I should know about?"

"Newport's sending someone over to help you out. You'll get a little time off tonight."

"Good. I need it. Gotta love that Newport crew."

"So how's Tony doing?"

"Stable for now. They're keeping him in a coma for a while to prevent any more brain swelling. But they think he's gonna be OK."

"Thank goodness. I'm praying for him."

"Well, keep it up. I think it's working. See you soon."

The car was silent, except for the swish of the wiper blades. *That bullet was meant for me*, he thought. *I was supposed to take that call. But what did I do to provoke it? Where is the hornets' nest?* He had no answer to that.

He reached the station and pulled his car in next to Chiara's. He entered the building and shook the rain from his coat and hat and hung them on the hook. Water was dripping into the pots in the far corner. "Let me empty those," he said.

"Hi, Charley." Her face was downcast. "So sorry about Tony."

"Yeah." He grabbed the pots and dumped them into the sink in the restroom. After replacing them in the corner, he returned to his desk and sat heavily in the chair. "I'll call tomorrow and find out when we can go to see him. I just wish I knew what was happening."

"What do you mean?"

"There was a note in the motel room telling me to back off. I have no idea what I'm supposed to back off from. Would you please pull a list of all the parolees released in the last two months? Maybe somebody has it in for me."

"Sure thing, Boss."

As Chiara entered the search on her computer, Whitehorse unlocked the cabinet behind his desk and withdrew the diamond ring. The band was scuffed and dirty from its sojourn on the beach, but the stone still sparkled. He held it close, turning it over and over, hoping to find an inscription with some kind of identifying information inside the band—a name, a date, anything that he might be able to pursue further. It was blank.

Chiara looked up from the computer screen. "That's quite a rock, all right. I'd let my boyfriend give me something like that any day."

Whitehorse took out his notebook and reviewed what the cab driver had said. *"I ask her what her groom is like and she mumbles something like* cow chez spay fud. *"*

Just then the phone rang. "Driftwood Police Department. How may I direct your call?" She put her hand over the mouthpiece. "It's the M. E."

Whitehorse picked up. "Hi, Amy. So what's the news? We got a match?" His face fell.

"What?" Chiara couldn't contain her curiosity. She got up from her chair and leaned over Whitehorse's desk.

"You're sure?" He exhaled. "Yeah. That catches me completely by surprise. Thanks for all your help." He hung up the phone and looked at his receptionist. "Goddamn it," he hissed between clenched teeth. "It wasn't our woman in the waves. The arm wasn't hers." He shook his head back and forth, still not believing what he had just heard. "We've got two bodies in the water."

23. The Stew (and the Plot) Thicken

Hey, Hammer! Wanna go out for a short walk?" Peter stood in the doorway and put down his briefcase as the dog came racing to him, tail wagging, body shimmying, Peter's slipper dangling from his mouth. "Sound like a good idea? I thought so. Let me change my shoes first." He reached out and scratched the dog behind the ears. "And thanks for the slipper, buddy."

A quick trip to the bedroom and he slipped into his walking shoes. Hammer eagerly presented his collar as he leaned over to fasten the dog's leash. "You're in luck. It's stopped raining for now. Let's go."

They went to their favorite route, along the edge of the woods. The air smelled clean and fresh from the day's rain. "In a couple of months we'll be able to do this in the daylight, Hammer. That'll be fun." The dog relieved himself against a small shrub and trotted happily beside his master.

"It was a good day, boy. Classes went well. Every student handed in papers on time, for once. I just wonder what's going on with my friend Sterling."

Hammer looked at him and cocked his head.

"Well, I'll get to the bottom of it. I'm going to call that policeman myself."

A wet fog began descending over them, drawing halos around the streetlights and adding to the eerie quiet that enveloped the small community of houses. Droplets from the trees clicked onto the pavement. Hammer picked up the scent of something, but Peter was able to pull him back on his leash.

He looked at his watch. "Time we turn around, boy. I'll get you some dinner."

Looking as though he understood completely what his master had just said, Hammer spun around and tugged Peter toward home.

"Hungry, huh? Lead the way."

Once back inside, Peter dried Hammer's paws with a

towel. "How about a treat tonight? A can of the chunky wet stuff?"

Hammer bounced eagerly at Peter's words. In moments, he was muzzle-down into what was described on the label as "Steak 'n' Gravy."

Peter used the time to call the police station. "May I please speak with Officer Whitehorse?"

"Is this an urgent matter?" Chiara asked.

"Oh, no. I'm Peter Bristol. I'm the guy who reported the woman swept out to sea. Found the arm."

"Of course. You caught him just as he was leaving. I'll put him on."

"Hi, Professor Bristol. Please don't tell me you've found something else on the beach."

"No, no. I was just curious. Any identification of the arm? Was it the woman I saw?"

Peter heard him hesitate for a moment. "I'm really not at liberty to say, Professor. It's still an ongoing investigation."

"Oh, sorry. I don't mean to violate protocol. Just one more question, if I may. Is there any truth to the rumors I've heard at school?"

"What kind of rumors?"

"That you searched Dean Wasserman's office illegally last year and harassed a professor while he was teaching a class?" He heard a long silence on the other end.

"Those rumors aren't exactly accurate." More silence. "I had a warrant to search the Dean's office. And I had a question about a salamander that I wanted to ask a biologist about."

"A salamander?"

"Yeah. The Rough-skinned newt."

It was Peter's turn to be silent. Finally, he said, "Thank you for your time, Officer. I won't keep you any longer."

"Call me any time, Professor."

Peter put his phone back into his pocket. "What do you suppose is going on, Hammer?" The dog didn't look up from his dinner. "I know. You've got more important things to do right now. But I'm puzzled. If the arm did belong to the woman, don't you think he would have just said so? And he did say he had a warrant to search the Dean's office. Why? And what the hell is a Rough-skinned newt? This is getting curiouser and curiouser."

On impulse, he called Chris. "You had supper yet?"

"Gonna take my break in about thirty minutes. Why? What's up?"

"Interested in going back to The Barnacle?"

"Sure. Mack makes a killer Irish stew, and it's a good night for that. When I don't have a Reuben, I go for the stew."

"OK. Sounds good. See you there in half an hour."

A thick lamb stew did sound good tonight. He let the dog out for his after-dinner business and changed into a pair of jeans. He had just enough time to go through his emails before leaving, but Hammer was scratching at the back slider. When he let him in, the dog followed him into the office. Peter logged onto his account and promptly deleted all but two messages. "Do you believe the crap I get on here, boy? I'll save those two for later when I have time to respond to them."

As he was about to log off, an idea struck him. He opened Google and looked up Rough-skinned newt. He skimmed the article he found. "This salamander is the most poisonous amphibian in North America. Its skin, ovaries, and eggs contain tetrodotoxin (TTX), the same neurotoxin found in pufferfish. It causes paralysis and death by asphyxiation."

"What the fuck? Oh, sorry, Hammer. I don't usually talk like that. Not into f-bombs. But why is a policeman searching a dead man's office and asking about a lethal salamander? Tell me, boy. What's happening?"

He logged off and stood up. "I'm going out for my supper. I'll only be an hour or so. Hold down the fort."

In moments, he was in the garage. He decided to take the X-5, the "family vehicle." He smiled at the thought of how well Hammer took to riding in the rear of the bigger car. It was indeed Hammer's BMW. As he pulled out and shut the garage door, he saw a fine mist hanging in the air, congealing on his windshield, obscuring his vision. He turned a switch, and the timed wiper began to scrub the glass clean every few minutes. Before long, he saw the Coronado Cab as he drew into the small lot at The Barnacle.

"Hey, buddy." Chris stood and extended his hand as Peter approached. "This was a good idea. Mack says the stew is great tonight, and Billy will be bringin' over a couple of beers."

"Good to see you, too. It's definitely a night for comfort food." He took off his coat and hat and sat down across from his friend. Billy arrived with their drinks. "Here's lookin' at you kid," Peter said in his best Bogart imitation. They clinked their glasses together. As each downed a long draft, they heard the TV over the bar. A blonde-haired woman stood under an umbrella and talked into the microphone she held at her mouth.

"In local news, a police officer was shot this morning at the Blue Whale Motor Inn in Driftwood, apparently during a domestic dispute involving a husband and wife. The couple fled the scene. Anthony Esperanza is in critical but stable condition at the town's hospital. Anyone with information that could lead to the apprehension of the couple is asked to call the police. We will keep you updated as we receive more details. Back to you, John."

Peter and Chris stared at each other.

"Our little town is gettin' big city troubles. Can't remember the last time a cop was shot here," Chris said.

"And just listen to what happened to me today." Before Peter could begin, Billy brought them their bowls of Irish stew and then returned to the bar. "Wow! That smells wonderful." He spooned a hearty chunk of lamb into his mouth. "OK. Time out." All conversation paused as they both satisfied their hunger.

With his bowl half-empty and his glass drained, Chris signaled Billy to bring another round. Then he looked at his friend. "So what was it you wanted to tell me?"

"Just some crazy stuff at school. My friend Sterling started ranting about Officer Whitehorse."

"I know Charley. He's a good guy."

"Not according to Sterling. He claims Whitehorse

searched Dean Wasserman's office illegally after the Dean's death and then harassed Sterling during a class he was teaching."

"That doesn't sound like Charley."

"It gets worse. I called the police station and asked the man himself about it. He said he had a warrant to search the office and that he had gone to the class to ask a question about a salamander."

"A salamander?"

"The Rough-skinned newt. Turns out the little beauties are everywhere and they're toxic as hell."

"Are those the little brown guys with the bright orange bellies? Move in slow motion?"

"The same. Sterling has a painting of one in his office at school."

"Sheesh! I've touched 'em. Picked 'em up. I never got sick."

"Well, you have to eat them to get sick. In fact, the poison's worse than cyanide."

Chris put down his spoon and looked into Peter's eyes. "So how'd the Dean die? You're not sayin' he ate a salamander, are you?"

"We were told he died of a heart attack. But doesn't it seem strange for the police to be searching his office and asking about toxic newts? I mean, am I just being paranoid or what?"

Chris picked up his spoon and resumed eating. "Paranoid. No effin' way an educated man is gonna eat a salamander. Period." He began chewing a hearty mouthful. "And nobody's gonna make him eat one either." He emphasized his words by swinging his spoon like a baton. "Your stew's gettin' cold."

"Yeah. You're probably right. I'm off the deep end with this." With his spoon he searched through his bowl for a potato. "But what do you expect from a guy who finds body parts on the beach?"

24. Chaos

It was too early for anyone to be dancing, but heavy rock music filled the lounge like an invisible tide anyway. The low lighting lent a twilight feel to the space between the stage and the bar. Two customers tried to chat with the bartender over the roar and nursed warm beers. The only active place was the video poker room off to the right side of the entrance. Each of the twelve machines had a worshiper sitting before it, testifying that this next hand would be the winner, rewarding him many times over for all the money he had sacrificed to the hungry machine. Every ten minutes someone stood up and stretched and went to one of the three ATMs to draw out more cash with a debit or credit card. In what looked like an act of penance, the latest petitioner leaned his forehead on the machine and whispered as he inserted his bank card.

In the back office, Abram Sokolov sat at his desk and stroked the scar on his left cheek. His sports jacket was draped over the back of his chair, and the sleeves of his white shirt were rolled up to his elbows. His predator's eyes bored into the man and woman standing nervously before him. "Tell me again, Iosif. How did you and Varvara make such a mess of this?" He glanced at the woman and she averted her eyes.

"It wasn't the right cop, Boss. The Indian. It was his partner. Esperanza, I think his name is. I was already swinging when he walked in. I knocked him over, but I didn't hit him square. He got up and was grabbing for his gun. Varvara here reached hers first and got off a quick shot."

"You damn near killed him, *idiot*! We don't kill policemen. Not in this shithole of a town. Not in Portland. We get too much heat if we do. We're supposed to stay off the radar."

"It all happened so fast, Mr. Sokolov. I didn't want him shooting Joey." Varvara's excuse fell on deaf ears, and he dismissed her comments with a motion of his hand.

"What's his condition?"

"The hospital isn't saying much. He's alive. In ICU."

"What about that orderly friend of yours? He have any more information?"

"Says the bullet didn't go in, but there were some bone fragments. Some swelling."

Sokolov scowled. "Any chance he'll recognize you two when he comes around?"

"He got a good look at Varvara when she opened the door. I came at him from behind and we were pretty much in motion the whole time."

"You." He pointed at the woman, who was visibly trembling. "Iosif will drive you to Whitey's in Salem. Keep your head down until I call you back here. Now get out of my sight."

"Thank you, Mr. Sokolov," she said as she ran out the door and closed it behind her.

The walls seemed to draw inward. The office grew dimmer as light seemed to be sucked from it. The bass sound from the music outside only emphasized the silence in the cramped space. Finally, Sokolov looked up at his soldier. "So what do we do, Iosif? Your mistake wakes up and ID's the *suka*. She'll cop a plea so she doesn't have to go back inside for violating her parole. And that leads the police to our operation." He shook his head back and forth. "You've threatened our business. Volkov in Portland will not be pleased."

The big man shifted his weight from one foot to the other. He withdrew a handkerchief from his jacket pocket and wiped his forehead. "I'll—I'll take care of it, Abram. I'll fix it."

Sokolov smiled. "Of course you will. That's why I trust you." He stood and extended his hand. "When you're done with that, I have another little job for you. Get hold of that little *mudak* Frankie. I want to know how he found out about Whitehorse in the first place. I want the whole story on that." He suddenly slammed his palm on the desk. "More nonsense! The bank wants pictures!"

Iosif looked at him without comprehending.

"The bank called me. New regulations. They have to take a picture of each of my machines. And the front entrance of every

business with one. They're sending someone over here
tomorrow."

"The ATMs?"

Sokolov nodded. "It's getting harder and harder to make a
dishonest living in this town." When his soldier didn't respond, he
added, "That was supposed to be a joke, *idiot*." He made a
dismissive gesture with his hand.

Iosif bowed his head and left. Varvara was waiting for him
at the bar. "Well, that was fun," she said.

The man grunted in response. "Need anything to eat or
drink before we go? My car is parked around back."

"No, I'm fine. Let's get out of here."

Back in the office, Sokolov was planning his next move.
He had learned from hard experience that telling Vasily Volkov
something directly was always preferable to letting him find out
things on his own. He placed the call.

"Why, Abram, to what do I owe the pleasure? You seem to
call me only when there's trouble. Is there trouble, Abram?"

"Yes, Vasily, but it's been contained. I wanted you to hear
about it from me first." He hated the sound of the man's voice—
oily and menacing. Pretending to be cultured. He hated his own
voice for toadying to him.

"It wouldn't have anything to do with that dreadful story I
heard on the news, would it? The police officer in your town that
was gunned down today?" He paused briefly. "We never shoot
policemen."

"One of my crews got carried away. They were just
supposed to rough him up a little. Give him a warning."

"A warning?"

"Yes. My boy at the college said the cop was asking
questions about him. That college is an important market of ours
and we don't want anything to happen to it."

"So you hired incompetents to solve your problem?" The
tone became vicious.

"As I said, it's been contained. That crew is no
longer...working for me. Word down here is that the policeman

will survive. We're good. I wanted you to know that our operation is safe."

"I'll take your word for it, Abram. After all, I'd hate to think what would happen if I had to send one of my own teams down there to...help you. Let's have no more of this ineptitude." The call ended.

Sokolov stared for a moment at the phone in his hand. How he despised the man. He gritted his teeth. *There was a time when no one would talk to me like that and live.*

He opened a drawer and withdrew a Cuban cigar from a silver humidor. Tobacco always relaxed him and helped him think more clearly. He snipped off the end and ran the cigar under his nose. With well-practiced gestures, he closed his lips around it, reached for the lighter on his desk, and ignited the tip, filling the office with huge plumes of fragrant smoke. His mood began to improve.

How had Frankie found out Whitehorse was inquiring about him? It didn't sound as though the police had ever talked directly to the boy. So who had said something? And how did they know? The more he thought about it, the less he liked it. Perhaps he had acted too aggressively—without enough research first. He blew a cloud of smoke toward the ceiling. He'd get to the bottom of it.

An hour later, he was still behind his desk when the phone rang.

"It's done," came the voice. The call ended.

Sokolov smiled. He could always count on Iosif.

25. A Visit to the Hospital

The days crawled by. All Whitehorse wanted to do was to see his friend. He had called Effling at the college several times to keep him up to date. Today he had favors to ask.

"So you still can't get in to see Tony?" Effling asked.

"Maybe Saturday. Now it's just immediate family—wife, two sons. Diana called me to say he's still in the coma. She sits with him. Reads him the paper. Says she's sure he knows what's going on."

"I'll keep him in my prayers. How are you holding up?"

"OK, I guess." He drummed his fingers on the desk and motioned for Chiara to get him another cup of coffee. "But this case is driving me crazy. Did I tell you I tried to contact that Dreams Come True Modeling Agency in California you told me about? The one Marisa went to as a kid? Out of business. Couldn't track down any records. So our woman in the waves is still a mystery. And there's something else now that maybe you could help me with. Something I should have told you about sooner."

"What's that?"

"That arm didn't belong to her."

"Christ Almighty! Are you saying we've got another body out there?"

"Yep." He knit his brows. "I suppose chances are a million to one that it's another of your kids, but could you check? Would have gone in the water around the same time. Not much decomposition. Young."

"I went over stuff pretty thoroughly when I came up with Marisa."

"Yeah, so this would have to be different. Not somebody missing. Somebody with reason to be gone. A girl expelled from school. Or maybe dropping out. Somebody that wouldn't have raised a red flag in your first go-round."

"Will do, Charley. I'll get right on it."

"And one more thing." He wasn't sure how to begin. "Remember I told you about that note to me they left in the motel room?"

"The one that told you to back off?"

"Yeah. I've been wracking my brain trying to figure out who I've pissed off. I had my gal Chiara check all the recent releases. Cons I sent up that might like to get even. Parolees that are out and about from back in the day. I've come up empty. Except for one name. You could say I went out of my way to piss this guy off."

"Let me guess. None other than our one and only Sterling Friese?"

"You got it. The man who wanted tenure so bad he killed for it." He took several deep breaths. "I don't know if I've told you enough how thankful I am that you believed me when I laid it all out for you."

"I told you before, Charley. I was a cop long before I was running security for a fancy-ass college. That guy's dirty and I keep an eye on him all the time."

"I appreciate that, Philip. So maybe keep both eyes on him for a while."

"But what does he want you to back off from?"

"Maybe anything to do with PCU? Anything that might get him back in the spotlight?"

"Makes sense. The little scorpion wants to crawl back under his rock."

"If I could find anything on him. Jaywalking even! I'd exploit it for all it's worth. I want to be the mosquito in his tent at night. The pebble in his shoe."

"I hear you, man. I'll keep you posted."

"Thanks, brother."

He ended the call and unlocked the evidence cabinet again. His shoulders slumped as he withdrew the ring and put it on his desk. He lowered his head and stared at the stone.

"You look like you expect it to talk to you," Chiara quipped.

"I know it's got a story to tell, if only I could hear it."

"Do you ever get to keep unclaimed evidence?"

He laughed out loud. "Not a snowball's chance in hell, girl!"

"I figured. Oh, well, it doesn't hurt to ask. My boyfriend and I are shopping for a ring. He's gonna propose to me."

"So you already know he's going to propose before he's bought the ring? Isn't that the cart before the horse?"

"He needs me to help pay for it. We try to be real careful about money."

"I guess it's a brave new world. We didn't do it like that in my day." He wrapped the ring in a small patch of cloth and put it in an empty match box he found in the back of a desk drawer. "I'm going out. Any jewelry stores besides Caruso's down on 101?"

"My boyfriend and I found a little shop on Kirkwood. Augustino's. Tiny place but pretty stuff. I think that's all there is in town."

"Well, I'll check them both out. And I'll hit up the pawn shops. See if anyone sold this ring or knows anything about it. But I guess it's a needle in a haystack."

"Worth a try. Maybe it'll talk to you."

But the search was fruitless. No one recognized the ring. Caruso's offered to clean it, but he decided not to, given its status as evidence. He chalked it up as yet another unyielding clue in a series that evaded his closest scrutiny. Disappointment was becoming his default mode. Chloe told him she could hear it in his voice when he called her that evening.

Finally, it was Saturday. A fellow policeman came up from Newport to help out and Whitehorse had the day to himself. He called Chloe at about 11:00 that morning.

"Would you come to the hospital with me?"

"Of course, honey. How about taking me out to lunch first? See if I can shake that glum mood out of you."

"Sorry, sweetie. I don't mean to drag you down. It's just that I can't seem to get a break. The pieces of this thing just don't fit together."

"Maybe you should stop thinking about it for a while. You know, give it a rest so you can come at it fresh."

"You're probably right. It's got me so jacked up I'm losing sleep over it."

"OK. So I recommend Tsunami in Depoe Bay. Then we'll get to the hospital."

"I'll pick you up in a half-hour."

The drive was pleasant. Although February had come in roaring with wind and rain and even the hail of January, the weather had warmed quickly, and today the sky popped with sun breaks, some of which lasted as long as an hour. In protected places, the temperature rose into the high 60's. Spring was trying to force its way into the coastal town. The view from their table overlooked surf crashing on a jagged ledge of rock. In another month, the gray whales would be here, on their annual trip from Mexico to Alaska. Some of them would stay and become residents throughout the summer.

"So talk to me," Chloe said after their grilled salmon arrived.

"And say what? That I'm worried sick about my partner? That I have another case I can't solve?"

"What if we talk about ourselves instead?"

He hung his head. "I'm sorry, honey. I'm not being fair to you."

"I just want you to be happy. And you haven't been."

"A shot partner, two missing bodies, a diamond ring...and a dead Dean have a way of making me unhappy."

She reached over the table and stroked his hand. "I love you, mister—happy or unhappy. We're in this together."

"You don't know how important that is to me." He smiled and raised a forkful of savory salmon to his mouth. "Tsunami never disappoints."

They talked no further of police matters. As the waiter came around with coffee afterward, Whitehorse asked, "Want to buy a house together?"

Chloe dropped the napkin she was touching to her lips. "What did you say?"

"Sell the little houses we have and buy a nicer one. Start fresh together."

A broad smile creased her lips. "That's still not a proposal," she said as she shook her head, "but I kind of like the idea."

Whitehorse paid the bill and soon they were on their way to Driftwood Hospital. They steered around the construction that would become the new Emergency Department and drove into the parking structure in the back. Covered walkways led them to the front desk.

"Charley Whitehorse and Chloe Denhurst to see Tony Esperanza," he said to the receptionist behind the computer screen.

The young woman made a few key strokes. "They've just moved him from ICU to B203. Down that hallway to the elevator and take a right."

He nodded his thanks and took Chloe's hand.

"Your hand is trembling," she said.

"Just a little nervous is all. Don't know what I'm going to see when I walk in."

He had his answer in three minutes. Esperanza's wife Diana leaped from her chair and ran to embrace him. Her eyes were red. She hugged Chloe.

"I'm so glad you could come. He's been asking for you." She stepped back to allow them to approach the bed.

The policeman's head was covered in a white helmet of bandages. An IV hung by the side, dripping clear liquid into the back of his right hand. He smiled.

"Like the new look? Quite the fashion statement, huh?"

"There's easier ways to get time off, partner."

Chloe's eyes brimmed with concern. "How are you feeling, Tony?" She turned to Diana. "And how are you doing, for goodness sake? I can't imagine the ordeal you've been through."

Diana walked to the bed and rested her hand on her

husband's left shoulder. "We've had better days, for sure. But I think we're out of the woods. He'll be under observation for another few days, but then we're homeward bound. My mother's been a saint with the boys."

"Doc says I'll have a permanent part in my hair. That'll make things easy for combing it after I shower."

"You must be feeling better by the sound of it."

"And I can identify one of 'em. A guy and a dame. Get the sketch artist from Newport up here. I got a good look at the broad's face." He squinted at his partner. "She said the strangest thing when she opened the door. Something like, 'You're not the Indian.' Like she was expecting you."

Whitehorse frowned and turned away for a moment. When he came back around, he said, "It was meant for me, Tony. It was all a setup, not a domestic at all. They left a note threatening me and my friends."

The big man whistled. "That explains it. But why? Whose toes did you step on?"

"I got some ideas. We'll talk more when you're back on your feet. For now, you're supposed to be resting."

"I'm ready to get back to work."

Diana slapped his arm playfully. "You're on bed rest for as long as the doctor tells you."

"Yes, my love." He faced Whitehorse. "I'm serious about the sketch artist. Please."

"Why don't you let yourself heal a little bit first?"

"Strike while the iron is hot. You know the drill, Tracker."

"But I thought people were supposed to lose their memory when they've been through stuff like this."

"Not if you've got a head like a brick, I guess."

"OK. I'll call them first thing Monday morning."

They visited for about an hour. Chloe could see that Tony was getting tired. "We should be on our way. Let you rest. We want you back on your feet."

"Thanks for coming by, guys. I appreciate it."

Another round of hugs and the two departed. As they

entered the elevator, Whitehorse thought, *Maybe this is the break I've been looking for. We'll ID that perp and finally start solving this thing.*

26. Mona Lisa

I *was too rough last night. I don't want to scare her away. Not yet.* Sterling poured himself a second cup of coffee and tossed the newspaper aside. Grace had left an hour ago, but not before commenting about how "wild" he had been in bed.

He knew he was using sex to get his mind off the ring. Ever since Peter had told him he had found the diamond, he couldn't stop thinking about it. Of course, his first thought was, *Is there any way they can trace it back to me?* He decided there was not. His second thought was, *Is there any way I can get the damn thing back?* He doubted it. Breaking into a police station did not sound like a very good idea. Better to give it up as lost, just as he had originally.

He left his cup on the table and walked down the hall that led to his bedroom. There on the wall was the picture of his mother, hands in her lap, displaying the diamond for all to see. Her gray hair fell over her shoulders in a gentle curl. Her lips were slightly parted in that enigmatic expression of hers. On days when Sterling was feeling energized and happy, she was smiling at him. On days when he was angry and frustrated, she smirked at him in the belittling way she did throughout his childhood.

"Mother, I'm going to have to take you down for the time being, at least until interest in your ring blows over. Can't take the outside chance that someone might see it here, can we?" He carefully lifted the framed picture from the wall, but not before opening it one more time. He had had the frame specially made. It was hinged so it could be opened like the face of a clock. There in the lower right corner, out of sight when the frame was closed, was the small case in which he had stowed his treasure. *"Consider it a gift for your retirement, Sonny,"* she'd say on one of her better days. On her lesser days, the ones when the madness gripped her, she'd snarl at him, *"I'm never giving this to you, you conniving little weasel. You'll have to pry it from my cold, dead fingers."* Which, as it turned out, is what he had done.

"You'll live in the back closet for a while, Mother. It's

substantially larger than the one you locked me in, so I think you'll be comfortable enough." He placed the picture behind a row of sports coats and closed the door. Then he returned to the kitchen to finish his coffee.

SUNDAY, MARCH 16, 1986. His mother was winding up again. Ever since last year, after his ninth birthday party, he had begun to see a pattern to her illness. At first, she would be happy, laughing and making jokes, buying him special treats at the store, making huge bowls of popcorn for their late-night TV watching, devising extravagant travel plans for his summer vacation. And then, as though falling from a great height, her mood would darken and she would rage at him. He'd overhear her carrying on conversations with people he couldn't see when she stood in the kitchen, unsure what to do with the knife she had just picked up. She'd refuse to answer the door or the phone. Unless he were quick and got out of the house, she would lock him in the closet for hours at a time *"so the spies don't kidnap you."*

He was afraid to tell his teachers. He loved his mother and didn't want her to leave him or be taken away. His father had tried to help, but had finally given up and left them two years before. *"Genevieve's a whacko, Sonny. She tries to hurt you, you call the cops."* Those had been his final words of wisdom as he closed the cab door and sped away. Sterling never saw him again.

Today his mother's hands were shaking. She hadn't showered in three days, and he could smell her unpleasant body odor. Her hair, normally pulled back in a neat ponytail, was dirty and disheveled.

"Help me with this aluminum foil, Sonny." She handed him a roll. "Tape it to all the windows. That'll block their radio waves."

"Whose radio waves, Mommy?" It was a straightforward question for a ten-year-old boy.

"The men in the black coats and dark glasses, dummy! The ones that want to kidnap you and do medical experiments on your body. You don't want them cutting you up, do you?"

136

"No way!"

"Then seal up these windows. Hurry!"

He worked alongside his mother to cover all the windows in the house. Her lips never stopped moving, and once she turned around and shouted, "You can't have him!"

"It'll be OK, Mommy," he pleaded. "Please calm down." It made him afraid to see her this way.

"It won't be OK until you're safe. Now go get in the closet."

"Can we have lunch first? I'm hungry."

"No time. Quick like a bunny. After I'm sure they're gone, I'll bring you something to eat."

And so he had gone into the little space again. He heard the lock click behind him. His mother had long since removed the single light bulb, so he found himself in total darkness. The terror of his first detention had given way to a deep sadness, which he tried to allay by recalling his mother's protests of love for him.

"I love you to the moon, Sonny."

"I love you to the moon and back, Mommy."

"I love you a googolplex, Sonny!"

He was stumped. "That's not fair. What's a googolplex?"

"I heard about it on TV a long time ago. It's a number so big it won't fit in the universe if you try to write it down."

He was happy his mother loved him so much. He just wished he didn't have to pee so badly.

SUNDAY, AUGUST 4, 1991. "You're crazy, Mother. Do you know that? You're the reason Dad ran away."

"Watch your mouth, you little shit. He ran away because he was sick of the fairy princess you're turning into."

"He ran away because you took all of his savings and all of the insurance settlement he got and bought that stupid ring. Have you looked in the refrigerator? We have no food. You can't eat diamond rings, you dingbat!" He ducked as she threw the frying pan at him. It thudded into the wall, punching a hole in the sheetrock. He spun on his heels and ran out the door.

Ten minutes later, he caught up with his buddy Kip, just as his friend was about to walk downtown to get a milkshake.

"C'mon along. I got a few extra bucks if you're broke. You know I've been working at Steakland since school got out, and I rake in the tips. Must be my movie star looks."

Sterling gave him a playful punch in the arm. "You're a few months older than me and you can get a real job. I'm stuck with a nutcase mother who won't give me a cent."

"Like I said, the shake's on me."

"Thanks."

"So what gives with your ma?"

"She threw a frying pan at me." He pulled up his T-shirt. "She did this a couple years ago. I never showed you before."

Kip stared at the little round scars on Sterling's chest. "Jesus! You can report her for that kinda shit. Child Protective Services. They'll haul her ass outta there and into a hospital so fast the ink won't be dry on the commitment papers."

"How do you know about that stuff?"

"Ex-girlfriend. Her old man is schizophrenic. Mother had him hospitalized twice before she finally divorced the bastard."

"But what would happen to me if I reported her?"

"Oh, shit. That's right. They'd probably send you into foster care."

"Could I come live with you?"

"That'd be cool, but they got a lotta rules and regulations about that stuff. Wouldn't fly." He thought for a moment. "I suppose you could run away. Not sure if that would be any better than a foster home."

Sterling took a deep breath and sighed. "I think I'll take my chances with the old lady. Just keep my head down."

"Good luck with that, man. I mean it. You don't think she'll come and get you in your sleep, do you?"

"I installed a lock on my bedroom door."

"You're good then. Unless she decides to burn the house down."

"Stop it already! You're not making me feel any better."

"Sorry. That was supposed to be a joke."

They walked in silence for several blocks. "Hey, wanna go to a movie tonight? My treat." It was Kip's way of apologizing.

"What movie?"

"Terminator 2. Supposed to be fantastic. Seen the trailers?"

"Yeah, with that liquid metal guy that fights Arnie. And Guns N' Roses does a song on the soundtrack. I'm in."

The day had changed and Sterling was smiling.

27. Consulting the Therapist/Priest

The weather had turned a corner in March. The rains seemed gentler, warmer somehow. Tulips and crocuses burst from the ground. Rhododendrons were set to pop into bloom within a month. Peter liked the lengthening of daylight as the earth approached the vernal equinox.

He and Hammer were thoroughly bonded. Taking the dog for walks after returning home from school had become the favorite part of his day. Hammer's boundless energy was contagious, and Peter's mood had morphed from morose to genuinely happy. "You're the best therapist a guy could have, boy. You know that?" As always, the dog barked his affirmation.

Sunday morning walks on the beach, rain or shine, were the highlight of the week for both of them. He no longer thought of the woman in the waves, the severed arm. Even his thoughts of Helen had changed. When he did think of her, they were pleasant memories—vacations together, her artwork and photography, trips to the wine country in the Willamette Valley, as well as to Napa and Sonoma. The guilt that had haunted him was finally gone, absolved by the sea and the sky and the love of an orphaned dog.

This Sunday was no exception. "I guess you're my priest, too, Hammer," he said, as he hurled a ball as far down the beach as he could. The dog barked in delight and bolted down the shore, kicking up sprays of sand with his galloping paws. Sun peeked through clouds and hid again, as if playing a child's game with the lucky beachcombers.

In moments, Hammer returned with the ball, eager for another romp. Peter threw it again and watched his pet speed away. When the dog came back, Peter held the ball before releasing it once more. "Walk with me, Hammer." The animal fell into step beside him.

"Help me with this new thing." He stroked Hammer's head, and the dog gave a quiet woof in response. "I'm not trusting my friend Sterling, and that's making me really uncomfortable.

Chris told me I was just being paranoid, but I can't shake it. If Officer Whitehorse had a warrant to search Dean Wasserman's office, why did Sterling lie and say he didn't? What was Whitehorse looking for? And then he goes into Sterling's classroom to get information about a poisonous salamander. I mean 'Whoa!'—that comes out of left field. Why does a cop snooping around the Dean's office want to know about a toxic newt? What's the connection?" He exhaled noisily. "Yeah, I know. I know. It's the question I'm afraid to ask." He stopped and cupped his hands around his dog's face. "Did Sterling Friese poison Dean Wasserman?"

When Hammer didn't respond, Peter listened to the gentle surf scuffing the sand. A wedge of three brown pelicans flew low over the water past him. A Black-backed gull strutted slowly away from something it was worrying at the water's edge. The dog barked at it, and the bird leaped into the sky.

"What do you think, Hammer? Sterling seemed upset a few weeks ago when I mentioned the diamond ring on the arm's finger. Think he knows anything about that?" Hammer cocked his head and woofed. "Yeah, I think so, too."

Peter threw the ball and launched Hammer down the beach. When the dog came back, Peter said, "I don't think I told you, boy, but when I was looking up Rough-skinned newts on the Internet, I found a story about three hunters camping out here in Oregon about fifty years ago. They found all three dead with no physical signs of injury. When they checked the campsite, they found a newt in the coffee pot! The article said the salamander's poison is 10,000 times more potent than cyanide."

The dog positioned himself in front of Peter, making him stop. Hammer looked at him with an expression that Peter interpreted as, "Enough talk. More ball."

"OK, Hammer. You win." He pitched the ball and laughed as the dog hurtled down the beach.

The next morning, he had a free hour after his first morning class. He walked over to the Security Department and asked for Philip Effling.

He was greeted by a dark-haired man with a bearing that spoke of military and law enforcement. "What can I do for you, Dr. Bristol?" He extended his hand. "You're the one who found the arm? Saw that woman swept away?"

Peter nodded and shook hands. "May we speak privately?"

"Of course. Come into my office and have a chair." He closed the door behind his visitor and took a seat behind the modest desk. "What can I help you with?"

"I've heard some stories about events surrounding Dean Wasserman's death. I don't know if you're free to tell me anything, but I need to ask. Did a policeman come here without a warrant to search the Dean's office?"

Peter saw the man hesitate, wondered if he were deciding whether to be honest or politically correct.

"Officer Whitehorse had a warrant, but the university had the judge void it before he could complete his investigation."

"Do you know what he was looking for?"

"I do not."

"Given that aborted search, is it reasonable for me to assume that there are some questions about the Dean's death? Might it have had something to do with an unusual poison?"

He saw the man stiffen ever so slightly, then relax again.

"Please, Dr. Bristol. I can't engage in any speculation about Dean Wasserman's death. It was ruled to be natural causes —heart attack, aneurysm. The family had the body cremated without an autopsy."

Peter decided to go for broke. "Is Professor Sterling Friese involved in this in any way?"

Effling stood up. "OK, I'm not sure where you're going with this, Dr. Bristol, but with all due respect, we have to wrap this up. I hope you can understand."

"Of course, Mr. Effling. Thank you for your time."

28. Tolstoy Goes to College

The next week was almost over when the big man, acting on his boss's instructions, pulled into the visitors' parking lot at Pacific Crest University. He was wearing his best suit and tie and was carrying a package wrapped in brightly colored paper. His short brown hair, chiseled face, and stiff posture gave him the look of a general or admiral as he walked into the administrative offices and addressed the red-haired young woman behind the desk.

"I have an early birthday present for Franklin Wise. Is there any way I can deliver it personally...Amelia?" he said, as he looked at her name tag on the desk.

"Of course. Please sign this register and write down the make and model of your car. And I'll need to see some photo ID. We've increased our security a lot over the last year. When you walked through the entrance, you passed through a metal detector that displays here at my desk."

"Then I'm glad I locked my gun in the car," he said with a smile and a wink.

She chuckled. "I like your sense of humor. We pride ourselves in maintaining a safe campus for our students."

"Of course," he said, "Can't be too careful nowadays." He scrawled *Iosif Tolstoy* in the book and withdrew his driver's license from his wallet.

"Oh, wow! Like the famous writer? Are you related?" She made a photocopy of the license and handed it back.

"No."

When he said nothing further, she took the ledger from him. "I'll call his room and see if he's in."

While she busied herself with the call, he looked around the office. *Smells like money*, he thought. *Where the rich pricks go to school.*

"Franklin, there's a Mr. Tolstoy here to see you." He saw a disconcerted look pass over her face. "He says he doesn't know any Mr. Tolstoy."

"Tell him Joey wants to see him."

"Joey wants to see you, Franklin." She paused. "I'll tell him." She hung up the phone and turned to the man. "He says he's very sorry to keep you waiting, and he'll be right over. He'll be coming from the Nestucca River Dorm across the way."

A moment later, Joey saw Franklin running toward the Administration Building. He smiled when he saw the frightened look on the boy's face. *Good. Keep the little shit in line.*

"H-hi, Joey," he managed as he burst through the door.

"Hello, Frankie. I brought you an early birthday present. Maybe we could take a little walk and you could show me around the grounds."

"Sure thing, Joey. Anything you say."

They walked out into the warm afternoon. The sun had emerged from gray clouds and reflected off the silver rings that pierced Franklin's brows. His black hair escaped in little tufts from the edges of his blue hoodie. He jammed his hands into his pockets as he quickened his steps to keep pace with the large strides of the man beside him.

Once out of sight of the receptionist, Joey dropped the package he carried into the first trash receptacle he saw. "Nice place you got here, kid. Be a pity if you had to quit or get expelled." He let the threat settle into the boy's psyche. He knew the first strategy of real muscle is to always keep your opponent off guard. "Boss wants more information. How'd you find out that cop Whitehorse was after you? He talk to you? Did you see him on campus?"

Franklin swallowed hard. "Um...a professor wanted to do me a favor. Said he heard the guy was asking questions about me."

"What professor?"

The boy's face blanched. "I-I don't want to get anybody in trouble. Like I said, he was doing me a favor."

"What professor?" Iosif repeated, completely disregarding his charge's objection.

"Sterling Friese," he spat out, squirming as though his

shirt and pants were too tight. "In the Biology Department. Please, man. He's an OK guy. He's given me another chance to pass his class."

"Relax. Abe is curious is all. I just want to talk to the guy. Find out what he knows."

"You guys didn't have anything to do with that other cop getting shot a couple weeks ago, did you?"

"Hell, no, Frankie. That was somebody else. We never shoot cops. And we don't kill people. We're business men."

"I knew it wasn't you. You've always treated me fair and square. So you're not going to hurt Professor Friese?"

"Like I said. We're business men. We just need to know what Friese knows so we can stay on top of things. He needs to keep us in the loop." He gave the boy a paternal pat on the back. "We don't want anybody bothering you, Frankie. We like you." The look on Franklin's face told Joey the boy wasn't sure if he should be comforted or concerned by that declaration. "Things are gonna be just fine. Don't worry. Go back to your dorm."

Franklin took off at a trot without looking back. Joey chuckled. *I love my job.*

He decided to meet with Friese while he was there on the campus, rather than try to find him at his home. He strolled back to the Administration Wing, relishing the reprieve in the weather, taking deep breaths of air perfumed with the orange scent of Douglas firs.

"Is Professor Friese here today?" he asked Amelia.

"Let me pull up his schedule." She made a few key strokes. "He's just finishing a class. Looks like he has office hours for students until 11:30 and his first appointment canceled. Shall I write you in there as a friend of Franklin's?"

"By all means. Thank you, Amelia."

"Done. Why don't you sit here? He always calls me when he gets back to his office, then I'll direct you."

"You like working here?"

"I do. It's just part-time. I work it around my class schedule." Her phone rang. "Yes, sir, I'll send him right over." She turned to Joey. "His office is in Rainier Hall, across the way," she pointed out the doors. "I'll phone the desk there so they let you in. "Nice meeting you, Amelia. Have a good day."

He walked deliberately, enjoying the knowledge that her eyes were on the body he had so carefully sculpted with his personal trainer. *Want a piece of this?* he thought, as he swaggered away.

In a few minutes, he was knocking on a door labeled **Professor Sterling Friese, Ph.D., Biology**.

"Come in," said a voice from inside.

He opened the door to find a lean, auburn-haired man sitting behind a modest desk piled high with papers. The man stood and extended his hand.

"I'm Dr. Friese, Mr. Tolstoy. My schedule says you're a friend of Franklin Wise. How may I help you today?"

Iosif felt the man's grip, almost as strong as his own. For a split-second, he considered squeezing to see who would say "uncle" first. He decided against such a contest and relinquished the hand. "You work out? I can feel it in the way you shake."

"I pride myself in staying physically fit. It looks like you do, too. Please have a seat."

He nodded. "I won't take too much of your time, Professor. I'm Frankie's uncle. I try to keep an eye on him while he's here. His father doesn't want him to screw up like he did in high school."

"I see. Has he told you that his performance in my class has been marginal the last several weeks? But we've had a good talk, and he seems to be coming around."

Iosif leaned forward in his chair. "He told me something else—that you warned him a cop by the name of Whitehorse has been asking about him, wondering about some kind of drug connection. He said he doesn't know where the police got that idea, but he wanted me to know in case they tried to contact me."

Sterling paused for a heartbeat, but it was long enough for Iosif to register it. "I gave your nephew a heads-up because I didn't want him to squander his promising career. The policeman walked into my lecture, and when I wouldn't leave the room, he sat there, glaring at me for the whole period. It was embarrassing. Once class ended, he took me aside and grilled me about whether I knew who was dealing drugs on campus, who the supplier was. I told him I knew nothing about it. Then he demanded I tell him everything I know about Franklin, claiming that it was common knowledge among a subculture of students here that Franklin could get them 'anything they wanted.' I told him I wouldn't violate any student's rights to privacy without a warrant or a subpoena. Then he threatened to implicate me for withholding evidence and obstructing an ongoing investigation. I had Security remove him from the premises."

Iosif sat there silently, studying the man's face.

"Just between you and me, Mr. Tolstoy, I think you should keep an eye on your nephew. As I said, his performance has been improving, but I wouldn't want him to get in with the wrong crowd. He's a talented young man with a bright future ahead of him."

Iosif stood up. "Thank you for your time, Dr. Friese. You've been most helpful. I'll have a good long talk with that rascal nephew of mine and make sure he stays on track to graduate." Just as he was about to leave, he said, "Do you have a scrap of paper? I'd like to write down my phone number for you. If you see or hear of Frankie doing anything stupid, will you please give me a call?"

"Most certainly."

The men shook hands again and Iosif left the office. He headed toward the parking lot.

In the distance, crows called from the forest. A wayward gull glided overhead, stark white against the blue of the sky. He heard surf rolling against the shore at the base of Cascadia Head. As he reached the parking lot and got into his car, he removed his pistol from the glove compartment and slid it into his shoulder holster. His final thought as he left the parking lot was, *What bullshit!*

29. The Indian, the Ape, and the Pumpkin Eater

W hat bullshit!" Sterling muttered to himself. "If that guy is Wise's uncle, I'm the Pope's love child!" He looked at his computer and saw he had another twenty minutes before his next appointment.

He tried to determine what his next move should be. More and more, it began to feel as though he were playing a game of chess, guessing his opponent's strategy, developing one of his own. *So who is Iosif Tolstoy?* he wondered.

He picked up the phone. "Amelia, we subscribe to that service so we can do quick background checks on people, right?"

"Yes, Dr. Friese. It's all part of our new security protocol."

"Great. Please run a check on my last visitor. I want to know if he is who he says he is."

"I'll have it for you in a minute."

When he hung up the phone, he thought, *That can't be his real identity. So what would I need to do to find out?* He was surprised when the phone rang so promptly.

"He's legit, Dr. Friese. Iosif Tolstoy, 47581 Periwinkle Court, Driftwood. Last known place of employment—Club Chaos. I'll email the information to you."

"Thanks." He was stunned. *He uses his real identity. And he works where Wise's band plays.* Sterling decided to exercise greater caution until he determined exactly what he was up against.

Is Tolstoy Wise's drug supplier? Franklin would've gone to him, worried that he was about to be arrested by Whitehorse, as I had led him to believe. Tolstoy wants to keep Wise working the university, so he wants to verify the story and get whatever other details he can before doing something to that infernal policeman.

Another possibility? Tolstoy is only the muscle for somebody else, somebody higher up the food chain. Either way, the little Indian will be getting his comeuppance in Spades.

Just as he was about to congratulate himself for his well-played gambit, another thought struck him: *What if that ape thinks I was lying to him? What if he thinks I know more than I was letting on about the drug traffic in Driftwood? Would that make me a loose end—another target on the list with Whitehorse? Shit!*

Bullshit! Iosif thought again, as he drove down Cascadia Head. "Call Abram Sokolov," he told the onboard communication system.

"Calling Abram Sokolov," the British-sounding voice responded.

"Abe, I'm on my way back."

"What did you find out?"

"Frankie was warned by his biology teacher, Dr. Sterling Friese. Guy claims Whitehorse hounded him for information. But I'm not buyin' it. There's something about that guy that rubs me the wrong way. He's hiding something. I don't know how much Frankie has told him about us, but I'm sure he knows more about our business than he should. The kid seemed too buddy-buddy about protecting him."

"*Blyad!*"

"Boss?"

"Come back to the shop and help me figure out what to do about this...nuisance."

"Right away."

Iosif guessed the trip to Chaos would take about fifteen minutes, so he turned on the radio and hummed along with the western song that was playing. He looked at his watch and decided he had enough time for a quick cup of coffee. Once he entered town, he made a detour to the Reef Coffee Shop. It didn't have a drive-up window, but it made the best brew in Driftwood, so the inconvenience was worth it to him. Besides, the Jolly Roger décor made him feel at home. *I'm a pirate, too,* he thought, as he smiled at the owner, Darby Gallaway, with the black patch over his eye and the broad-brimmed pirate's hat.

"Ahoy, matey!" Gallaway called. "Haven't seen you in a while. What'll it be?"

"Big and black, Darby. Need to stay awake."

"Excuse the get-up, by the way. Just had a gang of little ones and their mothers in here for cookies, and they love the whole cheesy routine. One kid even asked me if I was Jack Sparrow."

"What'd you tell him?"

"Argh!"

Iosif laughed. He handed Darby a five-dollar bill.

"Drinking it here, or do you need it to go?"

He looked at his watch again. "I can spare another few minutes. I'll drink it here." He hated paper cups and plastic lids.

"Here you go, Joey." Darby handed him a large black mug emblazoned with a white skull and crossbones.

Iosif walked to the small table in the corner and sat down. As he sipped the smooth but bitter beverage, he thought, *This is just what the Boss wants. Hiding in plain sight. In the fabric of the neighborhood. I buy coffee here. Shop for fish from Paul at Hook, Line, and Sinker. Get groceries at the SaveLots on 101. Nobody knows our real business, and everybody likes us.*

As if to confirm his thoughts, Darby called over to him, "So what's it like being a bouncer at Chaos? Enjoy your job? Young people sure seem to like your place."

"It's a good job. Boring sometimes. But you'd be surprised the guys—and the chicks—who try to pick fights with me. I know it's the alcohol talking, so I try to be gentle. Had to hurt somebody last week, though."

"Oh?"

"Yeah. Broke his arm. I can't stand it when a guy manhandles a woman. Know what I mean?" For a split second, an image of Varvara flashed in his mind, her eyes pleading with him, her mouth twisted in pain as he choked the life from her behind the restroom along the forested stretch of Route 18 known as the Van Duzer Forest Corridor.

150

"Ouch! That must've hurt!"

"Yeah." He took another sip of coffee. "I should probably be going, Darby. Nice talking to you. My best to your wife and kids."

"Thanks, Joey. Hope to see you again soon."

Sterling needed another cup of coffee. He walked down to the Faculty Lounge and saw Peter pouring himself a cup. The man waved him over.

"Hey, Sterling. Do you have a few minutes? Come sit with me."

"Give me a sec." He grabbed a mug and filled it, then walked to the table. "I have to admit, Peter, you're looking a whole lot happier than you have in months. Is it the dog, or have you started using dope to sweeten your mood?"

The other man chuckled. "It's my dog—my therapist-priest. He's absolved me of all my wrongdoing."

"Good for you." He took a sip of coffee. "I've got good news myself. Brady has approved my taking on three doctoral students for starters. I should be meeting them within the next month to work out the details. They'll be on board June 1. I'll throw a party to celebrate."

"Well, congratulations," Peter put down his cup and extended his hand, "to the rising star in our incestuous little club! You'll be a great mentor."

"Thanks for taking me under your wing when I arrived here. You were a big help."

"You took off on your own pretty quick. I guess cream rises to the top."

The younger professor smiled, basking in the glow of the flattering compliment. "So have you started dating? I hear a dog can be a great way to hook up with the ladies. Great conversation-starters and such."

"Not yet. But I could ask you the same question."

"Me? Confirmed bachelor. My ex taught me that. No more entanglements."

"Hey, mind if I ask? A few weeks ago you told me to be careful of that cop Whitehorse. What do you know about him?"

Sterling paused for a moment, taken aback by the sudden redirection of their conversation. Immediately, his guard went up. Then he smiled. "Like I said then, he's kind of a wild card. Very paranoid. I don't know how he got past Administration and into Rainier Hall. I just happened to be walking by when I saw him unlock the Dean's door and go in. I called Brady right away and he was there with Effling from Security in a heartbeat. Stopped that little sonofabitch from rummaging around where he didn't belong without a warrant. Brady reamed him a new one and kicked his butt off campus. Of course, the family went ballistic when they found out. Then a few days later he shows up in McCall, where I'm in the middle of a class. Makes snide remarks about my teaching. Clearly pissed about being kicked out because of me. Anyway, I called Security and had him escorted out again. Haven't seen him since."

Peter took a sip of coffee and shook his head back and forth. "I wonder what's with him? Why search the office of a guy who died of natural causes? What was he hoping to find?"

Sterling sighed and raised his mug. "I guess we'll never know."

"I actually talked to the guy myself."

Sterling stopped the cup just as it reached his lips. "Oh?"

"Yeah. I called to see if they had identified the arm I told you about. He wouldn't really say anything. I told him I had heard he went into a lecture hall here when somebody was teaching, and he said he was trying to get information about a toxic salamander, the Rough-skinned newt."

Sterling tried not to show any emotion, but under the table his left fist clenched. "He had seen a picture of one hanging on the wall of my old place when the ambulance came for Dean Wasserman. You did know he died in my home, didn't you? Poor man. I've since rotated my paintings, so now it's hanging in my office here if you'd like to see it."

"Thanks. Maybe I'll do that."

"Anytime." Sterling stood and took his cup to the sink. "Well, I've got a bunch of student appointments this morning. Catch up with you later."

"You bet."

It took all of Sterling's restraint not to slam the lounge door as he left.

That evening, he sat at home pondering the events of the day. *That goddamn ape.* More and more, Sterling was convinced that Tolstoy was an enforcer for somebody else. He couldn't help but think that Tolstoy had come to the university on a fishing expedition, looking for more information about the bee Sterling had put in Franklin's bonnet. *Are you scoping me out—assessing what kind of threat I pose to your operations? Damn! Maybe I shouldn't have started that snowball down the hill.* He cursed under his breath and shook his head back and forth. *Do I have to look over my shoulder now? Will you come gunning for me when I least expect it?* He promised himself not to give Tolstoy the opportunity.

And now his friend Peter. Former friend. Snooping around, asking questions that were none of his business. Why couldn't he leave well enough alone? "Peter, Peter pumpkin eater, had a wife but couldn't keep her," he hissed. He gritted his teeth and slammed his hand hard on the kitchen table, barely missing his glass of Pinot. "You nosy, prying sonofabitch! Now I've got to look out for you, too?" He thought back to Peter's lame attempt to interrogate him over coffee. He tried to collect himself by taking several deep breaths, but his temper still raged. He doubted there was any way Peter could find out about Wasserman's private investigation into Sterling's philandering. In fact, minutes after Brady, Effling, and Attorney Fairweather had had Whitehorse escorted from the campus last year, Sterling had slipped back into Wasserman's office and removed the offending report himself. Its ashes still lay in his fireplace.

But Peter was no longer an ally. He couldn't count on him to have his back. He'd be suspicious of everything Sterling did, looking for inconsistencies, trying to trip him up. Not supporting him in any faculty discussions or decisions. Perhaps even interfering with his doctoral students.

"Goddamn it!" His shout echoed off the glass slider to the deck. What to do? *First the Indian, then the ape, and now Peter.*

He took another sip of wine and willed himself to calm down. Finally, he managed a smile. What would the Don do in a situation like this?

He'd tell me to slow down and think. It's not time to go to the mattresses yet. There's nothing for Peter to find, no trace of my clandestine carrying-on, nothing to prove the Dean died of anything other than natural causes. Regarding the ape, let him show himself, show his true colors. If he gets pushy...he'll sleep with the fishes. And as far as the Indian goes, there's nothing to connect me to those girls on the beach. So what if Marisa took one of my classes? Lots of students take my classes. I'm a good teacher. In demand.

That seemed to work. He drained his glass and poured himself another.

That doesn't mean I don't stay prepared. Keep the guns loaded. Stay sharp. Very, very sharp.

He decided that he would place his pistols strategically in the house, in case Tolstoy came for an unwelcome visit. Even though he was in good physical shape, Sterling was no street-fighter and wouldn't want to go hand-to-hand with the giant. He arose and went to his bedroom, where he unlocked the gun safe in his closet. Withdrawing the 1911 Colt .45 and the Glock 17 9mm, he checked the chambers and magazines of both with the ease of long practice. The Glock he slid into the drawer of his bedside table, where he could reach it quickly in the event of Tolstoy's coming through the bedroom door. He took the stainless steel Colt to the den and stowed it behind the single pillow that graced his favorite upholstered armchair. Just the ticket for entertaining unwanted company.

He went back to the table and took a sip of wine. He brought the glass with him to the chair in the den and sat down.

Good. Not uncomfortable with the Colt behind the pillow. Not immediately obvious. I'm ready for their next move. The rage had left him at last, and the wine began to comfort him. With a smile on his face, he turned on *The Godfather* and settled into his chair, listening, as always, for the signature strain of the trumpet.

And it dawned on him. Why not stir the pot again? He pulled his phone from his pocket, glad that he had entered Tolstoy's information after his morning visit. He hesitated for a moment—this would give Tolstoy his own phone number. *What the hell*, he thought, and tapped the number on the screen.

A gruff voice answered after three rings. "Who is this?"

He could hear the pounding bass of dance music in the background. *He does work at Chaos. That's what I heard when I called Franklin.* "It's Dr. Friese, Mr. Tolstoy. You asked me to call you if I heard of Franklin doing anything stupid. Well, this afternoon Peter Bristol, a colleague of mine, came to me asking what I knew about him. Said he had reports from three different students claiming to have seen Franklin selling drugs to undergraduates. One even texted him a photo of a transaction he says happened in the Student Lounge. 'I'm keeping a file on that kid while I check all this out,' he says. 'If it's true, I'll take it to Chancellor Brady next week when he's back from his conference.' Looks like you'd better have that talk with that nephew of yours sooner than later."

There was silence for several breathing seconds. "Thank you, Professor. I'll do that."

Sterling smiled as he returned the phone to his pocket. *Hang on Peter. Freight train's a-comin'.*

30. Little Miss Sherlock

Whitehorse and Chiara, whose hair was pink today, had a cake and balloons on his desk when Esperanza returned to work for the first time since the shooting. They both clapped when he walked through the door.

"You look good, Tony," chirped Chiara.

"And where's that permanent part in your hair you were talking about?" his partner asked.

"Strategic combing, taught by my wife. Can hardly tell it's there unless the wind blows, then I just put my hat on."

"Well, welcome back. It's good to see you, old friend. We've missed you."

"I missed you guys, too. Ready to get back in the saddle. You'll have to bring me up to date on all that's been going on."

"Lots of the usual. A bunch of traffic stops, couple drunk and disorderlies. Pretty quiet overall."

"How's about our interesting case—the gal on the beach and the arm, if they're even related. And any connection to my little go-round?"

Whitehorse winced as though Esperanza had just poked an open wound. "I'll review what we've got, but it's not a helluva lot. Sit and cut the cake."

Chiara brought paper plates and napkins and plastic forks to the desk and withdrew a long knife from her desk drawer. "I made the coffee today, if you'd like to try it."

"Maybe I will, so long as my friend here had nothing to do with it. Wash down the cake with it."

Once everyone had a slice of cake and a cup of coffee, Whitehorse launched into his review. "So, as you know, our woman in the waves was Marisa Kennedy, who was very likely pregnant, according to the journal she kept. No 'shark week' in November and December." He saw the puzzled look on Esperanza's face and the smile on Chiara's. "Remember I told you how kids keep track of their periods?"

"Oh, yeah. Right."

"Anyway, they had a memorial service for her at the university. I heard it was real nice." He took another breath.

Chiara pursed her lips and looked up from her cake. "Charley, would you hand me the journal? I haven't really looked at it. If you don't mind."

"Sure." He opened the evidence cabinet and withdrew both the journal and the ring. He placed the ring on his desk and handed the slim volume to Chiara.

"Marisa is a cypher. Roommate didn't have much to say about her. No parents. No former place of employment. A dead end." He flipped through his notepad. "The cabby said she sounded drunk or high by the end of the ride. Probably took something just before she left the dormitory. When he asked her what her 'groom' was like, she said something like 'cow-chez spay-fud.' Mumbled some other strange-sounding stuff, too."

While he continued his report, Chiara was paging through the journal.

"DNA on the arm didn't match hers. No hits in the national database. I got nowhere with the ring. Philip Effling at the school's security searched every way through Monday and came up empty. She wasn't a student there. Another dead end and two bodies in the water." He frowned. "At least we kept it out of the papers."

"You're just full of good news. I guess you really did need me around to breathe some life into this investigation." Esperanza shoveled an enormous forkful of cake into his mouth. "Hey, it's second breakfast," he retorted to the looks from his coworkers.

"The forensic drawing you helped them create and fingerprints off the pen and phone ID'd the woman in the motel as Varvara Popova. Small time. Out on parole and missed her last visit. Hasn't been seen since the shooting. Waitress at Club Chaos here in town. Employer hasn't heard from her either. I interviewed him briefly. Abram Sokolov. He wasn't any help." He exhaled noisily. "I was hoping I'd see the guy that jumped you—you know, maybe he and Popova worked at Chaos together. But nobody else was around. Might have been hiding, I suppose."

"Did you ask Sokolov?"

"Yeah. He said on busy nights, he'll hire a bouncer or two, but they're all temps. Not sure if I believe him."

"What else do we know about Club Chaos?"

"A new lounge in town for twenty- and thirty-somethings. Loud dance music, bands on the weekends. Big on video poker in a side room." Whitehorse put down his fork and took a drink of coffee. "Well, any ideas? What am I missing?"

Chiara looked up from the journal. "Try saying 'cow chez spay fud' differently. You know, slow it down, speed it up. Then open Google and type in what you get. See if Google has any suggestions."

The two men looked at her as though she were a visitor from another planet.

"Use Google's autofill to see if you can get a lead." She returned to her reading.

"Cooww Chehzzzz Spaaaa Fuuud," Whitehorse began, to gales of laughter from his partner.

"Make it fast, Charley." Chiara turned into Coach Chiara. "What does cow-chez sound like? Could it be cowch's? How about changing the C-O-W to C-O-U? Couch's spayft. Here. Let me try." She put the journal aside and opened Google on her laptop. Her fingers flew over the keys. With a triumphant gleam in her eyes, she turned the machine around so the men could see it. "See what Google is suggesting under the entry line?"

And there it was. Couch's spadefoot toad.

"Holy shit, Chiara! She was calling her groom a toad!"

"And not just any toad, Charley," Esperanza chimed in. "You ever hear of a Couch's spadefoot toad?"

"Never."

"Know anyone who probably has?"

Whitehorse almost dropped the coffee cup in his hand. "Sweet mother! Sterling Friese! Finally a connection."

"I hate to rain on your parade guys," interrupted Chiara, "but all we've done is show that the bride took Friese's biology class. According to what you told me before, we already knew that. We still haven't proved she had anything special to do with him."

Whitehorse slumped back into his chair. "Since when did we promote you to detective, little Miss Sherlock?"

Chiara smiled. "I just keep my eyes and ears open."

"Well, keep doing it," said Esperanza.

"You know, for a minute, I thought we had something." The disappointment in the Native American's voice was clear to everyone in the office.

"Don't give up yet, Charley. I think I just found something in this book." Chiara was jamming her fingers into a small pouch on the back inside cover of the journal.

"I bet I went through that thing a hundred times."

"Well, it's folded up and taped inside the back pouch. Easy to miss. It's like she couldn't throw it away but didn't want anyone else to find it." She handed him a piece of paper about the size of a business card.

Whitehorse unfolded it carefully. "Dear God," he muttered. He cleared his throat and read it aloud.

Saturday morning, 6:00 AM

Hi, Marisa

Your dorm is locked, so I'm putting this in an envelope and taping it to the front door with your name on it. Hopefully, you've got some honest kids at your fancy school that will see that you get it.

First off, I'm not blaming you for what happened. It wasn't your fault and I don't want you to feel guilty about it. It's on me. I should have known better.

What I want you to know is that you're the best friend I've ever had. Thank you for that. But I guess it was one heartbreak too many. I'm done.

I'm taking the ring with me and hiking up to the LL. I've left him a note, too. Maybe I'm hoping he'll stop me? I don't know.

I'm so sorry.

All my love,

Emma

Esperanza whistled. "Jesus H. Christ! It sounds like a suicide note. Emma has to be the girl whose arm we found. And she knew Marisa. But who else did she leave a note for? And what the hell is 'the LL?'"

Whitehorse shrugged his shoulders.

"Really guys?" Chiara was shaking her head. "Every kid in town knows that. The LL is Lovers' Leap. Only they usually call it 'the Double L.' Kind of sounds like a train or something, don't you think? Anyway, you know at the very bottom of Cascadia Head how the road forks? The left fork takes you up to the university. The right fork takes you up this long winding road to a trailhead. Coast Crest Trail. Can't be more than a quarter mile or even less of pretty easy hiking to the cliffs at the end. Cliffs with a capital C. I'm talking about straight down, two hundred feet or more. That's the Double L. Beautiful views, by the way. You ought to check it out." She looked at her bosses with a smirk on her face. "And by the by, I hear from my friends at the college that the university considers that trail off-limits for students. Can't take the liability. They spell it right out in the student handbook."

Whitehorse ran his fingers through his hair. "I gotta hand it to you, Chiara. I don't know where we'd be without you. You're a lot more than a 'Girl Friday.'"

"Maybe I could be a 'Girl Monday-Through-Friday?' Could you run it by the City Council and see if you can get me approved for a paying job after I graduate in May?"

"You got it, girl."

"I keep telling my friend Hayley that this is the best job ever."

"She's the one with the job at the bank?"

"Yeah. When you mentioned the owner of Club Chaos,

you reminded me about something she told me in confidence a while back. I guess it's OK if I tell you. You won't get her in trouble?"

Both policemen raised their hands and shook their heads.

"Remember I told you there was something to do with ATMs? Turns out new federal regulations make the banks take pictures of every privately-owned ATM and a photo of the front of the shop or bar where it's parked."

"What's the deal? I never gave them a thought." Whitehorse knit his brows and Esperanza leaned forward.

"Turns out they're great for laundering money, like for drug dealers and such. I'm sure you guys know all about that kind of stuff. The bad guy puts his cash into the machine, the guy playing video poker uses his debit or credit card to take it out, and the bank deposits nice, clean money electronically into the bad guy's account, along with the ATM fee."

"Yeah, it's a pretty smooth deal," Whitehorse agreed. "And?"

"And so Hayley went with the bank manager to all the places in Driftwood with privately-owned machines. Some pretty spooky places, she said. Gave her the creeps."

"The point being?"

"All but two of the ATMs in town are owned by one guy. The owner of Club Chaos. I remembered because of that Russian-sounding name."

"The unhelpful Abram Sokolov. Employer of Varvara Popova." Whitehorse grimaced and scratched his head. Then he started smiling.

"Looks like the wheels are turning, Tracker. What have you got for us?" A broad grin spread across Esperanza's face.

"Let's say our boy Sokolov is a big-time drug dealer, and he has a sweet tooth for pretty young things. He entices Marisa into his bed with the promise of an unlimited supply of free drugs. But the girl plays a fast one on him and lets herself get pregnant. He drops her like a hot potato, maybe with a coda like 'You tell anybody that's my baby and I'll kill every friend you've ever had.'

She takes a handful of his pills and goes swimming. He hears about it and is afraid if we keep investigating, we'll find out about her connection to his drug operation. He sends Popova and another bad dude to persuade me to back off, only they make a mistake and bag you, Tony."

"And what about the arm?"

"Another of Sokolov's lovers. She finds out he's banging her best friend, Marisa. Impregnated her. She can't take it and throws herself off the cliff. Marisa reads the letter, is overwhelmed by guilt, and lets the wave take her the next day."

"And the ring?"

"The so-called engagement ring that Sokolov gives Marisa for extra sexual favors. He would have taken it back eventually, of course. It was just to sweeten the deal. Emma steals it from her in spite and takes it with her to her rendezvous at the Double L, where she becomes shark food."

Esperanza stood up and cheered. "You should be writing this stuff for Hollywood, man. That is the most entertaining script I've heard from you in a long time." He clapped furiously. "Crazy, but entertaining."

"Hey, you're the one who asked."

"Don't be hurt. It's just a little far-fetched."

"I'm open to any other ideas you've got."

Esperanza shrugged. "Fresh out of theories, buddy."

"So what do we do next?"

"Can we find out if Sokolov really does sell drugs?"

"How? Surveillance? Tough to do that with a two-man force. No time."

Chiara raised her hand, as though she were a child interrupting her parents' conversation. "I'm not old enough to go to Chaos, but my brother Perry is. He likes the place. Goes on Fridays and Saturdays with his friends. I'll bet forty dollars a night for drinks would persuade him to keep an eye out for anything going on."

Whitehorse and Esperanza looked at each other. "Couldn't hurt to do it for a weekend, could it?" said Whitehorse.

"Worth a try," his partner replied.

31. I Spy

Perry loved the idea. He was sitting at a table in Chaos, sipping a scotch and soda, shouting into his friend Mason's ear. The recorded dance music was just below the threshold of a jet engine at takeoff. The members of 3 Day Fish were setting up their instruments on the stage.

"These cops my little sister works for want to find out if this place is selling drugs. Especially up at the university. They're giving me forty bucks a night to sit here and keep my eyes open. It's a stakeout, man. Like in the movies. Pretty sweet gig, huh?"

"Tru dat. But how will you know it when you see it? I mean, what exactly are you looking for?"

"Hell if I know. The band up there is from the university, so I thought I'd go up before they start and take pictures of everybody." He pushed his long brown hair out of his eyes and scratched the week-old beard on his chin.

"Go for it. I'll just nurse my drink and check out the menu." Mason absently rubbed the inch-wide ring through his left earlobe.

Perry waded through the dancers on the floor and climbed the three stairs to the stage, where he got the group's attention by tapping Franklin on the shoulder. "I'm from Beachtown News," he shouted. "Can I take your pictures?"

"Sure, man. We'd love it. Any advertising is good advertising. I'm Frankie, by the way." He pointed to the man closest. "This is Mack, on bass. That's Jorge, on keyboards. And this is Larry, our drummer."

"Well, I'm Perry. Let me take a group shot first, then I'll get each of you individually."

"Using just your cell phone? I thought you guys all had fancy ass cameras." Frankie looked skeptical.

"Hey, we all got deadlines. This way I can get the pictures back to my office tonight. Now come on over here closer together."

He snapped several in fast succession, until he saw a

worried look wash over Frankie's face. Guessing someone was coming up behind him, he switched the phone to video record and turned around, holding it low, hoping to get images of whoever was approaching without their knowing it.

"Who are you?" The voice was loud and gruff and issued from a sour-faced man who towered over Perry.

"I'm Perry, from Beachtown News. Doing a photo piece on 3 Day Fish. And you are...?"

"Busy." Tolstoy looked around the man with the cell phone and addressed the lead guitarist. "Frankie, the boss wants to see you. Now."

"I'll be right back, guys."

Perry saw a frightened look on Frankie's face and kept recording as they walked off the stage into a back office. He turned to the remaining band members. "Let's do the individual pics while we're waiting."

Frankie returned five minutes later and Perry concluded the shoot. "I'm going back to my table so I can send these pictures in and watch your show. Come over after your set and tell me about yourselves." As he was leaving, he shouted, "And thanks, guys. Now go make some music."

He hurried back to Mason and took a big swallow of his drink. "Did you see that, Mace? Man, that guy's like a mountain on legs. I think I got a good video of him. They went into an office way in back that I never knew was there. I'm gonna send all this stuff to my sister and find out what the cops think about it." He drained his glass and raised his hand to get the attention of the cute mini-skirted server who was walking toward them with a tray of drinks in her hand. When she looked his way, he pointed to his empty glass on the table, and she nodded in response. A few quick motions of his fingers on the screen of his phone, and the pictures were sent on their way.

"Cool being undercover. Huh, buddy?"

"Sure, but I think you just burned through that forty and then some."

"Maybe I can get them to up the ante tomorrow. We

private investigators have expenses, after all."

"Tru dat."

Just then, the dance music stopped and the stage exploded in fire and fury. A piercing guitar riff shrilled through the smoke, as the drums crashed in a frenzied rhythm. Bass and keyboards launched into the fray, and the crowd shrieked its approval of the group's very own song *Zombies Rise.*

"Holy shit!" Perry grabbed his ears as waves of sound thudded into his chest with the force of a fire hose.

Mason was laughing at the bodies heaving on the dance floor. Conscious thought was impossible, blasted away by a tsunami of power chords and percussion. 3 Day Fish laid siege to the club and took it by storm.

Fifteen minutes into the set, Perry felt his phone vibrate. The message from Chiara said, "Great stuff. I'm sending it to my bosses now. I'll let you know tomorrow what they think."

The server arrived, set down the drink, and leaned over the table to talk directly into Perry's ear. "Let me know if there's anything else you want."

Mason tugged at her sleeve. "Could you bring us a large fry and ketchup? And a refill for me?"

"You got it." She zipped away to the bar to place the orders.

"I could get used to this spy shit," Perry quipped.

"You and me both, bro."

Thirty minutes later, Frankie announced to the crowd, "We're taking a short break now, but don't go away. Refresh your drinks, order some food, and we'll see you in fifteen."

The band members approached the table where Perry and his friend sat. "We gotta hydrate," Frankie said, as he waved his arm and got the attention of the bartender. "Ethan! Waters all around!" He made a circular motion with his hand and the man waved in response. "We never drink on duty. The music is everything." A server rushed to them with a tray of waters.

"You guys are fabulous," said Mason. "What a show!"

"Thanks. So what would you like to know?"

"Can I record this for later? I don't have my notebook with me." When no one demurred, he clicked the record button on his phone. "Don't know how well this will work with all the noise in here. I'll hold it toward each of you when you speak. So you all go to PCU, right?"

"Yeah. Juniors. This is how we get spending money. We can't even get close to tuition with our weekend gigs. That's what loans and parents are for."

"You guys native Oregonians?"

"I am. Larry is from Connecticut. Mack, Minnesota. Jorge, California."

"Quite a mixed group. Was it the music that brought you together?"

"And our shared distrust of politics and politicians," said Jorge.

Frankie smiled. "Jorge is our one and only anarchist, but he's of the peaceful persuasion. Content to watch the infrastructure crumble around us without lighting a match to help it along."

"Does your music address that?"

Larry burst in. "Our music is the epitaph on the grave of this corrupt society."

"Yow! That sounds pretty harsh."

"Have you been following what our country does to immigrants and their children? To other countries that aren't cookie cutter copies of us? To non-whites everywhere? Judgment day is coming, man. We're just the messengers."

"How is PCU dealing with all those issues?"

"PCU?" It was Mack's turn to chime in. "It's just another arm of corporate America. No world-saving going on at that place."

"You guys sound kind of grim. Given the doomsday feel of all this, do you think that mood contributes to drug use on the campus? I've heard it's a sellers' market up there." He saw Frankie stiffen.

"No way, man. School is really strict about that stuff. Zero tolerance policy." He took a long draft of water.

"So you're saying it's like a little castle up there, shielding the students from all the shit we have to deal with in the outside world?"

"No, man. I'm not saying that at all. It's the real world with rules. You get caught with drugs, they boot you out."

"So you gotta be real careful?"

"Look, it's time we get ready for our next set. Nice talking to you. C'mon, guys."

All the band members stood and headed toward the stage. When they were gone, Mason grabbed his friend's shirt. "You got pretty pushy. What was that all about?"

"Just seeing if he'd squeak if I rubbed him too hard. I think I hit a nerve. And it was just Frankie that was getting riled. The others looked like they could've cared less. I'm gonna text my sister."

"And tell her what?"

"We've identified suspect number one. Look. The bouncer guy calls him for a meeting with the boss in the back room. When he leaves, he looks like he's about to face a firing squad or piss his pants or maybe both. Then he's real antsy when I bring up drugs."

"Perry, you watch too damn much television. But I gotta admit, your interview was a piece of work."

They raised their glasses and clinked them together, just as the band blasted off.

"Spy times are high times!" Perry shouted. "This last round's on me."

32. Doing the Alligator Roll

Four days later, Peter called Chris at eight o'clock in the morning. "Any chance you could pick me up at school around 4:30 today? I had to bring my car in for service and didn't want to leave a rental in the school parking lot all day. If you can't, that's OK. I'll just have the dealership come and get me. They just usually take a long time doing it."

"Sure thing, Peter. I'll bring you to your car if it's ready, and then maybe we could go for a bite to eat."

"That works for me. See you this afternoon at the main entrance."

The day was very productive. Peter taught three classes, spent time with four doctoral students, and worked on the next exam for Abnormal Psych. As it got toward 4:30, he packed his brief case, put on his coat and hat, and headed toward the rendezvous with his friend.

After two days of sun and clouds, the gray deepened, and a light shower began. Mist curled up from the sea, feathering the edges of the campus as though seen through finely woven gauze. He walked down the sidewalk, looking for his friend's taxi. A black Mercedes sped into the traffic circle and intercepted him. A large man in a long, dark coat got out and came around the car toward him.

"Get into the car, Dr. Bristol," he snarled. "We have to talk."

"Who are you?"

"Someone who wants to be your friend. Now shut up and get in." He opened the passenger door and waved toward Peter.

A thrill of fear shivered through him. He looked for help, but no one else was close by. He backed away. "I'm not going anywhere with you."

"We can do it the easy way or the hard way, Professor. Get in now and I won't hurt you. Refuse to get in, and I'll break your arm. Either way, you're getting in. I imagine having an arm out of commission for a couple of months might be pretty hard for a teacher like yourself. Your call."

"What do you want with me?" His heart was pounding. The man was a giant compared to him and looked able to carry through on his threats.

"We need to have a chat about Franklin Wise."

"Who? Wise isn't in any of my classes this year. I don't know anything about him."

"Just get in the goddamn car!"

At that moment, the taxi turned into the traffic circle. Chris pulled up behind the Mercedes and sprang out of the vehicle. "What's the trouble here?" he called.

The man in the long coat turned and growled, "No trouble here. Just mind your own business. Drive away."

"Dr. Bristol is my friend, so this is my business. Drive away yourself, mister, unless you want to dance."

Peter saw his would-be kidnapper reach his hand inside his coat. He watched transfixed as his friend leaped into the air and pounced on the man. A gun clattered to the pavement as the two grappled together.

The terrified professor came to his senses and dialed 911. "Assault at the main entrance of Pacific Crest University! Hurry!"

The two men tumbled over and over on the ground. They reminded Peter of a news report he had seen of wildlife officers in Florida trying to capture an eight-foot alligator from a neighborhood porch. The reptile rolled itself around and around, wrenching the ropes from its would-be captors. So, too, the titans rolled, each scrambling to get a hold on the other. Chris freed an arm long enough to pound a punishing blow into the other man's ear. He responded by connecting with Chris's jaw, momentarily stunning him. Chris managed to pin the man's left arm behind his back, only to be thrown away by a herculean act of strength. He scrambled to his feet as the other man put his head down and charged. Feinting like a bullfighter, Chris allowed the man to pass by his side and came down with a double-fisted blow to the back of his neck. As the man's knees buckled, Chris hit him with a roundhouse kick that dropped him to the ground. The attacker tried to get up, but the former SEAL kicked him hard in the ribs, expelling the breath from him. It was over in seconds.

Chris picked up the gun and went to Peter. "You OK?"

"My knees are still a little shaky, but other than that, I'm fine."

"Who is this guy?"

"Damned if I know."

Chris pulled out his phone and snapped a picture of the fallen man.

"Did he say what he wanted?"

"Said we needed to have a talk about Franklin Wise."

"Who's that?"

"One of the students here."

"Getting up now, Dr. Bristol." The man in the coat had regained a sitting position on the wet pavement and was attempting to stand. His legs trembled at the effort. "You fight pretty good for an old man, Mr...."

"Harper. Chris Harper. Why don't you just stay down?"

"Oh, please. You won a fair fight. I don't have the energy for another round right now. But sometime, when I'm not held back by all this extra clothing..." He stood and shook the dirt from his coat. He rubbed his neck and ribs. "Just reaching for a handkerchief." He rummaged under his coat and withdrew a white handkerchief he used to stanch the blood from his lips and ear.

"We're pressing charges."

"Go for it. I'll tell my lawyers—who, I'm sure, are far better paid than yours—that you threw the first punch. Which is the gods' honest truth. I was merely trying to have a friendly conversation with a teacher who must've misunderstood my intentions. I'm worried about my nephew, Franklin Wise, and I want to do all I can to help him. I had heard Dr. Bristol might have some information about him."

"You threatened to break my arm!"

"Really? I don't remember that at all. I do recall your

saying you don't have time for anyone without an appointment. Not exactly the kind of attitude the university expects from its faculty, I'll bet."

Peter looked at Chris. "So it's my word against his."

"And may I have my gun back? I do have a permit to carry that, and I'd hate to have to accuse you of stealing it. It fell out of my holster when you tackled me."

Chris dropped the magazine out of the pistol and thumbed the cartridges out of it. Then he worked the slide and ejected the round from the chamber. He rammed the magazine back into the grip, and without saying a word, handed the gun back.

"Thank you, Mr. Harper. By the way, my name is Iosif Tolstoy. Feel free to take a picture of my license plate. You'll find I'm well-known in town. Lots of character witnesses." With that, he got into the car, started it, and pulled away.

"What the hell was that? Wise was a student of mine last year, but not this year. I could find out what classes he has and check with his profs." As he shook his head, he furrowed his brow. "Wait a minute."

"You thought of something?"

"Yeah. I had a conversation with Philip Effling, the head of Security here. He got pretty uptight when I asked about Sterling Friese. Suppose he and Friese are in cahoots? Covering up the murder of Dean Wasserman? Sending a little muscle to persuade me to stop looking for trouble?"

"Hold on, buddy. Listen to what you're saying. Murder?"

"Yeah, murder with poison from a toxic newt."

"I told you before, Peter. You're my friend and all, but that is just paranoid nonsense."

"Then why did Sterling tell me Whitehorse got into the Dean's office without a warrant, when even Effling admits he had one? Why did the university's lawyer have the warrant withdrawn before the search was complete? Avoiding a scandal? And why search the office anyway? What could he be looking for?"

"That's all circumstantial bullshit. You see that, don't you?"

"Is Mr. Tolstoy circumstantial? I'm telling you he threatened to break my arm if I didn't get in the car with him. What's that about?" He threw up his hands. "Sorry. I meant to thank you, by the way. You saved my bacon."

"Happy to do it, Peter, but I don't have a clue what's going on." Chris had an exasperated expression on his face.

"Something smells, my friend. I've got to get to the bottom of this."

"And what will you do if Tolstoy comes back?"

"Talk to him very nicely."

Chris bent over to pick up the cartridges from the pavement. He stuffed them into his pocket and looked up at the darkening sky. "Looks like the rain is getting more serious. I'm wet and cold."

Just then they heard a police siren approaching and saw the cruiser speeding up the drive. As the vehicle stopped and a policeman got out, Peter said, "Hello, Officer Whitehorse. We were just talking about you."

33. Joey Rides the Double L

L ater that evening, Sterling heard the wind rising as the rain rapped on the skylights like nervous fingers on a desktop. His second glass of wine stood half-empty beside the plate holding the remnants of his chicken dinner. He looked at his watch. Still plenty of time to clean up.

Grace had some kind of sorority dinner and couldn't come until about eight o'clock. He'd have the kitchen cleaned, a new bottle of wine open, and the candles lit in the bedroom long before she arrived.

He was startled by the doorbell ringing. "Grace, you're earlier than I expected. The place is a mess," he said as he turned the lock and opened the door. His jaw dropped when he saw the giant standing there. The man's coat looked as though he had rolled on the ground in it, and there were traces of dried blood by his left ear and swollen lower lip. The left side of his head was turning purple with a large bruise.

"Hello, Professor. We need to have a little talk." The man pushed his way into the house and took a seat on the couch in the den. "Come, Dr. Friese. Sit. Let's chat. Hope I don't get your furniture dirty."

Without taking his eyes off the man, Sterling closed the door and walked into the den, sitting in his upholstered armchair opposite him. He composed himself and asked, "To what do I owe the pleasure?"

"Relax. You look like a bunny rabbit staring at a rattlesnake. I just want to be in the loop is all—to know what you know. I had a little meeting with our mutual friend, Dr. Bristol, this afternoon. It didn't go well."

Sterling's eyes went round. "Did he do that to you?"

Tolstoy laughed. "That little prick? Hell, no. But he had a very competent friend."

"Would you like an ice pack?"

"Let's stop beating around the bush. I believe Bristol when he says he doesn't know anything about Frankie. What I don't know is what you know about Frankie. And about me."

Sterling fidgeted in the chair and reached an arm behind the pillow. He grasped the pistol and inserted his finger into the trigger guard. "Let's see. What do I know about Franklin Wise? Well, I know he smokes weed, but I haven't turned him in. Given the tenor of the times, that's small potatoes. Several students I'm...friendly with have told me they get more passionate and have better orgasms with some of the other stuff they've bought from him. Even had me try it with them, and they're exactly right." He smiled. "So yes, I know he's our pharmacy here on campus." He saw Tolstoy's jawline grow taut.

"What else?" he growled.

"What else? Well, the rest is speculation, of course. You don't strike me as intelligent enough to run a drug operation here in town. I'm guessing your boss, the owner of Chaos, does that, and you're his hired gun. Abram Sokolov. Looked him up." Sterling shrugged his shoulders. "Don't know if he's family with the Russians in Portland or just a private entrepreneur. Is that enough, Sasquatch?"

"What did you call me?" Tolstoy barked. He reached his hand under his coat.

Sterling leaped to his feet, gun in hand, and pointed it directly at Tolstoy's head. "You so much as twitch, you oaf, and I'll drill you a third eye. And don't think for a minute I'd hesitate. When the police get here, I'll tell them you broke into my house. Self-defense."

"Slow down, Professor. We don't have to be enemies." Sterling could see the fear in the big man's eyes. "You've been protecting our interests by not ratting Frankie out. It sounds like you benefit from that, too. Maybe a cut of Frankie's share to keep the gears running smoothly up here?"

"I'd consider that. How much are we talking about?"

"That's not my decision. You'd have to talk to the boss."

"Then let's do that. I have a guest coming later, so maybe we can wrap this up quickly."

Tolstoy seemed to relax. "Abe's at Chaos. I'll introduce

you to him."

"Excellent. But first I'll have to relieve you of your gun. After all, we're not exactly bosom buddies yet. So pull your hand out very slowly, and open your coat so I can see the gun."

Tolstoy complied.

"Good. Now with two fingers only, remove the gun and drop it on the rug." Again, the man followed orders. "Very good. Now your keys and your cell phone. Very slowly. OK. We'll be leaving through the garage. Any sudden moves and I'm afraid I'll have to ruin our budding relationship."

Sterling stepped back and out of the way of any quick rush Tolstoy might attempt. He picked up the key fob from a decorative bowl on a small table by the door to the garage. "OK. Open the door and hit the garage door opener on the right." As the door slid up, he said, "Good. Your car hasn't blocked me in."

Tolstoy reached for the passenger door, but Sterling corrected him. "Sorry, sweetums, but until we get to know each other better, you'll have to ride in the trunk."

"Crap, man. I'll barely fit in there. I won't jump you."

Sterling popped the trunk with the remote and motioned with the Colt. "Just get in. And don't get any ideas about picking up a rake or a shovel and coming at me. I'm a hell of a shot with this. I'll just wait in the doorway here until you're inside."

Tolstoy fumed but crawled into the narrow space. Sterling approached the trunk slowly and slammed it shut from the side, unwilling to present himself as a target for the giant to leap out at. Once the man was safely confined, he walked to the back of the car and spoke to him. "Sorry, Sasquatch, but I could only afford a used Lexus. This is a 2013, and they were notorious for having the inside trunk release break off. I'm afraid you're stuck in there. And in case you think about busting through the back seat to get me en route, know that the gun is beside me up front, and I'll pop you without a second thought. I'll tell the cops it was a car-jacking, of course."

"Just hurry up and get us down to Chaos," came the voice from inside. "I'm cramping up."

Sterling took a large lantern from a shelf and got in. He started the car, backed out, closed the garage door, and turned toward Cascadia Head. Twenty minutes later, as the car began bumping along the dirt road, Tolstoy shouted from the trunk. "Where the hell you taking me? This isn't the way to the Club."

"A little side trip. Wanted to show you one of my favorite places. You'll really like it."

The giant yelled a string of profanities at him.

"That's not the kind of example we want to set for our young people. Watch your mouth."

Another mile and Sterling braked the car to a stop. The rain had eased up again, but the air was heavy with moisture. The rich smells of salt air mingled with the loamy smells of deep forest. The surf was nearer, crashing heavily on the shoreline far below. Sterling picked up the lantern and the gun.

"Don't you jump out at me, now," he called into the trunk. But he knew Tolstoy would. He positioned himself off to the side, far from any possible attack. With the beam of the lantern full on the trunk, he pushed the remote button on the key fob.

Tolstoy leaped from the trunk as if shot from a carnival cannon. He tumbled to the dirt and rolled in a heap. Sterling was guffawing.

"You should have seen yourself! The look on your face! It was priceless! Now get up, you useless piece of shit."

"Where are we?"

"We're taking that trail there to Lovers' Leap. Or the Double L as the young ones call it. Great views."

"But it's dark, for God's sake."

"That way we have it all to ourselves. Start walking." Sterling held the lantern in one hand and his pistol in the other. He stayed far enough back that his prisoner couldn't kick dirt, snap a branch at him, or turn and pounce. He was taking no chances. "Mind your step, big fella. No guard rails and the path gets pretty narrow in places. Wouldn't want you falling off. It's a long way down."

The forest was silent but for the soft drum beat of

collected drops of rain that fell from the branches high above. Below, the waves broke on the rocks at the base of the cliffs. In the distance, an owl hooted.

"How much farther we got to go?"

"Not much. We're almost at the lookout. You'll be able to see up and down the coast for miles in both directions." He wished he had had the presence of mind to bring a coat with him when he left the house. *I was under duress,* he thought.

The beam of light bobbed as they walked. Soon the forest opened up, and they were in a sloping meadow. The surf became louder, more insistent. An occasional hole in the featureless clouds overhead winked with stars. On the horizon, they could see the lights of fishing boats plying their trade in the inky black water.

"OK, Friese. We're here. End of the line."

They stood on a table of rock, perhaps ten feet by ten feet. It was like the nail on a finger of forest that jutted into the sea. Sheer rock walls tumbled straight down into the Pacific.

"It's nice. Can we go now? I'm getting a little chilled. I'd like a drink."

Sterling shined the light into the man's eyes. "You'll get a drink, all right. I hope you don't mind, but I think you're out of a job. Suppose your boss will have a hard time replacing you, or does he have somebody waiting in the wings, ready to step up?"

"Hey, wait a minute. Wait a minute, Professor. You don't have to do this. I thought we had a deal. I was going to introduce you to Abe. If you need a bigger cut than just a piece of Frankie's action, I'm sure we could work something out. You don't wanna commit murder."

"Well, the thing is, Joey—isn't that what Wise calls you, at least according to Amelia?—the thing is, Joey, I already have committed murder. Fact is, I'm pretty good at it." He sighed at the memory. "I consider this place my own industrial strength garbage disposal. Watched a pretty young thing go over and nobody missed her! I scoured the papers, but nothing. That's when I figured it out. Nobody really gives a shit." He was shaking his head, frowning. "Will anybody miss you, Joey?"

"Hey, c'mon, Dr. Friese. We can work this out. We can cut a deal."

"Groveling doesn't become you, Joey. Stand up straight and take your medicine."

"I got a wife, man. And a teenage kid. And a mother in a nursing home. Please."

For a brief moment, Sterling waved the gun above his head, then he pointed it at the big man again. "Do you think there's a God above all this, Joey? Controlling everything?"

"What?"

"I'm inclined to agree with the French existentialists. Aren't you?"

"What the hell are you talking about?"

"The universe is indifferent to us. We're strangers in a strange land. Orphans in space. Maybe worse. Sartre said, 'Man is the disease of being.' If that's true, I guess that makes me the cure. Or maybe a vaccine. What do you say?"

"Please don't shoot me."

"I know that part. What about the rest? What do you believe about life?"

"It's a dog-eat-dog world, Professor. We gotta take what we need. Nobody's gonna give it to us."

"See. That's what I mean. Thank you. You didn't get that out of a textbook. You got that on the streets, from the hard knocks of life."

"Damn straight."

"So here's your last hard knock. You can either jump off the cliff of your own free will, or you can let me shoot you. Who knows? Maybe there's a one in a billion chance that you'd survive the fall, but there's zero chance you'd survive a .45 bullet to the head. Your call. I'll count to ten. One..."

"For Chrissakes, hold on! You can't do this!"

"Two..."

"I'll give you every penny I have stashed away. The deed to my house. The title to my Mercedes."

"Funny how, in the end, none of that stuff matters, does it? Three..."

"Goddamn it, give me a chance!"

"You've had what? Thirty-five, forty years of chances? Four..."

Tolstoy roared in defiance and charged him. A single shot rent the night, and he crumpled in a heap at Sterling's feet.

"Bad choice. Now I have to push your sorry ass over the cliff, and I bet you weigh a ton." He positioned the lantern on the ground to provide the maximum light. Then he sat on the ground and used his legs to roll Tolstoy's body over. He scooted closer and rolled the body again. Ten arduous minutes later, the body was perched on the edge of the precipice. He looked at his watch.

"I have barely enough time to get back and shower before my date arrives. Pray that she doesn't do anything stupid and have to wind up with you, asshole."

With that, he gave a final thrust with both legs and sent the body hurtling into the darkness.

As he drove back down the hill, he reviewed the events of the evening to make sure he had not forgotten any detail that might trip him up. *Of course. The ape's car. Should I just leave it on the street somewhere? Drop it off in a store parking lot? But why give the police a heads-up about a missing person?* He hastily formulated a plan.

Twenty-five minutes later, he was sifting through the contents of the Mercedes' glove compartment, looking for the registration. "*Voilà!*" he said aloud. "47581 Periwinkle Court, Driftwood." He entered the information into the maps app on his cell phone. Then he rushed back into the house, picked up Tolstoy's gun and cell phone, and, after wiping them down with a handkerchief to remove any traces of his fingerprints, stowed them in the car. With precious little time left, he returned to the house for a quick shower before Grace arrived.

"You've bought a new car?" she gushed when he greeted her at the door.

He stepped back to admire her short leather skirt and form-fitting blouse. "You look smashing tonight, darling. But I'm afraid the car isn't mine. Would you believe a friend asked me to drive him to the airport in Portland? We didn't think we'd have enough time to get his car back to Driftwood before we left, so I told him I'd take it back when I got home. I've got his keys. Would you do me the favor of following me in your car?"

"What's it worth to you?" she said, pouting with her bright red lips.

He leaned toward her and nuzzled her neck. "Up to half my kingdom," he whispered in her ear.

When Grace had returned to her car, Sterling got into the Mercedes and removed the phone from his pocket. He started the map to find Tolstoy's house and pulled out of the driveway.

They reached the house in less than half an hour. Sterling pushed the button to open the garage door, while Grace parked in the street and waited for him. Once inside the garage, he wiped the keys and put them in the center console. Then he wiped down the steering wheel as well. Using the same handkerchief to cover his finger, he pushed the button and ran out while the garage door closed behind him.

"There," he said to Grace as he got into her car. "Good deed done."

"Not hardly," she said. "Your good deeds haven't even started yet." She put a hand on his thigh.

He moved toward her, kissing her hard on the lips, relishing the whimper she made. "I have a very special wine for us tonight. I'm sure you'll enjoy it."

"I'm ready to enjoy everything."

34. Girlfriends

"More wine, Charley?" Chloe had fixed them a simple dinner—grilled pork chop, broccoli, a green salad. She smiled at the man she loved.

"Just a bit, thanks."

She poured half a glass for each of them. "You seem preoccupied. Cracking the case?"

"Maybe some movement. We think we've ID'd the guy that assaulted Tony. Chiara's brother Perry took some photos last weekend in Club Chaos. Big Russian brute—Iosif Tolstoy. Runs interference for the club's owner, Abram Sokolov." He took a sip of wine and returned his glass to the table. "Tolstoy showed up this evening at PCU, threatening Peter Bristol, the guy who started this whole thing. Wanted to know what Bristol knows about this student Franklin Wise, the kid we saw Tolstoy talking to in Perry's pictures. The Russian got in a helluva fight with Peter's friend Chris. Guy runs the taxi here in town."

"Coronado Cab?"

"Yeah. The cab that drove our swimmer to the beach. My friend Phil Effling, who's keeping tabs on Friese at the university, says this same Russian palooka paid visits to that student and to our famous Dr. Friese on the same day. On top of that, we've got a suicide note from Emma, the gal whose arm we found. She and the swimmer knew each other."

"Wow! What's next?"

"We're off to Chaos tomorrow to have a chat with Mr. Tolstoy. I'm sure he'll have an interesting alibi. Then back to PCU to talk with Marisa's roommate, Alicia, again. See if she can tell us anything about Emma."

"Never stops, does it?"

His eyebrows arched like question marks.

"The dirt and grime of death. I suppose a small town is better than a big city, but you still have to deal with the underbelly of things. The filth. The pollution of evil. Like mushrooms that grow in the dark." She became thoughtful for a moment. "How do you keep from becoming cynical? Or better, how do you keep from despair?"

Whitehorse took another sip of wine and exhaled a deep breath. "By reminding myself that evil is only an aberration—a perversion of life—not the heart of things. Evil is to mind and spirit what cancer is to flesh and bone. I excise it when I can. Isolate it when I can't." He put his glass down and chuckled. "Whoa! Where did that come from? Maybe that's just the wine talking. I guess I do my job the best I know how. Try to catch the bad guys and lock 'em up. Think you'll be able to bear it?"

"What do you mean?"

"When I make an honest woman out of you?"

Chloe smiled back at him. "I've learned not to hold my breath about that one." She reached across the table and stroked his face. "But yeah, I'll handle it." She ran a finger over his lips. "Kiss me?"

They both stood. Whitehorse leaned his face to hers and kissed her mouth. She responded in kind, pulling him close, feeling her body warm to his. She moaned in pleasure. "Stay with me tonight," she whispered into his ear. "For life's sake."

The next day, Whitehorse and Esperanza went to the university first, since Chaos didn't open until just before noon. Effling met them at Amelia's desk in Administration.

"Tony, I'd like you to meet Philip Effling. Runs Security up here. He's been an enormous help."

"My pleasure, Philip." They shook hands.

"Glad to see you're among the living. Heard you had a real close call. Find the perps yet?"

"One's disappeared. We're going to have a visit with the other one after we're through here."

"Well, good luck with that. Anyway, I've called ahead to make sure Marisa's roommate, Alicia, is there. C'mon with me."

They walked to the Columbia River Dorm under a sun-dappled sky. "Almost the equinox," said Effling.

"Yeah," said Whitehorse. "A day with equal amounts of

light and dark. And then the light keeps growing, overcoming the shadow."

"Hmmm, partner. If I didn't know any better, I'd say you were turning into a philosopher."

"Nope. Just haven't had enough morning coffee yet."

Effling and Esperanza laughed. The three men walked through the glass doors.

"Whitney, you know Officer Whitehorse. This is his partner, Officer Esperanza. Tony, this is Whitney, one of the RAs for this dorm. Whitney, I'll sign the register for us. Would you let Alicia know we're here? And key the elevator for us, please."

As they got off the elevator, Esperanza said, "Nothing like my school."

Whitehorse held up his hand and rubbed his thumb and fingers together.

"Yeah, I get it. Takes a lot of bread to go here."

Effling pushed the button labeled *Alicia Farmington*. "We're here, Alicia."

She buzzed them in, and they walked down the hallway to 210. Alicia opened after the first knock. The room looked brighter today. The curtains were open. No dirty clothes peeked out from under either bed, both of which were neatly made. Textbooks lay open on the small desk. "Big test today," she said, as if in answer to the unspoken question. "So what do you want?"

"Well, you talked about Marisa's boyfriend last time, but what about girlfriends? She have any that you know of? Any she was close to?"

"Emma. She was real good friends with Emma. Brought her here to the room for girls' night a few times. Just between us, I think Emma had the hots for her. You know? I don't think Marisa swung both ways, but it can be kinda hard to tell that stuff."

"But Emma didn't go to school here?"

"No way. It's like she almost sounded insulted when we told her she should apply for a scholarship here. Don't know what she had against this place."

"If she wasn't a student here, how did they meet?"

184

"At BeachStone Photo. Just like Marisa was old school with her journal, she was old school about taking pictures." Alicia was bouncing her head up and down. "Yep. Wouldn't think of taking pictures with her phone. Strictly camera. All these big lenses and attachments. Photography was a very special thing for her. 'I'm gonna be a real photographer,' she'd say. 'An artist.'" She took a deep breath and sighed. "Emma was her go-to girl at BeachStone. You know? Whenever she wanted a print made, she'd have Emma do it. Said Emma's attention to detail made her the best."

"And?"

"And one thing led to another. She started hanging with Emma whenever she wasn't with her boyfriend. You know? I wasn't needed anymore. Got sorta left behind."

"Why didn't you tell us this before?"

"You didn't ask. And I don't like talking about it."

It was Whitehorse's turn to sigh. "Sounds like that was hard for you. Losing a friend like that."

"I'm all right." There were tears in her eyes.

Esperanza put a hand on her shoulder. "Sorry we had to bring all this up. But now there's something else I have to ask. Is her camera still here? Maybe a portfolio of her work?"

"Administration boxed it all up. I'm gonna get a new roommate soon, and they had to clear all Marisa's stuff out."

Esperanza looked at Effling.

"I'm on it." He pulled the phone from his pocket and stepped out into the hall.

"Alicia, you've been very helpful to us today. Thank you." Whitehorse didn't know what else to say.

"Yeah. Sure. Anytime."

The men took their leave. Whitehorse could hear Alicia sobbing after she closed the door behind them.

When they reached the first floor, Effling's phone rang. "Got it. Perfect. Thanks, Amelia. We'll be right over."

"Marisa's stuff is locked in the basement of the Admin Wing."

They rushed across the courtyard and into Administration. After a brief check-in with Amelia, they hurried past her desk to the elevator. Amelia was right behind them and keyed the doors.

"Here we go," said Effling, as they filed into the elevator and hit the button for the basement.

When the doors opened again, Esperanza looked startled. "It's a lot bigger than I imagined it would be."

"Kind of reminds me of that room in Harry Potter's Hogwart's—the one with all the magic stuff in it," said Whitehorse.

"Or my grandmother's attic." Esperanza was shaking his head back and forth. "Watch my allergies kick in."

"Students get to store extra things here," said Effling. "Like suitcases, pictures they don't want on their walls anymore. Old knick-knacks. Used furniture. Out of date computers and other electronics. And often, they forget the stuff's here—like they've molted on the way to becoming something else. The skin they shed lies here gathering dust until the university cleans it all out—once a year on the first of July."

"Is everybody around here becoming a goddamn philosopher?" asked Esperanza.

"Maybe it's contagious in a place like this," quipped Whitehorse. "You better watch out."

"Fat chance," he chuckled.

They spread out to cover the area as quickly as they could. Several mattresses and bed frames were leaning up against the wall on the left. Along the wall on the right were rows of swivel chairs, three steel desks, and assorted furniture. Great stacks of suitcases, all with name-tags, occupied the middle of the room. Next to them was a heap of computer towers and keyboards, tangled in a bird's nest of wires. In a far corner were clocks and vases, scratched and dented file cabinets, framed pictures and cheap prints.

"Here's a bunch of boxes that looks promising. They're taped shut, but they have labels on them." Esperanza busied himself by pulling out the boxes one at a time and checking the names. "This could take a while." Twenty minutes later, he was still at it.

"I've found another pile over here." Effling's voice sounded daunted. "This is more of a challenge than I thought it would be. Is that you sneezing, Tony?"

"Dust gets me every time."

An hour later, their enthusiasm and their energy had diminished. "Not sure I can take much more of this, guys. Can we take a break?" Esperanza was blowing his nose again.

"Wait a minute. I think I've found something." It was Whitehorse, calling from the far western corner of the basement. "Boxes of clothes and books, photo albums, and a big camera in a case sitting right on top."

His colleagues rushed to his side. "Here's a Biology textbook with Marisa's name in it. This is her stuff, all right. Looks like there's eight photo albums. Why don't we each take a couple and go through them. See if there's anything we can use. They've got dates on them. I've got the latest. Sit on the floor or grab a chair from over there."

Whitehorse rolled a desk chair from the row by the wall and began to peruse an album. His partners did the same.

"She was really good," said Esperanza. "I've got landscapes here, portraits, even abstracts. Good as any stuff I've seen in a magazine or a museum."

"Ditto. Here's a series of portraits. Looks like classmates. It's like you can see their soul looking through their eyes." Effling was mesmerized by the pictures in front of him.

"Oh, dear God," murmured Whitehorse. "I've found Emma. Marisa has written her name on these pages." His voice was quiet, as though in the presence of the Holy. He tried to catch his breath. His eyes misted over. "She's so...so..." He was unable to finish the sentence.

There in his lap was a black and white study of a young goddess. Although in some pictures she was clothed, in most she was nude, the curves of her body proportioned exquisitely, as if she had been sculpted by a master from the purest marble. She disregarded the eavesdropping camera, as one might a stranger of no consequence. Self-possessed, she was at once erotic and innocent, seductive and naïve. Her face was an enigma, neither smiling nor frowning, lips parted as though at the end of a spoken word. Her eyes, deep and dark, riveted Whitehorse to the spot. He heard them say, "I have seen too much, hurt too much to bear..."

Esperanza gasped. "If Michelangelo had had a camera, those are the pictures he would have taken."

"Emma," whispered Effling.

Whitehorse struggled to speak, his voice catching in his throat. "We found the severed arm of this beautiful creature on the beach. Dear God in heaven."

The men were silent after that, each lost in his own thoughts, each knowing his job put him in contact with evil on a daily basis, knowing most of that evil was mundane, banal, as ordinary as ordering an overpriced coffee from a drive-up shop. But this apposition of the sublime and the sordid sickened them all.

Finally, it was Whitehorse who broke the spell and brought them back to the task at hand. "Let's keep going through these albums. See if there's anything else of importance."

Esperanza and Effling returned to their seats and opened their albums.

"I've got one from a year and a half ago. She was still refining her technique. Nowhere near what we saw in your album, Charley."

"Well, keep at it, Tony. You got anything, Philip?"

"Just more of the same. Any idea what we're looking for?"

"Maybe some divine intervention?" Whitehorse harrumphed.

"Well, holy shit! We may have just got it." Esperanza ran to his partner. "Take a look at this."

Effling looked over his shoulder. "Looks like a picture taken in a bedroom. Couple pictures hanging on the wall. That's the headboard of a bed."

"Tell him, Charley."

188

"Goddamn it! When we went through Friese's old house in Driftwood last year—that's his bedroom! He had those paintings of birds on the wall. Said some student of his did them. So Marisa was in Friese's bedroom—that's more than just taking a class from the sonofabitch." He stopped as if thunderstruck. "Double Goddamn it!"

"What? What've you got, Tracker?"

"Can you read the labels on those bird paintings? He had them all labeled. He spent the morning trying to impress us with the Latin names of his stuff and odd facts about them."

"Sorry. No can do. The image is too small."

"Hey, give me a try," interrupted Effling. "I got a bird feeder at my house. Spend a lot of time identifying them with a book I got." He leaned in closer to the picture. "Sure. The bird on the right is an American Goldfinch. The one on the left is a Varied Thrush. So what?"

Whitehorse opened Google on his phone and searched for Varied Thrush. "Got it!" His voice was triumphant. He showed the phone to his partner. "Try saying the Latin name."

"Ix-oh-ray-us—"

"Stop! What does that sound like?"

Esperanza shrugged his shoulders. Effling looked confused. Whitehorse pulled out his note pad.

"That's the 'weird shit' the cab driver said Marisa was spouting when she got out of his cab and started down to the beach. The Latin name for the Varied Thrush—*Ixoreus naevius*. And watch this." He Googled American Goldfinch. "There it is. *Carduelis tristis*. Car-do-ellis—the other thing she said. What she saw when she was in his bedroom, riding that sonofabitch. What she saw when everything went wrong."

Esperanza shook his head and grimaced. "Friese is Marisa's groom—the guy who impregnated her."

Whitehorse nodded in agreement. "Friese is Couch's spadefoot toad."

35. Like Mushrooms That Grow in the Dark

It was two o'clock by the time they left the university. Esperanza rubbed his belly. "Let's stop for a quick burger before we go to Chaos. I'm starving."

"Sounds good to me. Why don't you check in with Chiara and see if anything's going on."

Esperanza called while Whitehorse drove.

"Hey, Tony." It was Chiara's cheerful voice. "All's quiet on the western front. How did you guys make out at PCU?"

"Very productive morning. We'll brief you when we get back. We're gonna stop for a bite and then head over to Chaos and pay Mr. Tolstoy a visit."

"Be careful, guys. Oh, by the way, my boyfriend and I picked out my diamond last night. I'll have to tell you all about it later."

"Copy that. Guard the fort."

Whitehorse pulled into a drive-through and ordered burgers, fries, and drinks for both of them. "You're buying next time," he told his partner, who nodded in response. Their meals were gone in minutes.

"That's gonna sit in my gut like lead for the next two hours."

The Native American smiled. "It always seems so good when you're hungry, and it's always so bad after you've scarfed 'em down. We should know better."

In ten more minutes, they pulled into the small parking lot behind Club Chaos.

"I am so looking forward to this guy's alibi. I want him to be looking right into my face, remembering how I kicked him in the balls."

"We'll just play it cool. I'm sure he's got quite a story. Depending on how it goes, we can decide if we want to bring him down to the station for questioning. Maybe even book him on suspicion."

They entered the club and felt the pounding of the

recorded music.

"Are people in here deaf?" Esperanza shouted at his partner.

"If they aren't already, they will be." Whitehorse looked over at the video poker room, where supplicants sat before their idols. He shook his head. "Never understood the appeal of that." He walked toward the bartender and got his attention. "We're here to see Mr. Tolstoy."

"He ain't here. Let me call the owner, Mr. Sokolov." He picked up a phone and turned his back on the policemen. As he finished the call, he turned around and said, "He'll see you. Go down that hall to the right of the stage. His office is down in back. Can't miss it."

The men followed the directions and were soon knocking on the Russian's door. They were invited in and closed the door behind them, blocking out some of the club's ambient sound.

"I'm Officer Esperanza. I think you've met my partner, Officer Whitehorse, before."

"Good afternoon, gentlemen." Sokolov did not stand or offer his hand. "What can I do for you today?" He sat behind his desk, tie loosened at the throat, sleeves of his white shirt rolled up to his elbows. He ran a finger down the scar on his cheek, just as Whitehorse had seen him do at their previous meeting. *His tell*, the policeman thought. Then the man stroked his short beard. Stacks of papers covered the desk and a large ledger was open in front of him.

"We'd like to speak with your employee, Iosif Tolstoy." Esperanza acted as their spokesperson.

"So would I. He hasn't come to work today. Hasn't called. Very unlike him. May I ask why you want to see him?"

"We have reason to believe he's the one who assaulted me at the Blue Whale Motor Inn a while back. With another of your employees, a Miss Varvara Popova, who also seems to have conveniently disappeared."

"Oh, dear. How unfortunate. I've never completely trusted those two. Always seemed to be scheming behind my back. I'm certainly glad you weren't hurt more seriously."

"It was bad enough—take my word for it. Do you know where Tolstoy was yesterday?" Esperanza studied the man's eyes, hoping he would lie about Tolstoy's adventure at the school. The man never flinched.

"I think he was going out to Pacific Crest University. He's very solicitous about his nephew."

"And who would that be?"

"Franklin Wise. Plays in a band we sometimes feature here." He looked at a schedule on his desk. "In fact, he'll be playing here this weekend, Friday and Saturday."

"Well, Tolstoy left the college about five o'clock. Any idea where he was going after that?"

"Let me think. Yes, he called me to say he was going to meet with one of Franklin's teachers. The man had already left for the day, but agreed to meet with him at his home."

"That's pretty unusual for a university professor, isn't it?"

"I should say so. But he's a pretty unusual man. Very dedicated to his students."

"And that would be...?"

"Dr. Sterling Friese."

Esperanza heard Whitehorse cough. "How long has Tolstoy worked for you, Mr. Sokolov?"

"I told your partner when he last visited me that Iosif is a temp. That's not totally accurate. He started as a temp, but he's been part-time for me over the last year. I'll especially want him here this weekend when the band plays. The crowds can get pretty boisterous. Young people dance and get thirsty, so they drink more. But we've always maintained a safe club. That's one of the reasons we're so popular."

"With that and your video poker machines, I imagine you must turn quite a profit. Good thing you've got all those ATMs in town to help with your cash flow." From the look in Sokolov's eyes, the barbed communication was not lost on him.

"Can I help you gentlemen with anything else? I must get back to business." His tone sounded dismissive.

"May we have Tolstoy's home address? Maybe see if he's there. Save us the time of looking it up."

"Certainly." The Russian opened a drawer, removed a file, and wrote the address on an index card. "Here you go."

"You've been most helpful, Mr. Sokolov. We'll show ourselves out."

Once they were back in the cruiser, Esperanza said, "So first he's a temp, now he's part-time. What do you think, Charley?"

"He may be a part-time bouncer, but he's a full-time hired gun for Sokolov."

"My thoughts exactly. What now?"

"Let's run by his house, though I don't think we'll find anything."

"Think the toad got him?"

"At this point, nothing would surprise me."

Within ten minutes, they were pulling into the driveway on Periwinkle Court.

"Pretty nice house for a part-time bouncer," said Whitehorse. The ranch-style dwelling was painted in subtle earth tones that complemented the stonework around the garage and front door. The lawn and gardens looked as though they were professionally maintained.

The policemen walked up to the front door and rang the bell. When no one answered, Esperanza said, "I'm gonna look around back."

"I'll check the windows here and on the side. See if I can see anything." Whitehorse shielded his eyes and looked through the glass panes surrounding the front door. Then he walked to the nearest window, peering inside, looking for anything out of order. His partner came back around.

"Everything looks OK. Doors are locked. Can't see anything out of place. Should we try to get a warrant from your judge friend and search inside? Tell him we got a possible assault subject that may be on the run?"

"Let's call it attempted murder. That'll get his attention."

"Sounds good to me."

Sokolov looked at his watch for the fourth time in the last half hour. Four-thirty. He had not heard from Iosif all day and feared the man was either locked up somewhere or dead. He presumed the latter. Should he call Volkov? *Blyad!* He picked up his phone from where it lay on the desk and tapped it. A few rings later he heard the voice he hated.

"Hello, Abram. Always good to hear from you. I trust you're enjoying the break in the weather?"

"Yes, Vasily. Of course, it's always a bit chillier here at the coast."

"Indeed. Good news to report, I trust?"

The man was silent for several moments, trying to decide how to describe what had happened in a way that would not make him look like a fool. He gave up on the effort. "I've lost my number one man."

"Iosif Tolstoy?"

"Yes. Iosif. He went to check on Sterling Friese, the man who told my boy Frankie that the police were looking for him. That was last night, and I haven't heard from him since."

"Dead?"

"I presume so."

"This man, Friese. Who is he?"

"A professor at the university here." He was greeted by gales of laughter.

"A professor—a teacher! An effete intellectual!—took down that giant? I find that hard to believe."

"I think we underestimated him. I think he's very dangerous."

"Then take him out! We can't afford to look weak to our competitors." He paused. "No. Better yet. I'll have my men deal with him. They'll be in your club Friday night by 8:00 P.M. Give them all the particulars then." He terminated the call.

It was all Sokolov could do to refrain from throwing his phone across the room and smashing it on the far wall. Volkov's men here? *Blyad!*

Would the university still be open? He looked online for the number of the Administration Office at PCU and called.

"Pacific Crest University. How may I direct your call?"

"I'm trying to get hold of Dr. Sterling Friese. Is he still at the school or has he left for the day?"

"He had a meeting late this afternoon, so he may still be here. I'll try his office. Who shall I say is calling?"

"This is Iosif Tolstoy. Franklin Wise's uncle."

"Why, Mr. Tolstoy. I didn't recognize your voice. You sound so different over the phone. This is Amelia."

"Oh, hello, Amelia. People have told me that."

"Let me put you on hold while I ring his office." The phone went silent for a moment.

"This is Dr. Sterling Friese. To whom am I speaking?"

"Ah, Dr. Friese. Abram Sokolov here. I'm the owner of Club Chaos. I wanted to make sure you accepted my call. Have you seen my employee Iosif? I think he intended to pay you a visit yesterday."

"Big brute of a guy? Not too bright? Not since he visited me at school the other day, inquiring about his nephew, Franklin Wise. Why do you ask?"

The Russian expelled his breath between clenched teeth. "Iosif has not come to work today. Do you know anything about that?"

"I'm sorry, Mr. Sokolov. I really can't help you."

Sokolov was silent for several moments. He disliked being lied to. "We need to talk."

"My sentiments exactly. We want the same thing."

"And what would that be?"

"Each of us wants to carry on his business without any troubles. No inconveniences. No...loose ends, so to speak."

"Indeed. You are no trouble to me, Dr. Friese." He spoke as if addressing a child unable to comprehend adult affairs. "And tell me. What exactly is your business in all of this?"

"I want things to run smoothly here at the university. I

want to take full advantage of the tenure I've worked so hard to get. I presume you want things to run like a well-oiled machine at your club."

"Of course. Anything else?"

"You may know I've taken a special interest in Franklin, even before Iosif came asking about him. I'm doing my best to keep him out of trouble."

"What kind of trouble has he been getting into?"

"You've heard his band. That boy can be a wild one. But he's got a good heart. I'm trying to keep him focused so he earns passing grades. I'd like to see him graduate next year."

Sokolov chuckled, a sound devoid of humor. "I'm afraid you're being a bit disingenuous, Professor. He said you told him Officer Charles Whitehorse has been looking into his selling drugs on campus."

"As I told Iosif, that policeman came into my lecture hall, making absurd accusations. I wasn't about to violate any student's rights. And I didn't want Franklin to get blindsided."

Sokolov was silent for a moment, as though digesting this latest deceit. "Shall we meet? Sometimes these things are best discussed face-to-face."

"I'd like that. I can be available any time I'm not teaching a class."

"I'll check my schedule and get back to you. Please give me your cell phone number."

Sokolov called fifteen minutes later. "Can we meet Friday night around nine o'clock?"

"Certainly. I'll drive down to your club."

"Don't trouble yourself. I'll send my representatives to pick you up."

"OK. Nine. Friday. I look forward to it."

As he put the phone into his pocket, Sterling frowned. He wiped the perspiration from his brow. Things had gone much further than he had anticipated. His hands were trembling.

For a minute—for just a minute—I thought I might be able to reason with that man. Had he asked me to meet him at

Chaos, I would've. We might even have come to an understanding. But it's all a ploy. He's sending his goons to get me.

He poured himself another glass of wine and sat in his favorite chair. *Talk to me, Don Vito. I handled the ape, but Sokolov is upping the ante. Things have gone too far.*

And he imagined the raspy voice in his ears, reassuring him. *"It's not personal. It's business. Be ready."*

Of course. Be ready, as I was for Tolstoy. He took a deep breath and exhaled it slowly. *I will be,* he promised himself. *I will be.*

36. Peeping Tom

E xcuse the mess. I just moved into this office last week and I still haven't unpacked all my boxes yet." The sign on the door said, MARTIN WEST, PRIVATE INQUIRIES.

"Your sign doesn't say private investigator or detective." Peter was doubtful.

"I just wanted somethin' that sounded more discreet. Know what I mean? But yeah, I'm a private dick. Retired from the police force a year ago and retirement drove me crazy. I mean, how many times can you mow the lawn in a week? And what do you do when football season is over? Gained twenty pounds just sittin' around. Then I started smokin' again after bein' off the cancer sticks for three years. Wife told me to get a job or she was leavin'. So here I am."

Peter looked at the man behind the desk. His hair was thin and gray, his craggy face a mass of wrinkles born of a lifetime of smoking tobacco. Suspenders over his shoulders helped to keep his pants from sliding down his bulging belly.

"Well, I'm not even sure if I should be here. I just can't shake the feeling that a man I used to call a friend is into something bad. Very bad."

"And you want to see what I can find out?"

"Exactly. If I'm just being a paranoid nutcase, then so be it. I'll relax. But unless I know one way or the other, it's going to drive me crazy. It's getting harder to stay focused on my teaching."

"Teaching?"

"Psychology at Pacific Crest."

"You gonna psychoanalyze me?"

Peter laughed. "You're safe with me, Mr. West."

"Whew! That's a relief. No tellin' what skeletons are hidin' out in my closet."

Peter pursed his lips. "I don't mean to be indelicate, but can you give me a ballpark idea of what you charge?"

"I charge by the hour for the short jobs, by the week or by

the month for the longer ones. Here you go." He opened the middle drawer in the desk and withdrew a sheet of paper. "I think you'll find my prices very reasonable, especially when you compare them with Invictus Investigations, the big outfit in town." He handed Peter the page.

Peter frowned. "Ouch! This'll max out my budget."

"Why don't you give me the details, and maybe I can figure out about how long it'll take. That way I can give you a fair estimate."

"Okay."

"Start with what you know. Then tell me what you think. I'll take notes."

Peter told him what he knew about Sterling Friese. Then he shared his speculations.

"So you think this Dean Wasserman had some kinda dirt on Friese? And Friese killed him for it?"

"It happened right around the time he was coming up for tenure, a big step for a university professor. I think the Dean was going to scuttle his bid. Maybe get him kicked out of PCU."

"What do you think the Dean had on him?"

"Haven't a clue. But my paranoia says it had something to do with his love life. Friese is very secretive about it. Denies dating. Handsome guy, but says his ex made him a confirmed bachelor."

"And you think it was poison?"

"I think so." Peter did not mention the Rough-skinned newt. "And something else." He shared with West the stories about the bride on the beach, the arm and the ring. "I don't know if those are connected in any way, or if Friese had anything to do with them. I just know he seemed startled when I told him about the diamond ring."

"Tell you what, Mr. Bristol. Or is it Dr. Bristol?"

"Peter is fine."

"OK, Peter. And you can call me Marty. I'm not very busy right now. Give me a week and I'll see what I can do. I'll find his ex-wife and talk to her. Maybe stake out his house for a few days.

I'll even give you a discount." He wrote a figure on a piece of paper and handed it to his client. "Half now for operatin' expenses. Half when I give you my report."

Peter sighed. "I have to do this. I gotta get my life back. Let me write you a check."

West watched his client leave. *With any luck, I'll have this done in three or four days and still have a little cushion.* He was pleased that he could conduct a substantial portion of his business from the comfort of his desk, using his computer. Stakeouts could be difficult, especially in bad weather. The only perk was that he sometimes got very compromising pictures of some very pretty women, a personal collection of which he kept in a locked file cabinet for his own enjoyment later. His wife wanted him to work. It wasn't his fault that his job sometimes made him take pictures of ladies in various degrees of undress.

It wasn't long before he tracked down the ex-wife. Sabrina Haydn, a.k.a. Sabrina Friese, residing in Chino Hills, California. He debated whether he should call or just take a flight to L.A. and speak with her personally. He opted to try the call first, since flying there and back would eat up a whole day.

"May I please speak with Ms. Sabrina Haydn? This is Martin West, callin' from Driftwood, Oregon. I'm not a telemarketer."

"This is Sabrina Haydn. I'm not interested in getting a lower interest rate on my credit card or applying for a vacation offer from a time-share. So talk fast. I'm hanging up in ten seconds."

"I'm a private investigator, Ms. Haydn, trackin' down information on your former husband, Sterling Friese."

"That cheating, lying sonofabitch! A private investigator was after him last year, too. What's he done this time? Rape a minor?"

"Somebody was investigatin' him last year? Do you remember who?"

"I dunno. Started with an *I*. Invisible? Invincible?"

"Invictus?"

"Yeah, that's it. Anyway, I'll tell you what I told them."

"You sound pretty angry. Was he unfaithful to you?"

"Unfaithful doesn't cover it. He'd screw anything with boobs. Developed a real taste for co-eds. University threw him out, but then covered it all up. Didn't want a scandal scaring away their benefactors."

"How many women are we talkin' about?"

"I don't know. Ten? Twenty? And some of them disappeared afterward. I think he paid them to move away and keep quiet."

"So he was never a family man?"

"He was a shit to our daughter, but I protected her."

"Anythin' else you think I should know about him?"

"Be careful. He's a real gun-nut. Says he got it from his years in the military. 'Trained sniper' he called himself, but I don't know if I ever believed him."

"Ms. Haydn, you've been very helpful. May I leave you my number in case you think of anythin' else you want me to know?"

"Sure."

He concluded the call and sat back, congratulating himself on a job well done. *This calls for a drink. I think I'm halfway home.* He checked the weather for the rest of the week. No rain until Sunday. A little surveillance might be in order.

The next day, he called PCU.

"Pacific Crest University. This is Amelia. How may I direct your call?"

"I'm Lawrence Driver. I was callin' to see if Professor Friese will be at the university today. I'm doin' a feature story for TV 6 in Portland and will be out there today or tomorrow."

"Mr. Driver, we have to clear all those things through Chancellor Brady. But yes. Dr. Friese will be here all day today from 8:30 A.M. till about five tonight. Would you like me to go ahead and call Chancellor Brady to get your interview arranged?"

"Tell you what, Amelia. Let me call you back. I have to solidify my own schedule first. You've been very helpful." He hung up the phone, looked at his watch, and pulled up a page on his computer. "There you are, Professor. 9730 Grenadine Drive, Neskowin. I think I'll check out your house in the daylight when you aren't home."

It wasn't hard to find. He parked in the street and walked up the driveway toward the house. The garage was off to the left, and a large covered entryway provided visitors with escape from inclement weather. The bright red front door contrasted with shingles the color of clam shells. Around either side of the home were sweeping vistas of the blue ocean below, dappled with sun and cloud. Before he reached the front stoop, he saw the doorbell. It was one of the new variety, incorporating a camera that broadcast an image to the owner's cell phone. In his experience, residents who used this system seldom installed other cameras around the perimeter. Nonetheless, he decided to be careful. Staying out of range of the doorbell, he walked toward the right side of the house and then around to the back. The home took advantage of the ocean views with large windows on every suitable wall. Visibility would be good for his camera work. Low shrubs would provide some protection, but he would still blacken his face and wear black clothes. He walked farther, and there was the bedroom. It would be perfect.

Nine-thirty that night found him approaching the house, a deeper shadow against the darkness of the night. There was a car in the driveway. He assumed Friese would have pulled his car into the garage, so this would be a guest. He took a photo of the license plate. He kept low as he rounded the house. He knew that sudden movements would be his surest giveaway. Through the windows of the den, he saw two figures. The man he recognized as Friese from pictures he had seen. The other figure was a young woman, twenty-something. Blonde-haired. Attractive. He clicked pictures of them standing there, sipping wine. Friese put his arm around her and kissed her neck. She put her glass down and raised her

202

face to his. They kissed long and hard. Then Friese put his own glass on a coffee table and took her by the hand out of the room.

West crawled on his hands and knees to be able to peep through the bedroom windows. "Take it all off, baby," he whispered as he watched her disrobe. The camera was an extension of his fingers. He imagined himself caressing her young body, touching her as only a lover could. His heart pounded, and his breath came in quick gasps.

He finally lay back on the ground, staring up at the stars overhead, letting his heart rate return to normal. He had everything he needed.

Once back at the car, he placed the camera on the seat beside him. He patted it like a beloved pet. "Got some great ones for my collection," he said aloud. On the drive home, he wondered if he should return tomorrow. Would the same girl be present? Another one? He decided it would be only professional to do a little more surveillance. He would come back, perhaps a little earlier...

The next day he decided to call in a favor. "Hey, Tim."

"Hi, Marty. It's been a long time. How's business?"

"It's good. Keeps me just busy enough. Out of the house, away from the little lady. And I'm not dodgin' bullets like before. How's Invictus?"

"I wouldn't have believed a little burg like this could generate so many investigations. We're a little hotbed of gossip and suspicion. I love it."

"I wonder if I could ask a favor from an old cop buddy?"

"Sure. What can I do for you?"

"Well, I know your reports are sealed, but could you tell me if you guys investigated somebody by the name of Sterling Friese sometime last year?"

"Geez, man. You want me to lose my job? That stuff's confidential. You know that."

"Yeah. I don't want you to get canned. But can you just tell me if a file was opened?"

There was silence on the other end. Then the man harrumphed. "You're stretching our friendship, Marty. But I'll see what I can do. I'll call you back."

Half an hour later, West's phone rang.

"Yeah. A guy by the name of Wasserman hired Ozzie—you remember Ozzie?—to check Friese out. Guy's a real womanizer. That's all I'm gonna say. And don't ask me to do anything like this again." He terminated the call.

Damn, I'm good! That calls for a drink.

Friday after nightfall, he was parking in the street well below Friese's house. He grabbed his camera from the front seat and locked the car. He was eagerly anticipating another show, and had even brought along a flask of whiskey to further his enjoyment. He toyed with the idea of taking a video.

As he approached the driveway, he froze. Voices—male voices. At least two. Maybe three. He couldn't make out what they were saying. Then two gunshots in rapid succession.

That's a Glock 9mm.! Forty years on the force had taught him to differentiate between the sounds of certain guns. *I'm outta here!* He had retired from the police, glad to be alive. He wasn't about to risk his life now.

He ran as fast as his diabetic, nerve-damaged feet would carry him. Before he could leap into his car, he heard two more shots.

37. Hanging Out With Orestes and his Mom

S UNDAY, MAY 11, 1997. He sat by her bedside in the den, which he had converted into a makeshift hospital room, watching the slow rise and fall of her chest. The extended care facility had been reluctant to release her to his care while she still had an IV line and a Foley catheter inserted, but he had been very persuasive. Her Medicare made it possible to have a Hospice nurse in the home every day, and they would monitor all medical interventions.

The regular furniture in the room had been pushed to the periphery to accommodate the large electric hospital bed. Sterling had brought in a portable bookshelf for the blankets and towels and IV solutions. He placed a small TV on a table in the corner so she could watch her soap operas in the afternoon. The remote sat on the bed covers by her functional left hand.

Sterling looked at his mother, a shrunken ghost of her former self. The stroke had been debilitating, paralyzing her right side and her ability to speak, but she still retained awareness. She wasn't eating, so the IV was her primary source of hydration and nutrition.

Katrina, the Hospice nurse, had stepped outside for a quick smoke. He had assured her that he would keep careful watch over the old crone.

"What am I going to do with you, Mother? Why won't you give me the ring? What use can it be to you in the grave?" He leaned over her in the bed. She thrust her left hand under the covers, away from his intruding eyes. "You do know you're dying, right? It's just a matter of time. Why not let me have it? I could use it as an engagement ring when I find the right woman." He thought for a moment and chuckled. "Or bait to lure the wrong woman into my bed."

She followed him with eyes the color of volcanic glass. He saw hatred in them, unreasoning malice that could not be appeased.

"You said I'd have to pry it from your dead fingers. I'll do that. I promise. When Katrina takes her next break, I'm going to kill you." He said it without emotion, as though he were ordering a coffee from a bored barista. "I wanted you to know so you'll have some time to think about it—work yourself up to it. It'll be a big event in your life. Prepare yourself."

He could see that the loathing in her eyes had succumbed to fear. He liked that. She began to struggle to speak, thrashing her head back and forth, flailing with her left arm and leg.

When the nurse returned, Sterling ran to her. "She just started doing this. I don't know what upset her. Does she need more pain medication?"

"She's not due for another half-hour, but let me call her doctor. Maybe we need to increase her dose if it's not holding her."

While she stepped out of the room with her phone, Sterling leaned over the bed again and smiled at his mother. "Ah, Genevieve, I've finally gotten your attention. After all these years of neglect, you're finally ready to listen. But it's a little late, don't you think?" He nodded his head slowly as she continued to thrash. "I mean, how many hours did I spend in that dark closet? It would add up to weeks, wouldn't it? Months maybe? And think about all the times you put your cigarettes out on my chest. I never told the teachers, never took my T-shirt off in gym class. All to protect you." For a moment, his eyes went far away as another memory shook him. "How old was I when you began starving me? But I could get food at school. And I think spanking me gave you a thrill." He felt his heart begin to pound. His breath began to catch in his throat. "And the other things," he hissed. "The unspeakable things."

Just then Katrina returned. "All set. The doctor has agreed to an increase in your pain meds, Genevieve, so I can give you another shot right now."

The old woman's eyes went wild. She swung her good arm and leg and threw her covers off. She tried to form words, but could only manage unintelligible grunts.

"Easy, honey. Let me draw up the syringe. It'll only take a

minute. Here we go." She injected her patient and stepped away from the bed.

Sterling faced his mother, with his back to Katrina. He smiled broadly at her. "There, there, Mom. You'll feel better soon." He watched as his mother's eyes began to glaze over. "It won't be long now."

Two hours later, Genevieve appeared to be sleeping. Katrina motioned to Sterling.

"Can you keep an eye on your mom for a few minutes while I go outside for a smoke?"

"Sure. Go ahead."

As soon as she left the house, Sterling approached the bed. "Wake up, Mother. It's time."

The woman's eyes popped open, round and wild with fear.

"You look terrified, Mother. This won't hurt. I'll just pull this plastic bag over your head and you'll suffocate. It won't take too long. I guess it must be a little like drowning."

Genevieve withdrew her left hand from under the covers and tried to strike him. He easily dodged the blow. Then she swung her leg out in a clumsy kick.

"You show real spunk, Mom. I like that. I may have to lean on you a little to keep you from thrashing about too much. But I'll try not to hurt you." He exhaled a long breath. "You know, I was thinking about injecting air into your IV line. Makes what they call an air embolism that gets stuck in your heart. Causes a heart attack or a stroke. But you might survive that."

He withdrew a large plastic bag from his pocket and shook it to open it up. "Suppose the Furies will pursue me like they did Orestes? He killed his mother, Clytemnestra, and the Furies went after him to drive him mad. It's a great painting by Bouguereau." Sterling chuckled. "Gotta love those Greeks. Always whacking each other." The smile vanished. His voice was a feral snarl. "Orestes killed his mother because she had killed his father, Agamemnon. You didn't exactly kill Dad, but you drove him away. Kind of like the same thing to a little kid, isn't it,

Mommy?"

He became aware of the pounding of his heart, as he watched the terror grow in his mother's eyes. It excited him. "Here we go," he said. "Just breathe normally, Mother."

Katrina returned a few minutes later, smelling of tobacco smoke.

Sterling met her at the entrance to the den. "She seemed uncomfortable, so I turned her on her side, facing the wall, and propped her there with a pillow. As soon as I did that, she fell right back to sleep."

"OK. I don't need to poke her or prod her with anything for about an hour or so. I'll just let her sleep and catch up on my record-keeping."

"I'm going out for a bite to eat. I won't be long."

He decided a celebratory dinner would be in order. He would dispose of the plastic bag in the restaurant's men's room and admire the ring over cocktails. As he reached his car, he withdrew the diamond from his pocket and let the rays of the early evening sun ignite its fire.

Its beauty was breath-taking.

208

38. A Proposal

You look particularly lovely tonight." He found himself staring at the way her blonde hair cascaded over her shoulders. "And that white T-shirt takes my breath away."

Chloe smiled at him. "Why, Charley Whitehorse. And here I thought you were more of a leg man. I'll remember the T-shirt the next time I want to work my feminine charms on you." She stood up from the dining table. "Let's just leave the supper dishes for now and take our wine into the living room."

"Sounds good to me. We can do clean-up later."

As they took their seats on the couch, she turned to him. "How's your daughter doing? I haven't seen her since she visited you last spring. Things have been so crazy around here we haven't talked about her."

"Sally's doing great. Would you believe that after bouncing around in southern California for a year after she graduated, she got offered a job at Microsoft? Yep. Moves up to Seattle the end of May. I'm so proud of her."

"Will she stop here on her way? We should have a party to celebrate."

"Great idea. I'll call her so we can plan it."

Chloe smiled at the man she loved. "I've got news, too, Charley. It's official. They're letting Kaitlynn out on June first."

"That's terrific!" Whitehorse put his glass on the coffee table and took Chloe's hand.

"She's racked up a bunch of college credits, so she'll have a head-start at McCall Community College in Newport. She's applying for the fall semester."

"Good for her. Does she know what she wants to do?"

"She'll matriculate into PCU if she can snag a scholarship. Wants to work with traumatized kids. Probably get a degree in Social Work."

"Did you tell her about Friese?"

"No. I didn't think I needed to burden her with that. If he's still there when she gets in, I'll give her a heads-up so she steers clear of him."

"*If* he's still there?"

"Sure. You'll get him. The Tracker always gets his man."

He laughed. "Will Kaitlynn be getting her own place?"

"If her friend Tessa is ready to move out, they'll get a place together. Otherwise, she'll stay with me to save money. It's a short commute to Newport. I'm guessing she'd like to stay in the dorms at PCU if she can get in."

"Those are big plans." He turned his head and became thoughtful for a moment.

"Where'd you go?"

"Oh, just making some plans of my own."

"Like what?"

"I haven't been able to stop thinking about what you said when you asked me to spend the night with you last time. 'For life's sake.' After you talked about the evil I face in my job every day. It occurred to me that I get so caught up in what you called the 'mushrooms' that I miss the wildflowers." He leaned toward her. "You're my wildflower, and I want to spend the rest of my life with you." He stood up from the couch, then got down on one knee. "I need to make something else official. Will you, Chloe Denhurst, marry me and make me the happiest man on the planet?"

Chloe almost spilled her wine. "I—I..." She put down her glass with trembling fingers.

"Just say, 'Yes.'"

"Yes! I will, Charley! I will! I will! I will! Stand up and kiss me!"

The two embraced as though they were trying to make their bodies occupy the same physical space. He felt her surrender to him, offering her mouth, closing her eyes, allowing him to lower her onto the couch. He gently lay on her, stroking her hair and face, kissing her neck, feeling his heart pound in sync with hers.

"I love you, Charley Whitehorse," she whispered, her voice hoarse with desire. "Let's go to the bedroom." Her lips curled in a broad smile. "Just to make it official."

Whitehorse stood and helped her up. Then she took him by the hand and led him to her room.

An hour later, Chloe was snuggled in his arms, halfway between sleep and wakefulness. Whitehorse watched the rhythmic rise and fall of her breathing, certain he had never felt happier or more content in his life. He ran his fingers through her hair and down her shoulder.

"How did I get so lucky?" he said.

Chloe stirred. "What?"

"How did a scar-faced flatfoot like me win a lady like you?"

"Scar-faced?"

"Sure." He pointed to his chin. "That one's from Billy Bonheur in sixth grade. Hit me with a sucker punch. My left cheek, up by my eye? Jerry Dartmouth, eighth grade. Said he didn't like 'Redskins.' Got my nose broken twice in high school. I just never fit in."

"What do you mean?"

"I was a wild child as early as I can remember. Neighbors called me 'Geronimo.' Always getting into trouble, stealing toys from other kids. When beatings from my father didn't seem to straighten me out, he 'got religion.' Decided the only cure was to bring me up in the Native ways."

He saw the confusion on Chloe's face. "My family wasn't big into the whole Native American thing. Just tried to get by. My grandfather sold car tires. Dad worked in a lumber mill. Anyway, he diagnosed my problem as 'trying to be too white.' Said it was the whole family's problem. So he started teaching me to speak Chinook Jargon—what the Confederated Tribes call Chinuk Wawa nowadays. Made me grow my hair long and wear a braid."

"Yikes! I can't imagine that would help you fit in."

"It didn't. Made things way worse. The more I kept trying to fit in, the more he kept trying to make me stand out. 'You're special,' he'd tell me. I wanted to believe him, and then I'd take another punch. Middle schoolers and high schoolers don't like 'special.'"

"So what happened?" He could hear the concern in her voice.

"It all came crashing down when I was thirteen years old. Dad took me to a Sun Dance ceremony in Canada. He had friends up there and got us invited. Thought it would be a kind of coming-of-age thing for me to see the real deal." He sighed. "Long story short, it scared the crap out of me. I had nightmares for a month. He finally gave up. Said I was a lost cause. A hopeless case."

"I'm so sorry, Charley." She reached out and stroked his face. "What did you finally do?"

"Decided I better learn to defend myself. So I took martial arts lessons. Got into maybe two more scraps after that, then the kids left me alone."

She kissed the scar on his cheek. He began to smile.

"The Police Academy was just what I needed. It centered me when nothing else was working. And it only took me a year of boozing to figure that out. Of course, Tony has been a real lifesaver." He let out a deep breath and nodded his head. "And now I'm so happy with my heritage. I sit on the Tribal Council and I love it. And despite what you white folks might say about the casinos—'We gave you liquor and you gave us gambling addiction'—they do a whole lot of good for us."

"This 'white folk' doesn't say that," Chloe snorted with a smile. "And I'd like you to teach me what's best about your heritage. I want to understand."

"It would be my honor, honey. To share it with the most beautiful woman I've ever met."

"Most beautiful? That's a bit lavish. Don't you think?"

"Not at all, sweetheart. You turn heads." He caressed her face, then changed the subject. "Is it weird for you, knowing that I have a cordial relationship with my ex?"

"No way. She's the mother of your daughter. Happily married to somebody else. I'm glad you get along with her. I hate

212

it when divorced couples are still at each other's throats years later. Of course, I don't have quite the relationship with Bruce that you have with Cindi, but we're working on it. He's been very good about visiting Kaitlynn."

"We both have a lot of years in prior marriages. With other partners. Suppose that will screw us up?"

"I think of it as working out the kinks. We're both more mature than we were the first time around. Dispelled some illusions. Refined some expectations. Second time will be a whole lot better." She pecked his cheek. "Well, OK, Prince Charming. So where's my engagement ring? You said this was going to be 'official.'"

"Hmmmm. About that. I thought I might borrow a page from our phone gal at work. She and her boyfriend got engaged and then they went shopping for a ring together. Would you be up for that?"

"I think that's a lovely idea. We could start this weekend."

"Start?"

"You don't think I'm going to choose the very first ring I see, do you?"

"Uh, I guess not. So this is a process? As in, lots of stores?" The thought filled him with the dread that only a male non-shopper can know.

"I think we should take a special trip to Portland this weekend and do it right. Hit a bunch of jewelry stores. Have dinner out in a nice restaurant. Maybe even spend the night in a classy hotel."

He wasn't sure what to say. "Okay. So this is turning into a much bigger deal than I expected."

"Don't worry, lover. I've got your back. And we'll have combined incomes. Remember?"

Just then his phone rang. He reached for it on the bedside table. "This is Whitehorse. What's up?" His expression went from playfulness to perturbation. "When? What's the address? Whose house is that?" His eyes went round. "Holy shit! I'll be there as soon as I can."

He leaped from bed and grabbed his clothes. "Sorry, but I gotta run. Really bad timing."

"Can you tell me?"

"Shots fired in Neskowin."

"Where? Somebody you know?"

"At the house of Sterling Friese!"

"Oh, dear God. You be careful. I don't want you to get shot now that I've finally gotten you to propose to me. Did Friese get killed?"

"We can only hope, darling. We can only hope."

39. The PI Speaks

P eter, I'm done with this case. There's been some new developments and I want out. I'm sure I got more than you need. Can I come by and drop off the file tonight?" Martin West sounded agitated.

"It's a little late, but sure. What's the hurry?" Peter couldn't conceal his surprise.

"Well, I got some great pictures last night, so I thought I'd go back one more time tonight. Just as I get to the driveway, I hear gunshots, so I call 911 and clear out as fast as I can. I'm not riskin' my life for this kinda shit. His ex says he's a gun-nut, so I'm not takin' any more chances."

"You talked to his ex?"

"Sabrina Haydn. Gave me an earful. I'll fill you in when I get there. I can be at your place in half an hour. Chinook River Estates, right?"

"Yep. Just hit the buzzer and I'll open the gate for you."

True to his word, West arrived thirty minutes later. Hammer raced to the door and began to bark excitedly. Peter grabbed him by the collar as he opened the door. "Don't worry about Hammer, Marty. He's a cream puff. Just happy to have the company."

"He's a good-lookin' dog. How long've you had him?"

"Got him in January. A stray. He found me on the beach."

The investigator looked around at the home as he patted Hammer on the head. "I guess he got real lucky findin' you."

"It's mutual, I can assure you." Peter scratched behind his dog's ears. "We're best buds. Here, let me take your coat."

"A little chilly out there tonight. But at least it's dry."

"Rain'll be back this weekend."

"So I hear."

Peter led him to the kitchen table, where his visitor set down the large manila envelope he was carrying. "Can I get you a cup of coffee? A beer?"

"Coffee will keep me up, but a beer would be nice."

Peter opened an IPA and poured it into a tall glass. He brought it back to the table and handed it to West. "What do you have there?" he said, pointing to the envelope.

"Pictures I took last night. Your man was playin' hide the salami with a barely legal. Take a look."

Peter winced at the crudeness of his speech. "I recognize that girl. Don't know her name, but I've seen her on campus. I'm sure she's a student there."

"Grace Kaiser. Aren't there rules against this sorta thing?"

"Damn straight. In this '#MeToo era,' this could cost him his job."

"There's more. His ex unloaded on me. Told me he got kicked out of his last job cuz he was bangin' the co-eds. Then the school hushed it up so they wouldn't lose their backers."

"That doesn't surprise me." Peter shook his head. "Universities aren't exactly models of good behavior and sexual integrity. I'm sure you've seen it on the news."

"She told me he got investigated last year by Invictus."

Now Peter sat up straight and looked hard at the man. "That's the big outfit you mentioned to me before?"

"The same. Got a buddy there. Former cop like me. The report is sealed, but he told me your guy Wasserman paid for it."

"Sonofabitch!" Unable to contain himself, Peter stood up and began to pace the room. "Wasserman found out! He was gonna kick that womanizing bastard out. So Friese killed him."

"Whoa. I don't know nothin' about that. I'm just sayin' this guy can't keep his pecker in his pants."

Peter took a deep breath. "Marty, you've been worth every penny. Let me write you a check for what I owe you." He left to get his checkbook and returned to the table. "I can't begin to tell you how helpful you've been. Now I know I'm not crazy."

"My pleasure, Peter." He folded the check and stuffed it into his wallet. "I guess I'll be on my way. Thanks for the beer." He stroked Hammer as the dog escorted him to the door.

As soon as the man had left, Peter got on the phone with Chris. "I'm not paranoid! I was right!"

216

"About what? Bring me up to speed."

"About Friese. He's screwing his students. It's been his MO for years."

"You got proof?"

"Right in my hands."

"Can I come over?"

"Please. I'm jumping out of my skin."

Twenty minutes later, Peter let the Coronado Cab through the gate. Hammer announced Chris's presence at the front door.

"Hey, big guy. Glad to see you, too." He scratched behind Hammer's ears as the dog wiggled every part of his body in his excitement at seeing his friend. "Hi, Peter. I brought along a little libation. I hope you don't mind." He held up a bottle of Scotch. "It's not Macallan, but it's pretty decent."

"I'll get the glasses. Just put your coat on the hook. One ice cube, right?"

"Right."

Peter set the glasses on the table, and Chris filled them with two fingers of the amber liquid.

"Here's to your not bein' a nut," he said, raising his glass and clinking it against Peter's. "Now show me what you've got."

"Well, I hired a private investigator. These are pictures he took last night at Friese's place." He handed the glossies to his friend.

"Holy shit! Is your detective into porn? These leave nothin' to the imagination."

"That's a student. Grace Kaiser."

"What else?"

"His ex-wife told my PI that Friese was kicked out of his last teaching job for screwing his students. I'm sure that's why he didn't get tenure before he came here. She said the university hushed it up, so PCU wouldn't have known."

Chris took another drink. "So he's a bad egg, accordin' to these pictures and his ex."

"There's more. The report is sealed, but my guy says that

Dean Wasserman hired Invictus Investigations last year. Wasserman found out and Friese killed him to prevent getting kicked out of another school before he got tenure."

"Okay, that seems like a bit of a stretch."

"What do you mean?"

"Let me play devil's advocate. Wouldn't Friese's attorney claim that the pictures have been faked or altered? Or that the girl manipulated Friese so she could blackmail him into giving her passin' grades?"

"Would that work?"

"Ultimately? I don't know, but it could get dragged on for months."

"But what about the ex?"

"You mean the angry woman he left behind, bitter over the divorce, willin' to say or do anythin' to get even with her intelligent, community-minded husband?"

"C'mon, Chris. You can't be serious."

"This guy hasn't gotten this far by bein' stupid. You don't think he'd hire the biggest hot-shot lawyer he can find to defend himself?"

"But what about the previous university?"

"The one that will stonewall any investigation—for years, if that's what it takes—that might hold them liable or might implicate them in any way in what's goin' on here? What do you think?"

Peter was getting desperate. "What if I just bring these photographs to the Board of Trustees? Wouldn't they throw his ass out?"

"Not before he sued your ass for defamation. You'd be— what's that cliché they use now?—livin' under a bridge, in a cardboard box, eatin' dog food. Wanna go there?" He reached for his friend and put his hand on his shoulder. "I'm tryin' to save you from gettin' hurt. I'm not sayin' any of this is right or fair. It just is. You've got no body. You've got a partial investigation that was closed down last year. Give whatever evidence you've got to the police. Let them try to untangle it. Let it go."

Peter leaped from his chair. "I can't let it go!" His shout echoed off the kitchen tiles. Hammer barked and poked his master with his muzzle, as though worried what this outburst might mean. "I can't let that lying, cheating, murdering bastard get away with it!"

"Give it to the cops, Peter. You're not a judge and jury. You can't bring him to justice by yourself."

"Yeah? Well, we'll see about that."

40. Gunfight at the Not OK Corral

S terling looked at his watch again. 8:15. He pulled his black sweats over his clothes for concealment and warmth. A black baseball cap completed his outfit. He drew his Glock from his bedside table, again a choice based on its black finish as opposed to the shiny stainless steel of his .45. He switched his phone to silent and slid it into his pocket. When Sokolov's so-called "representatives" arrived, he would be waiting for them outside.

Previously, he had unplugged his flat screen TV, removed it from the wall, and leaned it against the couch in the den. His receiver and blu-ray player sat next to it. Then he had disconnected his desktop computer tower, keyboard, and speakers, and brought them to the den as well. Rounding out the collection of electronics were his laptop and a new phone he had just purchased today, still unopened. The last items were in a small pouch—his Rolex watch and the few hundred dollars he had had in his wallet. As a final preparation, he opened the glass slider in his bedroom and pulled on a pair of latex gloves. The stage was set.

Sterling slipped out the front door and locked it behind him. He ran down the driveway and hid in the shrubs across the street, affording him a perfect view of his house. The cold night air began to seep through his clothing as he kept his silent vigil. *Will this work?* he wondered. *Are they really this stupid?*

Time dragged on. His legs began to ache, and he found himself shivering as his core temperature dropped. At 8:45 a black Toyota pulled into the driveway. Two men got out and approached the front door. When they rang the bell, their picture was transmitted to Sterling's cell phone. The screen gave him a good image of his visitors, in their long, dark coats.

"Dr. Friese," said one. "We're here to take you to see Mr. Sokolov."

Sterling spoke into his phone, and his voice was broadcast from the speaker in the doorbell. "Just give me a minute. You're a

220

little early."

"We can't keep Mr. Sokolov waiting, so please hurry."

Across the street, Sterling couldn't help but chuckle as the two men grew more and more restless with the delay.

"Dr. Friese. Please come with us. We have a schedule to keep." They began pacing on the front stoop.

After almost five minutes had elapsed, he saw one man draw a gun from under his coat. Sterling tensed in readiness.

"Friese! Open the goddamn door now!" The man nodded to his partner, who drew his gun as well. Without another word, the leader slammed his boot into the door. Sterling heard wood splinter as the door crashed open. Both men rushed in.

Sterling leaped into action. He ran across the street, crouched by the front of the car, and let the air out of the driver's side tire. Then he sprinted to the side of the house. In moments, he heard the gunmen burst back out the front door, cursing at each other.

"How could you let him get away, you idiot?"

"It wasn't my fault. You're the one standing around, making sweet talk with him. And there's no way we coulda chased him down that steep hill in the dark. He shoulda had a bullet in his head by now, and we shoulda been back at Chaos finding a whore and a stiff drink."

"So what are we gonna tell Vasily?"

"We'll tell him it's no problem. We'll get the sonofabitch tomorrow. This is all that dumb Sokolov's fault anyway. Can't deal with his own team."

While they continued to argue, Sterling raced around the side of the house and slipped through the door into his bedroom. He tiptoed toward the open front door. The men's voices were louder.

"What the hell is this? A goddamn flat tire?" The taller one was yelling now.

"Shit! How could we have a fucking flat tire?"

"Because you drove over something sharp, dumbass!" He popped the trunk and withdrew the jack. "Here. You start while I get the spare out."

Sterling emerged from the house, aiming his gun at the men. "Hello, gentlemen. Before you get any ideas, I'm very fast, and I'm very good. I'll drop both of you before either of you gets your gun out. Are we clear?"

The men nodded.

"Good. Now, you at the trunk. Get up here with your buddy. Everybody keep their hands where I can see them. I'm just gonna walk around the side of the hood so we've got the car between us. There we go."

He watched the men, their eyes shifting back and forth, their fingers twitching. The taller one said, "Can we make a deal?"

"Of course we can. The deal is to shut up and listen. Shorty, you stay put and don't move. You, big guy, open your coat and pull out your gun with two fingers. Very slowly. Don't make me kill you. Lay it on the hood of the car and then take two steps back. Excellent. Now, shorty, you do the same."

"You don't know who you're messin' with, man," the shorter of the two said.

"Enlighten me."

"Vasily Volkov. Very big. Very powerful. He'll squash you like a bug."

"Shut up, Nikolai," the taller man said.

"Let him speak. OK. So you're Nikolai," Sterling pointed his gun at him. Then turning his gun toward the other, he said, "And who might you be?"

"Yevgeni," the man answered in a voice seething with rage.

"Nikolai and Yevgeni—Keystone Cops for big, bad Vasily. Out of Portland, I presume?"

Both men nodded.

"So what's Volkov doing down here in Driftwood? You can tell me. I'll be dead soon anyway. Right?"

"Vasily is helping Abram tie up loose ends," Nikolai said. "We don't want anything to interfere with our business."

"And I'm a loose end?"

The men's silence answered his question.

Sterling picked up one of the guns from the hood of the car. "Just like mine," he commented, as he tucked his own behind his back. Then he picked up the other. "Just to keep this straight. This one's yours. Right, Nikolai?" He motioned with the gun in his right hand.

"Yeah."

Sterling fired both weapons in rapid succession, striking each man in the heart. He ran to their crumpled bodies and tucked each pistol into its owner's hand. Then he fired each gun again to assure that powder residue could be discovered on the hands of the thugs. Once he accomplished that, he rushed through the front door and began to carry out all the items he had stowed in the den. He thrust his belongings into the back seat of the car, sliding the flat screen in last. The task was completed in less than two minutes. Surveying the scene one final time, he darted back into the house and stripped the rubber gloves from his hands. With trembling fingers, he pulled off his black sweats and cap, and stuffed clothes and gloves into a large plastic bag for disposal later. When his own gun was restored to his bedside table, he called 911.

"There's dead men in my driveway! My house has been broken into!" He mimicked breathless excitement.

"Are you hurt, sir?"

"No. I was out walking."

"Give me your address, please."

"9730 Grenadine Drive in Neskowin. I'm Dr. Sterling Friese."

"That incident has already been reported, Dr. Friese. Police are on the way. Are you at the house now?"

"Yes."

"And how many men are there?"

"Two."

"Did you kill them?"

"No! Of course not! I told you I was out for a walk. I just

found them. When I got back into my house, I saw that they had taken all my stuff—my TV, my computer—"

"Could there be anyone else in the house?"

"Er...I don't know."

"Please get out of the house immediately and wait down the street for the police. Stay on the line with me till they arrive."

Sterling did as she requested, a broad smile lighting up his face. *This just might work*, he thought. It was necessary for both Sokolov and Volkov to believe that it was the incompetence of their men, and not Sterling, that had gotten them killed. If they believed he did it, he would spend the rest of his short life looking over his shoulder, awaiting the inevitable reckoning.

His smile only grew larger as he heard the wail of an approaching police siren. He hoped it would be Officer Whitehorse.

The next morning, Sterling Friese, Abram Sokolov, Vasily Volkov, Charley Whitehorse, Tony Esperanza, Chris Harper, Peter Bristol, and Chloe Denhurst each shared something in common. They were all watching the morning news when a most unusual story broke:

"This just in from the coastal town of Driftwood." The brown-haired anchorman looked directly into the lens of the camera. "In what may be the most bizarre burglary in recent memory, two thieves were found dead last night after apparently shooting each other in an argument over a flat tire. The two had broken into the home of Dr. Sterling Friese—a professor at Pacific Crest University and seen here in this recent photo—who was out walking at the time. It looks as though they had filled their car with Dr. Friese's possessions, only to discover that they were going nowhere fast with a flat tire. Whatever was said between them, the gunfight ended quickly, leaving both suspects dead at the scene. Their identities have not been released pending further police investigation."

"Would that be some form of road rage, Ted?"

"You've got me, Sheri. Driveway rage? I guess this notice

would apply to any other would-be thieves in the area: have your car serviced before you go out on your next job. Now for our weather, let's go to Caroline."

41. Diamonds Are (Sometimes) Forever

With his mind churning, Whitehorse had been impossible company over the weekend. Chloe told him she understood that he wasn't in his best mood to go shopping for an engagement ring. She made him promise that next Saturday was their time, come hell or high water. To Portland in mid-morning, a light lunch, and serious ring-shopping until a romantic dinner in the early evening. Then it would be cocktails and dancing until checking into a nice hotel for the night. Chloe had it all planned.

On Monday morning, Whitehorse was still fuming as he drove to the station. Friese had somehow outsmarted him once again. He didn't believe for a second that those Russian thugs had killed themselves, but he couldn't come up with any other scenario that made sense. As he had told Effling, he didn't believe in coincidence. So how had they wound up dead in Sterling Friese's driveway? Of all the houses on that lane—and Friese's was far from the most opulent—how had they selected that one for their bungled burglary? And Russians, no less!

Not only that, but Russians from Portland, associated with Vasily Volkov, who had been on the radar of every policeman in Oregon for the last two years. Sokolov had to be taking his marching orders from him. Volkov must have sent his henchman to Driftwood to clear up a mess he felt Sokolov was incompetent to handle.

And suddenly lightbulbs began flashing in his brain. Friese was the mess Sokolov couldn't handle! And that mess had to involve Popova and Tolstoy. He was convinced that Tolstoy was also dead, since their search of his house had revealed his Mercedes in the garage with his keys and his phone in it. Four dead Russians, with Friese as the link between them! How had a university professor in a podunk little town become involved with the Russian mob?

At the station, Whitehorse had to get his mind off it and let it simmer. He often did his best "tracking" by not focusing on the evidence directly. He would discuss it later with his partner to plan their next move.

When Chiara arrived—she insisted it was a green hair day —he decided to ask her about her shopping for an engagement ring.

"It was terrific, Charley! And very educational. They have a new guy at Caruso's and he gave us the whole scoop. Have you got the time?"

"Sure. Tony's not here yet. Go for it."

"OK. So it's about clarity, color, and cut." She pulled a small piece of paper from her purse. "The GIA—that's the Gemological Institute of America—has a scale for rating clarity. At the top is IF—internally flawless. From there it goes to VVS1 —Very, Very Small Inclusions 1—all the way down to I2— Inclusions 2."

"It sounds like you took a class in this."

"I was so excited, I took these notes!"

"So tell me more."

"We learned that for normal human beings like us, VS2— Very Small Inclusions 2—is perfectly adequate and the best bang for our buck. Most of the inclusions and blemishes at this level are invisible to the naked eye."

"What about color?"

"It's graded from D—colorless—to Z—easily seen yellow or brown tint. G to I grades look as colorless to the naked eye as the D to F range. And of course, they're cheaper."

"And cut?"

"Ideal cut if it's the classic round shape. Makes the diamond sparkle more. Excellent cut if it's a fancy-shaped diamond. Shape is just personal taste."

"So if I shop for a ring with Chloe, we should look for an Ideal or Excellent cut, VS2, in the G, H, or I grade?"

"A ring for Chloe? Are you guys getting engaged?" She threw herself at Whitehorse and embraced him in a bear hug. "Congratulations, Charley! I'm so happy for you!"

"Am I interrupting something?" Esperanza closed the door

behind him.

"Charley and Chloe are getting married!" Chiara shrieked.

"Holy mackerel! That is not what I expected to hear when I walked in." He smiled at his partner. "Gonna do the deed, huh?"

"Yep." He was nodding his head. "What have I been waiting for?"

"That's what I've been telling you, man."

"Chiara has been educating me about diamond rings. Chloe and I are going to Portland next weekend to shop for one."

"Oh, I forgot one thing, Charley. Our diamond was already laser-inscribed by the company, but we're adding our own inscription, too. A little heart with the words *C & S Forever.*"

"What do you mean laser-inscribed?"

"Lots of times the company that sells their diamonds to the jewelry store burns a laser inscription on the 'girdle.' That's like the circumference of the stone—the edge. It's usually an icon of the company and a code number that has all that GIA info I just told you about. How big the stone is. Clarity. When you buy your diamond, the jewelry store registers your personal info with the company. That way there's a record of who bought that particular stone, where, when. It's all kept in the company's database."

"Hmm. I never knew that. I wish there was a laser inscription on our evidence ring. That could give us something to work on. But I looked at it every which way. There's nothing there."

"Oh. You can't see it without a microscope."

"What did you say?"

"I said a laser inscription is invisible. You need a microscope to see it."

"Holy shit! You mean we might be able to find out who bought this ring and when they bought it?"

"Yep. I'm surprised they didn't look when you brought it to the shops in town."

"They just gave it a quick once-over. Never looked at it with a microscope. Felt like I was getting the brush-off."

"Who knows, Charley. Maybe you'll get lucky."

"Just for the sake of argument, better get your judge friend to grant you a warrant," Esperanza said. "In case the jewelry store has qualms about releasing information they think is personal."

"Good idea. I'll get right on it." He turned to their receptionist. "Again, what would we do without you, Chiara?" He shook his head and chuckled. "I'm going to do everything I can to get you a full-time, paying job here. We need you!"

The young woman beamed. "Thanks, Charley. Thanks to both of you. I'm so glad to be on your team."

Judge Harowitz was taking a much-needed holiday, so Whitehorse was unable to get the warrant he needed for several days. On Thursday, he walked through the door of Caruso's Fine Jewelry.

"Good afternoon, Officer. I'm Thomas Caruso. Only been on the job a couple weeks so I haven't met everyone in town yet." The young brown-haired man extended his hand. He was dressed in a dark blue suit, with a white shirt and a blue-striped tie. Whitehorse saw an appealing innocence in his face.

"Charles Whitehorse." He shook hands. "Family member?"

"Harold's son. Finished college last year. Did my wild oats thing for a few months in Europe, and now I'm home to earn a living and pay off my student loans. Dad invited me to come on board, and I took him up on it."

"I wish you every success, Thomas."

"So how can I help you today?"

"Well, I have a diamond ring in evidence. I need to find out if it's been laser-inscribed, and if it has been, what it says."

The young man paused. "Officer Whitehorse, that's protected information."

"I thought you might say that. Here's my warrant."

Thomas looked at the document. "Perfect. Let's take a look at the ring."

The policeman withdrew it from his pocket. "Here you go."

Thomas placed the ring under the lens of the microscope that sat on the small desk behind the counter. He fiddled with the focus and the angle of the ring. "It's very faint, but I think I can make it out." He took his eyes from the microscope. "Inscriptions can be polished off. Looks like your ring has been buffed pretty hard."

"We're thinking a week in the sand and the tides."

"That'd do it, all right. Let me take a closer look." He jotted notes on a small scrap of paper. "Yep. It's from Lazarus Karlan. They're very big into laser inscription. That's their logo and an eight-digit code number." He pushed away from the desk and stood up. "Here's the ring back. Let me pull this up on the computer and see what we've got."

Whitehorse leaned over the counter. *Am I really going to get a break in this case? Can I hope for so much?* He was not prepared for what the jeweler had to say.

"Here we go." Thomas pointed at the screen he was reading. He turned it so Whitehorse could see it, too. "It was purchased and registered by a Genevieve Friese on January 20, 1984, from Schroeder's Jewelry in Los Angles, California. 2.1 carats. IF, D." He looked up from the screen. "That's a fabulous stone. I can sell it loose for about $100K. Put it in a flashy setting with a lot of extra sparkle around it, and you'd definitely have a high-ticket item."

The policeman almost fell over backward. His face turned ashen. "Did you say Friese? Genevieve Friese?"

"Yep. F-R-I-E-S-E. See?"

"Oh, my God!" His eyes went far away as he started to do the math. "It's gotta be the sonofabitch's mother or grandmother!"

"Someone you know?"

"Thomas, I couldn't begin to tell you how helpful you've been. Would you please print that screen page for me?"

"Sure thing. Give me a second." He tapped a couple of keys. "There it is on the printer now." He handed the paper to Whitehorse.

The policeman's fingers trembled as he folded it and

stuffed it into his shirt pocket. It wasn't Sokolov's ring after all. It was Friese's. He was the link to the women on the beach. He had either given it to Emma or she had stolen it from him. And Friese must be the "he" that Emma mentioned in her note. She wanted him to go out to the Double L and stop her from committing suicide.

And he hadn't done it.

42. Just Like Rhode Island

Larry's cousin had come through. The stage where 3 Day Fish would play was now flanked by several big "gerbs"—what July Fourth revelers called "fountains"— cylindrical fireworks that produced a controlled spray of sparks. His cousin's were significantly larger than what the band had been using, and all the members were excited. They finally had pyrotechnics worthy of their reputation as the new alpha band on the coast.

Frankie and Mack were tuning their instruments, while Jorge ran through some chords on the keyboard, and Larry twirled his drumsticks. Chaos was packed. Dancers could do little more than shimmy on the floor in the tight press of sweating bodies. The light man was practicing with the spots, shining first on band members, then panning over the crowd. The sound man in back was whispering prayers over his board. Smells of fried food, alcohol, and marijuana perfumed the darkness. The tension in the air was palpable as the time for ignition approached.

Mini-skirted servers were rushing through the throng, trying to deliver drinks and food before the opening number. The three bartenders were mixing their potions with the quick and deliberate ease of seasoned professionals. The mood was festive. The biggest party of the week was about to begin. Only the video poker players seemed oblivious to all of it, feeding their unresponsive gods money while the uproar kept building in the main room.

Meanwhile, in his rear office, Sokolov was restless. He missed having Tolstoy to watch his back. And were Volkov's men really so stupid as to kill each other over a flat tire? Or had Friese pulled off another masterful deception, as he must have done with Tolstoy? Should he be worried? Would it be better to have this upstart college professor as a friend than an enemy?

At times like this, he could talk to Tolstoy, bounce ideas off him, and the giant would listen patiently. Hearing his own thoughts spoken aloud would clarify his mind, relax him. Now he

232

was stuck gibbering to himself, getting nowhere. *Blyad! If Friese killed Tolstoy, I want him dead! I'll kill him myself!*

He took a breath, calmed himself, and called Friese's cell phone. "Dr. Friese? I hope I am not interrupting."

"Not at all, Mr. Sokolov. I'm actually here in town doing a little shopping. How may I help you?"

"I wanted to extend my sympathies. I hope you weren't too traumatized by those dead men in your driveway the other night. You and I never got a chance to meet."

"Your 'representatives' apparently tried to loot my house."

"I can assure you they were not my men. When my men arrived, the police were already there. They just turned around and came back to the club. Things have been so busy I haven't had the opportunity to call you until now."

"Well, I appreciate your concern. I'm not used to seeing dead people at my house."

"I can imagine. That would be stressful for anyone. So shall we try again to meet?"

"I'd love to."

"Do you have some time tonight? I would like to meet sooner than later, but it will be noisy. Your student Franklin and his band are here."

"I'll be entertaining a guest later, but I'm right down the street. I can be there in a few minutes."

"Good. Park in one of the reserved spaces behind the club and call me when you arrive. I'll let you in through the private rear entrance."

When Sokolov terminated the call, he slid open the right-hand desk drawer and withdrew his pistol. A quick check confirmed the magazine was full and a cartridge was loaded in the chamber. He laid it on his desk.

Leaving the dry warmth of the liquor outlet, Sterling hunched over and held the brim of his hat against the wind and rain. He put the wine and liquor he had just purchased into the trunk and then slid behind the wheel of the Lexus. His hand found the holster nestled under his arm and took comfort in it. Since the events at his house last Friday, he took his .45 with him everywhere except on campus, where Effling forbade it, despite his concealed carry permit. He hoped the Russians wouldn't try for him in such a public place.

He started the car and put the defroster on to clear the windshield. What was his plan? He was convinced Sokolov wanted to kill him, so he would have to strike first. He remembered the phone call he had made to Tolstoy at the club, and how loud it was in the background. Loud enough to muffle a gunshot?

The club was only a half-mile down the street. He put the car in gear and left the lot. In minutes, he found a reserved parking place behind Club Chaos. Deciding against calling Sokolov, he got out of the car and walked to the rear entrance. He withdrew the pistol from its holster and put it in his right coat pocket. With trembling fingers, he tested the doorknob. It was unlocked. He let himself into the throbbing darkness.

"Showtime," he whispered.

After his second glass of wine, Peter was pacing his living room, complaining to Hammer. "Yeah, boy, I know Chris is right about all this. I'll hand over West's evidence to the police. But I have to do something more than that. I want to confront that bastard myself." Hammer woofed. "Yeah, he's dangerous. But what's he gonna do? Shoot me? He probably doesn't even own a gun. He poisoned Dean Wasserman. So I won't let him feed me."

He stopped long enough to pour himself another glass of wine. "I'll make copies of the pictures on my printer and rub his tenured little nose in them. What do you think?" Hammer barked an affirmation. "Good. So you're with me on this. I need your support." He put his glass down and took the envelope of pictures into his office. He decided against copying the whole collection, so he picked the two most damning ones and ran them through his printer. Then he folded the copies and inserted them into a business envelope. On a small scrap of paper, he jotted the missive, "I think we should have a little talk, Sterling. Your former friend, Peter." He put this into the envelope as well, then sealed it and wrote Sterling's name on the front. "I'll put this in his box at school on Monday. That should get a rise out of him, but not the kind he likes."

Peter walked back to the living room with Hammer close behind. "Did I tell you I checked out Grace Kaiser? Her Biology grade went from a C+ to an A- overnight. I guess she suddenly got smarter." He scratched behind the dog's ears and then stroked his neck and back. "What a world, Hammer. What a world."

He paused for a moment, remembering Chris's advice. *Hand it over to the police. Let them untangle it.* He sighed. "I know that's the right thing to do, Hammer. But what if they go after him before I get my crack at him?" The dog woofed. Common sense finally kicked in, overriding the alcohol. "OK. OK. I'll call Officer Whitehorse. Damn it. I suppose I shouldn't sit on this over the weekend." He pulled his phone from his pocket.

"We about ready to roll, guys?" Frankie shouted above the din. He looked at the mass of heaving bodies on the dance floor and smiled. He knew it was all sex and sweat, and it excited him.

"Gimme about two minutes. Gotta replace a string." Mack was moving as fast as he could to prime his bass.

"We're gonna give 'em a show like they've never seen or heard," chimed in Larry.

"I wanna start with *The Cemetery Shuffle*." Frankie was famous for last-minute changes.

"Good choice. That'll bring down the house." Jorge was ready to bang some heads.

3 Day Fish was poised on the razor's edge.

Sterling felt the pounding bass of the recorded dance music in his gut. It was loud, but not loud enough to mask a gunshot. He looked at his watch. When was the band supposed to start? He wrapped his hand around the grip of the pistol in his pocket and inserted his finger into the trigger guard.

To his left, the hallway led to the main room of the lounge. Ahead of him, he could see the band on the stage, fussing with their instruments. Sokolov's office must be to the right. He walked slowly in that direction down the darkened corridor. In the dim light, he could barely make out photographs of bands and singers pinned to the walls. He tried to remember what this building had been before Sokolov had bought it and remodeled it. A restaurant? Another club?

On the right was a door. It had to be his office. He entered without knocking, hoping to startle him.

The Russian was sitting at his desk, both hands flat in front of him. Sterling saw the man's eyes widen and dart toward the gun that was lying twelve inches from his right hand.

"Dr. Friese. I was expecting you to call." Sokolov took a breath. His hands began to shake.

"I think surprise parties are more fun, don't you? But enough pleasantries. Why did you send those two thugs to kill me? What possible threat can I be to your organization?"

"You killed my cousin! *Mudak!*"

"Tolstoy was your cousin? Well, he came after me first. It was self-defense." Sterling saw the Russian's eyes glance toward the gun again.

Just then the walls shook as an enormous burst of sound exploded from the stage. Sokolov reached for his gun. Sterling shot through his coat pocket. Two bullets struck Sokolov before he could close his fingers around the pistol. He fell back in his chair, eyes wide, blood spilling from his chest and mouth as he struggled to breathe. Sterling snapped the gun from his pocket and shot the man in the head. Then he started slapping the side of his coat where the cloth had begun to catch fire from the discharges.

With calm deliberation, he took a handkerchief from his pocket and wiped the doorknob clean. With the cloth around the knob, he opened the door and wiped the knob on the other side. Then he closed it and hurried down the corridor to the exit.

He immediately recognized something was wrong. Black

smoke was billowing from the stage. The music had stopped and people were screaming. Then fire alarms began their piercing shrieks. He couldn't look back. He reached the exit, wiped both sides of the doorknob, and ran to his car.

Frankie couldn't believe what he saw. As they slammed into their opening song—a roaring, screeching apocalypse of sound—the pyrotechnics erupted like volcanoes, spewing massive showers of sparks like lava over the walls and ceiling of the stage. The crowds howled in delight. But before the band had completed the first verse, the rivers of fire ignited the acoustic foam insulation. In a heartbeat, massive billows of black smoke engulfed the stage, as flames consumed everything combustible. People began to scream. Fire alarms shrilled. Sprinkler systems gushed. The band members leaped from the stage into the seething mass of bodies struggling to escape. Chaos had visited Chaos.

The electricity sizzled and went out as the wires burned through, plunging the club into total darkness. Then emergency lighting over the exits flickered on, casting a ghastly glow on the frightful agony, unfolding like a hellscape by Hieronymus Bosch. Blinded by smoke, the stampede toward the doors was unstoppable. People were trampled beneath stumbling feet, crushed against walls that would not open. Screams became frantic coughs as the toxic fumes choked the breath from the fleeing victims.

Frankie lost his friends in the melee. "Larry! Mack! Jorge!" It was useless. No single voice could be heard over the cacophony of sound that drowned out all else. He was squeezed into the moving crowd, inching toward the front. Water from the sprinkler system poured over him, gluing his hair to his face and his shirt to his back. His eyes smarted from the smoke, and his lungs burned. It became harder and harder to catch his breath. His heart pounded. "I don't want to die!" he cried, but his coughing stopped any further speech. He knew he would never make it to the front doors alive. He had heard of disasters like this—people stacked like cord wood by exits jammed with bodies. The Station

Nightclub Fire in West Warwick, Rhode Island. He was only six or seven when it happened, but he had read about it as a teenager, when he was going through what he called his "classic heavy metal phase." 100 people killed, 230 injured, when Great White miscalculated their onstage pyrotechnics.

So he was going to die. It didn't matter that he was young and had his whole life ahead of him. He prayed silently. "God forgive me for dealing drugs. For cheating in my classes. For having sex with Maryanne. I'm sorry! Don't send me to hell!" *Or am I already in hell? Have I died already? No, damn it!*

But knowing he was going to die if he didn't do anything different freed him. A kind of calm settled his racing heart. *Is there any other way out? Of course! The rear exit that we use to bring our instruments in and out. But that's back where the fire started. Have the sprinklers put it out? Would the smoke be too much?* It didn't matter. He was going to die anyway. He might as well try.

Using all his strength, he pivoted around and fought against the tide. As he suspected, he was near the back of the mass, so there were only a few rows of people to push through. He took off his wet T-shirt and tied it around his nose and mouth, creating a mask he hoped would protect him from the worst of the smoke. His eyes were tearing so badly he could barely see. With a jolt, he stumbled into the right hand wall. On all fours, he began crawling down the corridor. He felt along the wall, trying to find the door. How much longer would he retain consciousness before passing out from smoke inhalation? And there was the door frame! He held his breath and stood up. Fumbling for the doorknob, he burst outside, falling in a heap on the pavement. He ripped off his mask and took great breaths of fresh air. Rain washed over his face, cleaning his eyes, making white rivulets through the black ash smeared on his cheeks. Lying on his back, he threw up his arms and began shouting, "I'm alive! I'm alive!"

A sharp, mirthless laugh escaped his lips.

He rolled over and wept.

43. Living in the Labyrinth

FRIDAY, JANUARY 19, 2018. Marisa was fiddling with her camera. Emma lay naked on the couch, a flowered shawl draped lazily over her lithe frame.

"Are you ready yet? I'm getting chilly." She pulled the shawl tighter.

"It'll keep your skin tone better. Good for the shoot. I'll only be a minute. These will be beautiful." She pursed her lips. "*You're* beautiful. You're the best subject I've ever had, and these will be the best pictures I've ever taken."

A final adjustment of her lens, and she motioned to Emma that she was about to begin. Emma stretched cat-like on the couch, extending and withdrawing her arms and legs, turning to the side and back, pulling the shawl close and opening it wide. She pouted and smiled, opened her lips and closed them, flirted with the camera. Her youthful body was perfect, unselfconscious. Posing was as natural to her as writing the poetry that filled her journals. She looked through the lens at Marisa, trying to get her to see the love in her heart, all to no avail. Marisa was taken, besotted with an older man she refused to name or talk about.

Marisa snapped pictures in rapid succession, staring at her subject, moving up and down and around, making little noises of approval and surprise. "Oooh. Yes. Just right." Photographer and subject became one, each anticipating the other's moves and wishes. It was a sublime act of creativity and joy. Finally, they stopped, sated with beauty.

"That was wonderful, Emma. Let's print them and get them in the album today. Would you mind if I tried to get them into a juried show? The Bandon Gallery and the Elk Creek Gallery are having shows in March, and they're accepting submissions now."

"Go for it. I wonder what it would feel like to see myself on a gallery wall in my altogether? Little boys staring at my boobs? It's not pornographic, is it?"

"No way. It's art. You show what human beauty can be

like—the female form."

Emma sighed. "I wish I felt like that on the inside. But my beauty is only skin deep."

"Don't say that! I think you're a beautiful person. You're kind, generous, forgiving. You went on that missions trip to Mexico with your church and helped build houses for poor people, for heaven's sake. You volunteer three nights a week at that nursing home. You sponsored that food drive for the homeless here and in Portland."

"It just never seems to be enough. I don't know." She couldn't bring herself to tell Marisa she was in love with her. Marisa was already the best friend she had ever had, but she wanted more. She wanted to share the poetry she had written for her, the dreams she had for the two of them together. But she couldn't interfere with the relationship Marisa already had with the lover she wouldn't talk about—the lover who promised her an engagement ring in the spring. What to do to fill the hole in her heart?

"Let me throw my clothes on. I'll drive us to the photo shop and then bring you back here. I need the overtime anyway, and the boss'll give it to me."

The car she affectionately called "Rattle-Trap" protested when she turned the key but did start, complaints notwithstanding. Marisa sat in the passenger seat. She rolled down her window, insisting she could smell exhaust inside the car. It was a continuing argument between them. They were at the shop in fifteen minutes.

Although there were four other employees, Marisa would allow only Emma to process her work. "I just don't trust anyone else with my stuff." Emma was more than happy to oblige. She was three days late on her rent and a few extra hours would help make ends meet. While she worked, Marisa got on Facebook with her photographer friends.

When the task was complete, Emma rang up the bill and accepted Marisa's payment. She handed her the envelope of pictures. She then signed out and waved to the store manager as she and Marisa left.

"Do you think I'm pretty?" she said, as they got back into the car.

"You ask that all the time, and it throws me every time you do. It boggles me that you can't look in the mirror and see how gorgeous you are."

"Gorgeous?"

"You should work as a model, for heaven's sake."

"But people leave me. How can I be pretty if they always leave me?"

"What people are we talking about?"

Emma sighed. "It's nothing. I'm sorry I brought it up."

"It's not nothing. Who are we talking about?"

But Emma said no more. When the silence grew too uncomfortable, Marisa turned on the radio. They were soon back to the campus. Emma drove Marisa to the entrance of the Columbia River Dorm. "All ashore that's going ashore," she said.

"Thanks, Emma. I'll get these in the album by tonight and show you the spread tomorrow. Then you can help me decide which ones we might enlarge, which ones to print on aluminum or canvas for the galleries."

"You bet, hon." She watched Marisa walk to the dorm and enter through the glass door. As she turned and left the campus, a single tear trickled down her right cheek. *Why do I feel so incomplete? I have a best friend, a job I love. What's the matter with me? What do I need to do to make it right?*

It didn't take her long to reach her one-bedroom apartment on the southern boundary of Driftwood. It was an older duplex, in need of painting. Starlings made nests in the eaves every year, staining the siding with permanent white streaks. The interior sorely needed updating. Dark paneled walls and shag carpets were the least of the problems. Given the groans that the refrigerator and dishwasher were making, it was only a matter of time before they would give up the ghost and need to be replaced.

Once inside, Emma hung her coat on the rack by the door

and put on a tea kettle to boil. Then she opened her journal and let her pain shape words on paper.

Back at the dorm, Marisa laid out the pictures on the table. Once satisfied with the order and the groupings, she inserted them into the photo album. Then she decided to shower again to prepare for her evening. Tonight would be a big night. Tonight she would tell him.

Her life had changed so much since she had entered Pacific Crest. Gone were the nightmares of her father sneaking into her room at night, alcohol and tobacco smoke heavy on his breath, clumsily fondling her under the sheets. She no longer heard the shrill arguments between him and her mother, complaining about the daughter who should have been an abortion. She didn't have to make excuses to anyone about not feeling sorrow when her parents were killed in a head-on collision with a semi-truck on I-5 four years ago.

Sterling was a gentleman. He was good to her in ways boys had never been. Kind, considerate, listening attentively to the stories she'd tell, her dreams and aspirations. He supported her desire to become a professional photographer without hesitation.

And he made her feel beautiful.

Sterling put candlesticks on the table and set it with his best silver and china. Earlier in the day, he had purchased a pound of fresh dungeness crab meat and a quarter pound of salad shrimp at Hook, Line, and Sinker. From a chef friend, he had learned that the secret to the perfect crab cake was to puree salad shrimp into a pink paste and use it as the binder to hold the crab cake together, without resorting to eggs or potato. Six crab cakes, lightly covered with panko, lay on a plate next to the fry pan. The Sauvignon Blanc chilling in the refrigerator would be the perfect complement. Good food and good wine were the best aphrodisiacs, and Marisa was a champion in bed. Just the thought of her excited him.

Their routine worked well. Marisa would walk down the

hill as far as the fork to the Double L. He would be parked on the main road just before the turn-off to the university. She would call him on her cell phone, and he would be there to pick her up within sixty seconds, without risking possible exposure by driving up to the dorm. The clandestine nature of their rendezvous added an element of danger that his young women found stimulating. He owned the candy store.

With everything prepared, he got into his car and drove to the college. He parked and waited. Previous encounters with Marisa had taught him what she liked best, what turned her on the most. One night, when she was particularly passionate, he had called her "my favorite firework," and she all but exploded in some of the most frenetic love-making he had ever enjoyed.

The phone call came through on Bluetooth. "Is my lover-man ready?" cooed the voice.

"At your service, my darling. I'll be there in a minute."

The pick-up went without a hitch. On the drive back to his home, she said, "I have a feeling this will be a special night."

"Every night with you is special, Marisa."

He always felt more comfortable when the garage door closed and provided them privacy. "Come inside, my dear. I have a new wine I want you to try. Tell me if it's any good."

"First things first. Kiss me. Prove that you're glad to see me."

It was like waving a red flag at a bull—another thing he loved about Marisa. He willingly complied. Heart racing, he finally disentangled himself from their embrace. "Wine and food first," he laughed. "You're a tiger tonight."

She smiled at the compliment. "I want you."

"And you shall have me. I promise."

They entered the house, and he took her coat. "Sit here at the bar while I open this wine." He poured her a small amount in a long-stemmed glass. "Swirl it like I showed you. Inhale deeply to smell it. Then taste it."

The wine was the color of pale straw. She raised it to her lips. "Mmmm. I like it."

"What do you taste? Remember how we practiced?"

"OK. Citrus up front. Grapefruit, for sure. Maybe a little peach or mango? And melon. Oh, at the end, a hint of pineapple. It's yummy."

"Excellent! Let me fill your glass, and I'll get some for myself." It was more strategy. He knew she liked learning things that made her feel more sophisticated.

Dinner was simple but delicious. They ate and drank and laughed together.

"I have a berry tart to put in the oven for dessert."

"Can we save it for later?" Her face was flushed.

He reached over and put his hand on her breast. "Your heart is pounding, my dear."

"You know what I want, Sterling."

He stood and led her to the bedroom.

An hour later, they lay quietly, a patina of sweat glistening on their bodies in the flickering glow of the candle.

"You're wonderful, Marisa. My favorite firework."

She leaned over and kissed him on the lips. "I love you. I could stay here forever."

"Then I'd lose my job, and you'd flunk out of school. We can't let that happen to our aspiring photographer, can we?" He stroked her cheek. "Shall I put the tart in the oven?"

"Mmmm. I didn't think I'd be hungry again, but I am."

He got up from bed and put on a long plush robe. "And I'm hungry for you again. I'll be back in a minute."

As he entered the kitchen to pre-heat the oven, the doorbell rang.

"Don't answer that, honey," Marisa called from the bedroom.

"I'm expecting something from FedEx that I'll have to sign for. I'm decent in this robe." His jaw dropped when he opened the door.

"Emma?" He stepped back as though he had been struck.

"Hi, Daddy. I wasn't sure you'd recognize me. It's been so long."

"But—but..." He blocked the doorway when she tried to enter. "It's good to see you, but this isn't a good time."

"We haven't seen each other in ten years, and this isn't a good time?" He could hear a note of disappointment in her voice.

"I'm entertaining a guest, sweetheart." He pointed to his robe. "You can see I'm not dressed. Could we schedule a time to meet? Maybe tomorrow morning?"

"Did you get the package? Is everything OK?" Marisa called from the bedroom.

"What? Is that—?" Emma pushed past her father and ran toward the voice she had heard. Sterling ran after her. She stopped at the bedroom door when she saw Marisa lying there.

"Emma?" Marisa pulled up the sheet to cover herself. "What are you doing here?"

"What am *I* doing here? What the hell! You're fucking my father? He's your secret lover?" She threw up her arms and began pulling her hair. Then she clawed at her face, gouging her cheeks with her fingernails. "My best friend! My father!" She wailed like an infant who would not be consoled. Her body shook in spasms.

"Calm down, Emma. It'll be OK. Let me explain." Her father lowered his voice and spoke slowly, trying to soothe her. He reached for her, but she batted his arms away.

"How could I be so stupid!" she shrieked. "Mom was right about you! You fucked every girl in your class then, and you're still doing it now." She turned to Marisa, cowering in the bed. "He promised you a ring? Never gonna happen! That's his mother's ring, and he just uses it for bait. He'll dump you like he's dumped all the others." She wheeled around at her father. "You're a pig—a fucking predator. You should be in jail, not teaching at a university." She spit in his face.

"Emma!" cried Marisa, sitting up now in bed. Tears were streaming from her eyes. "I didn't know! Please believe me! I didn't know he was your father."

Emma took a deep breath and wiped tears and blood from

her face. She reached out a hand to Marisa and gently touched a finger to her lips. "I know that, dear one. I'll always love you."

She looked at her father, wiping saliva from his face with a tissue.

"I guess I'll leave you two lovebirds to your own devices. I can show myself out." She shut the bedroom door behind her. On the way down the corridor, she spied the framed photograph of her mad grandmother hanging on the wall. She remembered it from her childhood. *Do you still hide the ring, Grandma?* she wondered. She opened the frame on its hinges and found the little box inside.

And there it was. She took the ring, slid it on her finger, and closed the case. "Goodbye, Daddy," she whispered.

Marisa was weeping. Sterling sat on the bed and took her in his arms. "I'm so sorry, darling. You didn't deserve that. My daughter is very...volatile."

"Is it true what she said? About you and other girls?"

"Of course not. Her bipolar mother poisoned her with lies from the time she was a toddler. 'Your father is a cheat. Your father sleeps around. Your father never loved you.' When she went off her medicine, she became delusional. And she went off her medicine a lot. I'm afraid Emma began showing signs of bipolar disorder herself in her early teens. Spent three weeks in a mental hospital after a suicide attempt."

"She never told me that."

"I'll bet there's a lot she hasn't told you. Like the time she tried to kill me in my sleep? Hit me with a baseball bat. Lucky for me she didn't have the strength to do any real damage. But I had a lump on my noggin for weeks."

"This is all too much, Sterling. My head is spinning. I don't know what to think."

"Don't think. All you have to know is that I love you. Let me prove it to you again." He stroked her hair and drew her face to his. After the first kiss, he felt her warm to him again.

Forty-five minutes later, Sterling sat up. "Now I'm really ready for that tart. I never did get it in the oven before. I'll go do it now. Be right back."

She grabbed his arm before he rolled out of bed. "Stay for a moment, honey. There's something I want to tell you."

He lay back down and wrapped his arm around her so her head lay on his chest. "What is it, darling?"

She let her fingers play with the hairs on his chest. "I've been meaning to tell you for a while now. I just never got the chance." She took a deep breath and plunged ahead. "We're going to have a baby. I know it's a little soon, but we can move up the engagement. And I'll graduate before the baby is born. I even found a wedding dress that I like. I hope you're not mad."

His whole body stiffened. "You're pregnant? I thought you said you were being careful about that. This isn't how we planned it." He sat up. "No, this won't work."

"What do you mean?" He could hear the alarm in her voice as she sat up next to him.

"The timing is all wrong." He shook his head. "You can't be pregnant now with four months of school left." He looked into her eyes. "OK. We can fix this. We can arrange for you to have an abortion."

"But I don't want an abortion. I want to have your baby." He heard a whining note that infuriated him.

"You can't have a baby! Do you know what the Chancellor would say if he knew I had impregnated one of my students? What the Board of Trustees would say?" He grimaced. "You watch the news. Universities are taking it on the chin for sexual abuse cases. That's what they'd call it. Sexual abuse! I'd lose my job!"

Marisa began to cry. "I thought it would make you happy."

"Happy? Are you crazy? You're getting an abortion. And that's final." He got out of bed and began to dress in quick, abrupt motions. "Get your clothes on," he snapped. "I'm taking you back to school."

She whimpered as she drew on her pants, pulled the

blouse over her head, and fastened her shoes. "Sterling, I..."

"No more talking. You've talked enough for one night. Don't forget your purse."

He all but pushed her out of the house and into his car. They made the drive in total silence. The rain had abated and the wind was still. When they reached the fork, Marisa got out, and Sterling turned the car around and sped away.

The walk up the hill seemed out of a nightmare to her. There were no lights for the first three hundred yards, and the darkness of the forest was total. The only sounds were the droplets of water falling from the branches above to the earth below. A large animal bounded away on the left and startled her.

Sterling had changed so completely. Was a different person. She had never seen him angry like that. *He doesn't want me or our baby! And Emma! I've crushed my best friend!* She clenched her fists and wailed into the night.

Guilt washed over her in great, smothering waves. She hadn't grieved for her parents. Never told Sterling she had stopped taking her birth control pills after those side effects. Kept the truth from Emma until it was too late. Now she had lost everything.

The closer she got to the school, the more bereft she felt. As the agony carved a hole in her heart, a spark of anger ignited and began to fill it.

Emma had no reason to lie. She had called her father a predator. Marisa hadn't wanted to believe that. Allowed herself to be seduced by him again. But in a flash of self awareness, she knew it was true. Sterling had been abusing women his whole life. He had never loved her. He had groomed her for his own lust. Flattered her. Told her things she wanted to hear. He had no intentions of marrying her. That was just another lie. The ring, the engagement—all strategies to get her to let down her guard. To let the monster in. She clenched her fists so tightly her nails dug into her palms. She shrieked in rage.

She would make it right with Emma tomorrow. She had to. Otherwise, there was nothing left to live for.

Sterling awoke Saturday morning to find a letter had been taped to the glass panel of his front door.

Dear Daddy,

By the time you read this, I'll be at the Double L. There's nothing left. You took my childhood, and now you've taken my best friend. I wonder how long before she winds up on the trash heap with all the others?

Two years ago I tracked you down and moved to Driftwood, imagining that when the time was right, I might make peace with you. "Make amends," as they say in my group. If I was going to stay sober, it was one of the Steps I'd have to take. But that was just a fantasy. I see that now. You can't make peace with a dragon without getting your arm bitten off.

There is some relief in knowing Mom was right. That my own memories are accurate—not the nightmares of a mentally ill child. I've spent so many years doubting myself.

I couldn't begin to tell you how many times over the past two years I've sat on that shelf of rock at the Double L wondering, "Do I launch myself into the universe today?" Each time the answer was no. Until today. This is the day.

I'm reminded of a poem I wrote when I was about 12 or 13. I was a pretty precocious kid, as you may remember. And depressed. I called it "Living in the Labyrinth." That was my life all right. You were the Minotaur, of course, hiding in the dark around the next corner. I guess you still are.

Anyway, it's a good day for a launch.

See you in hell,

Emma

P.S. I have Grandma's ring.

Sterling crumpled the letter in his fist and ran down the corridor to his mother's picture. He snapped it open. The ring was gone. He slammed his fist into the wall and roared his inarticulate rage. He'd have to get it back. Was it too late? Had she already jumped? With all the speed he could muster, he threw on a pair of jeans and a shirt, grabbed his coat, and ran to the garage. In seconds, he was racing toward Cascadia Head.

He looked at the time on the dashboard. 7:00 A.M. The day was supposed to be sunny, before a major storm moved over the coast tomorrow. When he reached the dirt road, he slowed down as he navigated the ruts and washboard bumps. He saw an old car up ahead. Pulling behind it, he leaped out. He sprinted down the forest path. Branches scratched at his face. Twice he tripped over roots and fell on the moist earth. Finally, he reached the small meadow.

"Emma!" he shouted. "Emma!" He saw a forlorn figure sitting on the ledge. At the sound of his voice, the figure stood and turned to him.

"Daddy!" she exclaimed, her face lighting up. "You came! You came for me!"

"Please come away from the edge."

She paused and frowned. "This is the day, Daddy. I have to. Why should I stay?"

"Please, Emma."

"Can you think of any reason I shouldn't return to the universe?"

"You're not returning to the universe. You're killing yourself." He tried to suppress his anger.

"So why shouldn't I?"

His frustration boiled over. "Emma, I can't play games with you. Please give me back the ring."

"The ring? Is that why you're here? All you care about?" She held up her finger to show him. "Grandma wanted me to have it."

"Don't be absurd. You never knew her."

"She came to me in a dream."

"Bullshit! Give me the goddamn ring now!"

She turned away from him, as though she were about to jump. He sprang forward and wrapped his arm around her neck, yanking her off her feet and back from the edge.

"Stop! You're hurting me!" She sank her teeth into his arm, as she kicked and squirmed in his embrace.

He howled in pain and flung her away from him. She tumbled to the ground and got back to her feet, just as he grabbed her again. This time, he had his hands around her throat. She fought his grasp, pounded at his face with her fists, pulled him with her toward the precipice.

"GIVE...ME...THE...RING!" His words were an animal snarl through clenched teeth.

Her eyes went wide as he tightened his grip, choking the breath from her. Before she passed out, she thrust her knee up between his legs. The sudden pain startled him. He loosened his stranglehold. She brought both feet up and kicked against his chest with all her might. Breaking free, she lost her balance, and plunged backward over the cliff.

"Daddy!" she wailed as she tumbled over and over like a leaf in the wind.

"My ring!" he screamed as he watched her fall. He raised both fists to the heavens and shrieked in fury.

He sat heavily in the dirt. His mind went blank. As the minutes passed by, his rapid breathing returned to normal, and his pounding heart slowed. There was nothing to be done for it. His ring was gone forever. Looking back toward the path, he remembered a deep ravine about fifty yards down the dirt road. Perhaps he could roll her car into it before any hikers came up the trail. The car would be invisible from the road. Wouldn't be found for months.

With grim determination, he stood and returned the way he had come.

44. Eine Kleine Newtmusik

The fire made national news. CBS declared it "eerily similar" to the Station Nightclub Fire of 2003 in West Warwick, Rhode Island.

"We interrupt our regularly scheduled programming for this breaking news," said the reporter. "A club for young people has suffered a catastrophic fire that turned deadly tonight. So far the official count is 54 dead and 87 injured, but those numbers may change over the next few days. Here is Sigmund Orre, our correspondent on site in Driftwood, Oregon."

"Thanks, Geoffrey. Here I am at what remains of Club Chaos. You can see the rubble still smoldering behind me. It will take a long time for this little coastal town to recover from its worst fire since the Driftwood boardwalk and carnival burned down on July 21, 1967. Most of the dead succumbed to smoke inhalation, and many of the injured were trampled in the stampede to escape. Police and fire fighters agree the losses would have been far higher had the club not had a state-of-the-art sprinkler system. All indications are that the pyrotechnics used by the band, 3 Day Fish, started the blaze. Two band members were killed, Mack Springer and Jorge Hernandez. In addition, the owner of the club, Abram Sokolov, was pronounced dead at the scene. We will keep you updated as more information becomes available."

"I'm sorry, Chloe. More than anything I'd like to go to Portland with you and spend a romantic weekend together. You know that." It was Saturday morning, and he was calling her from the police station.

"I understand, darling. Our time is coming. For now, you have to do your job. Just know that I love you."

He sighed. "We're still identifying bodies. Families have jammed the phones. They've gathered outside the station here and at the fire department. It's a madhouse. Tony and I are on overtime. We're headed back to the club in a few minutes."

"Please take care of yourself. Eat. Stay hydrated. Take breaks."

"Of course. I'll call you when I can. Love you."

"Love you, too."

He slid his phone into his pocket and turned to his partner. Before he could say anything, the station phone rang. Chiara, trouper that she was, had volunteered for Saturday duty and fielded the call. "Ted Ames, Fire Chief, on line one." She motioned to Whitehorse, who picked up the phone.

"Hi, Ted. What have you got?"

Esperanza saw his partner's face drop. "What?" he whispered.

"Goddamn it! Can you keep a lid on it? If the news gets this, they'll have a field day. It might even trigger a turf war with the Russians in Portland. OK. Great. I owe you big time. We'll be there in ten minutes."

He looked at Esperanza. "Fire Deputies took a good look at Sokolov. The fire didn't kill him."

Esperanza cocked his head, a look of confusion on his face.

"Three bullet holes in the sonofabitch."

"Christ Almighty!"

"They've gotten hold of Forensics from Newport. So far, they've kept it away from the press. Who knows what would happen if they got hold of it? Some bad actor down here takes out the local guy and Volkov in Portland goes berserk. I don't want any more blood on our streets. As far as anybody is concerned, the bastard died in the fire."

"Are you thinking what I'm thinking?"

"Sterling Friese? Let's see. If we count Tolstoy and Popova, that's five dead Russians, two of whom wind up in Friese's driveway. Think he's developing a taste for it?" He made a face that looked as though he had just bitten into a lemon. "Kind of boggles the mind."

"Shit! So much for life in a small, sleepy town."

"Well, let's get our asses in gear and get down there." As all three phone lines lit up, he called to Chiara. "You're in charge, girl. Good luck!"

Chiara gave him a thumbs-up sign and reached for the phone.

The scene at the wreckage of Club Chaos was surreal—a dystopian movie set come to life. Black body bags lined the street. Smoke from the ruins hung over the block like a noisome cloud, contaminating everything with the scents of death and burnt plastic. Crowds held back by yellow police tape stared silently or wept, coughing in the fumes. A Catholic priest led a group of mourners in saying the Rosary.

Whitehorse and Esperanza made their way inside the rubble, where firemen were extinguishing the last of the hotspots. They remembered where Sokolov's office had been, and encountered the Forensics team from Newport there.

"Hi, Charley. Tony. There's our friend. Haven't bagged him yet. Two to the chest and one to the head."

Whitehorse leaned over the body. "Pretty intact, Larry."

"He had a fireproof door on his office. Sprinklers really helped." The man held up a plastic bag. "Found only one shell casing. Been through this shit every which way but loose and only got one. Don't have a clue where the other two are."

"Fingerprints on it?"

"A pretty good chance. It bounced out of the way under his desk, so it wasn't exposed to the worst of it."

"Make it a priority. OK?"

"You got it, Charley."

On Monday morning, Sterling was surprised to see a young man sitting behind the desk in Administration. The man extended his hand. "I'm Neville. I haven't had the pleasure of taking one of your classes yet, Dr. ..."

"Friese. Sterling Friese. Biology. Where's Amelia?"

"She's in the hospital, recovering from smoke inhalation.

Four others, too." He frowned. "Five of our students died in the fire. Chancellor Brady will be addressing the school, and a memorial service is being planned for Wednesday."

"Dear God," he said, feigning concern. "What a tragedy." He shook his head and went to empty his mailbox. He had spent the weekend congratulating himself for a job well done and an escape well executed. Today he had only two classes and three student appointments, so an extra cup of coffee would be in order as soon as he opened his mail. At his office, he set his briefcase by the file cabinet and took a seat behind his desk.

One envelope looked curious. It had only his first name hand-written on the front. When he cut it open and looked inside, his heart skipped a beat. There were two pictures of him and Grace Kaiser that left nothing to the imagination. The brief note said it all: "I think we should have a little talk, Sterling. Your former friend, Peter."

"'Former' friend, old man?" he said aloud. "If you want to play hardball with me, bring it on."

Despite his bravado, he was worried. Pictures like this could ruin everything he had worked so hard for. Tenure, doctoral candidates, prestige. The Board of Trustees would have him removed for ethical violations of his contract, tenured or not. No appeal. All lost. He couldn't let that happen. No matter the cost.

Stir the pot had been his working MO before, and he would resort to it again, adding a little confusional tactic as well. He had Peter's number on his cell phone, so he texted him a message.

"Oh, my God! Thank you for showing me those pictures. I got a packet of them myself in the mail two weeks ago, demanding $250,000. I need your help. I think my ex has hired somebody to blackmail me, using those Photoshopped pictures. Please let me know when and where we can meet. I'm really scared."

He smiled as he sent the message off. *People believe what*

they want to believe. Have I given him another version of the truth he'd rather accept? Or at least planted a seed of doubt in his self-righteousness? He burst out laughing. Peter had no idea with whom he was playing.

Peter felt his phone vibrate, but was in the middle of teaching a class. When the class concluded, he returned to his office and looked at the message. It was not the response he had been expecting. Had he inadvertently fallen into the ex-wife's scheme by randomly hiring the very man she had paid to blackmail Sterling? Was something so far-fetched even possible? His head was spinning. No. Sterling was a lying bastard. A sexual predator. But how to explain the men found dead in his driveway? Had they been local muscle hired by the blackmailer to make Sterling pay? Then how did that giant Tolstoy and Philip Effling fit into it? Nothing made any sense.

He looked at his watch. Plenty of time before his next class for a cup of coffee. He decided to check the class rosters on his computer first. Grace Kaiser was taking a statistical analysis class with his friend Adrian Hauerbach. Class was almost over. Maybe he'd pay her a visit before his coffee.

Five minutes later, he was waiting outside the lecture hall for Grace to emerge. Students began filing out, and he easily spotted the attractive blonde in the short blue dress.

"Ms. Kaiser? I'm Dr. Bristol. I don't think we've met yet. May I have a moment of your time?"

"Of course, Professor. What can I do for you?"

"Please come to my office. I'd rather speak in private."

"Am I in some kind of trouble?" She looked worried.

"Oh, gracious, no. It's just a personal matter. Right this way."

Once they were in his office, he motioned her to the chair in front of his desk. He sat across from her. His expression became somber. "I'll get right to the point, Ms. Kaiser. Are you carrying on an affair with a faculty member?"

She looked shocked. "Of course not, Dr. Bristol. I'm a

serious student with long-term goals. I don't have time for that sort of thing. Besides," she smiled, "my father would stop paying my tuition...and chop the legs off the guy."

"I see. But Ms. Kaiser, we have pictures of you in rather compromising positions with a member of the faculty."

"They can't be me. No way. I'm not that kind of girl."

"You're sure?"

"Absolutely. What faculty member is it?"

"I'm afraid I'm not at liberty to say."

"OK. I understand. Do you have any other questions, Professor? I have get to class."

"Just one. Any idea who might want to ruin your reputation by creating these false pictures of you?" Her answer surprised him.

"It's something I've known my whole life. You can't be as pretty as I am without having enemies." She stood up and smiled at him. "Goodbye, Dr. Bristol."

He watched the door close behind her and sat there, unsure what to think. Did he know any more than he did before? Was she being truthful, or was she a great liar? He needed that cup of coffee.

As Grace walked down the hall toward her next class, she smiled to herself. Sterling had prepped her for just such an event. "Deny everything," he had coached her, "No matter what they say. No matter what proof they claim to have. Ours is a forbidden love that no one else would understand." They had even rehearsed a conversation like the one she had just had with Dr. Bristol. But she would get Sterling to close the curtains in their bedroom next time. "Open to the stars and the sea," he had claimed. That would change.

There sat Sterling in the Faculty Lounge when Peter walked in. The man stood and extended his hand. "Thank you so much for showing me those pictures, Peter. Please get your coffee and come sit with me."

Peter filled his mug and joined him. Sterling's lips were trembling. He sat wringing his hands, scanning the room as though he expected an unseen adversary to come bursting in at any moment.

"I thought they couldn't be serious. $250,000? What university professor has money like that lying around? So I didn't do anything. Then those goons show up dead in my driveway. I think they were sent to scare the money out of me. I haven't said anything to the police. I'm afraid to make things worse than they are." He wiped his brow with a paper napkin. "What should I do? Who else have they sent those pictures to? Brady? The trustees? It has to be my ex. I don't know anybody else with that kind of venom." He took a sip of coffee. "And now I'm worried she'll try to hurt you or my other friends."

Peter looked startled. "That may have happened already. Some big guy grabbed me out front, claiming he wanted to know what information I had about your student Franklin Wise. My friend Chris Harper fought with him."

"Shit! That must have been Tolstoy. The same guy wound up in my office. Told me he'd snap my neck like a toothpick if I didn't start paying." He grimaced and shook his head. "I'm so sorry you got dragged into this. Where will it end? What can I do?"

"You have to go to the police. Despite your feelings about Officer Whitehorse."

Sterling's eyes misted over. "I know you're right. It's just..." He turned his head away. "I stand to lose everything, Peter. Everything I've worked for all these years."

Peter reached out and put a hand on his shoulder. "We'll figure it out. I'm busy for the next couple of days, but come to my house after supper on Thursday. Let's think this thing through together."

Sterling swung around to face him. "Thank you so much, Peter. You don't know how much this means to me." He looked at his watch. "Gotta go, my friend." He reached for his mug to bring it to the sink.

258

"I'll take care of that, Sterling. Go to your class."

"See you Thursday, Peter. Thanks again." *And that's how we big boys play the game*, he thought, as he left the lounge with a smirk on his face.

Peter took the phone from his pocket.

On Thursday evening, Peter was just putting the last of his dishes into the dishwasher when he heard the buzz from the gate.

"Hi, Peter. Sterling here."

"Hi, Sterling. Come ahead." He pushed the button to open the gate. In moments, Hammer began barking as Sterling approached the front door.

"Easy, boy. This is a friend." Peter held the dog by his collar. When he opened the door, Hammer growled. Peter could feel the tension in the dog's body. "Sorry, Sterling. Hammer is usually very friendly. I haven't seen him act this way before."

"Probably senses I'm not much of a dog-lover, but that's OK." He bent toward the animal and slowly opened both hands to allow the dog to sniff them. "Hey, Hammer. Can we be friends for tonight?" Hammer sniffed a kind of harrumph and backed away.

"Strange. Well, have a seat at the table. Can I get you something? Beer? Wine? Coffee?"

"You know, a cup of tea might be nice. I'm kind of chilled. Think I'll keep my jacket on for a bit."

"You got it. I'll put the kettle on."

Hammer refused to leave his master's side. As Peter busied himself in the kitchen, Sterling looked through the glass slider. The light from the house didn't penetrate far into the darkness. "We got a warmer spell coming," he said. "And dry. I've gotta get out and do some yard work around my place."

"I'm glad the landscaping is taken care of around here. It was never my thing. Earl Gray OK?" He fussed with mugs and tea bags. The fragrance of the bergamot cheered him.

"Sure. That's my go-to tea. Take it straight. No milk or sugar or lemon."

"Fair enough. The water will boil in a few minutes." He

came out to the table and sat down. Hammer sat beside him.

"Is that the whole packet of pictures?" Sterling pointed to the large manila envelope on the table.

"That's them. Pretty hard core stuff."

Sterling opened the envelope and slid the pictures out onto the table. "But you have to admit, she's got great tits."

"What?"

"C'mon, Peter. Don't be naïve. That girl is a piece of work. Look at her." He ran his finger along the picture and smiled at the disgusted look on his colleague's face. Then he drew the .45 from under his coat. "I said look at her." Hammer began to snarl. "You keep that dog under control or he gets the first bullet." He waved the pistol in Hammer's direction, then brought it back toward Peter. "Are you a betting man, Peter? Because I'm betting you don't own a gun like this, much less know how to use one."

"So it's true? Everything?"

"Of course it's true, Peter. I'm a young man. I have needs. The cherries are ripe for picking." He smiled again at his former mentor. "I can tell you now because a crazed robber is about to break into your house and kill you when he discovers you're home. On top of everything else that's happened in our sweet coastal burg, the university will grieve the loss of one of its most beloved professors. Hell, I'll get up at your memorial service and deliver the eulogy. It's kind of poetic, isn't it?"

Peter stroked Hammer's head and neck, felt every muscle, tense and ready. "May I ask you a personal question? Just to put it to rest."

"Sure. Fire away."

"Did you kill Dean Wasserman?"

Sterling didn't hesitate. "Of course I did. He was going to deny me tenure and get me fired. Got pictures like you did of some of my earlier conquests." He pursed his lips and took a deep breath. "Wasserman's death was my masterpiece. My Monet of murder, if you will. My Van Gogh of vengeance."

"You poisoned him, didn't you?"

"Yes, but creatively."

The smirk on the man's face made Peter want to leap out of his chair and grab him by the throat. "OK. I'll bite. How so?"

"The Rough-skinned newt. *Taricha granulosa.* Tetrodotoxin is mostly in the salamander's skin. Just one of the little buggers has enough to kill twenty or thirty people. And it's heat stable and water soluble."

"I read on the internet about three hunters in Oregon found dead, a newt in their coffee pot."

"Urban myth. Never really happened. But I boiled my little beauty and made coffee from the water. It was a pleasure to watch Wasserman die so slowly and painfully."

"Do you know how sick you sound?"

"Face it. I'm a genius. Outsmarted everybody. You should have seen how I took out those two Russians Sokolov sent to kill me." He was on a roll, boasting about his accomplishments. "Let the air out of their tire. Got the drop on them while they were distracted and made them give up their guns. Shot them with their own weapons and then filled their car with my stuff so it would look like a burglary gone wrong. Pretty ingenious, if I do say so myself."

"Would you like to take a bow?"

"Now don't be a poor sport, Peter. It's just a big chess game, and I have you in checkmate."

Peter shook his head back and forth. "Check maybe, but not mate." His words were clear and calm."

"What do you mean? You have no moves."

"May I get something from my pocket?"

"Very slowly."

Peter withdrew a small plastic bag from his shirt pocket and dropped it on the table. It made a soft clunk like dropping a coin. "I wanted to thank you for bringing your gun tonight."

"What the hell?"

"Are you a betting man, Sterling? Because I'm betting that the police will be able to prove that the slug in this bag was fired from the gun you're holding. They pulled it from the body of Abram Sokolov. Told me all of your bullets didn't exit the corpse.

This one lodged against his spine. I guess he had some kind of metal in there. A Harrington rod? History of scoliosis or something."

Sterling clenched his teeth. Peter saw a gleam of sweat on the man's forehead. "And as if that weren't enough, I'm surprised how careless you got at the end. Police found one of your shell casings under Sokolov's desk. The fingerprints on it match the prints on the coffee mug I brought to them after our little meeting in the faculty lounge on Monday."

Sterling's face turned ashen and began to twitch. "How long have you known about me?"

"I've had my suspicions for a long time, but I haven't wanted to believe them. The pivotal moment was when I first told you about the arm I had found on the beach. You spilled your coffee when I mentioned the diamond ring. And then you went off about Officer Whitehorse. I knew something was wrong. Just couldn't put all the pieces together."

Sterling looked as though he might vomit. "That obvious, huh?"

"Afraid so." Peter nodded. "Oh, I almost forgot. The police arrested your student, Franklin, yesterday. Possession with intent to sell. What's the expression they use in the pulp detective stories? 'He sang like a canary?' Told them all about how you said Officer Whitehorse was after him. How he told Sokolov."

Sterling's shoulders slumped, as though some essential life force were draining from his body. He was moving his lips but no sound was coming out.

"The Russian thought you were a security risk, didn't he? Sent Tolstoy after you?"

"That stupid ape!" Sterling found his voice, snarling at the mention of the man. "He's at the bottom of the Double L," he spat. "With another of my slugs in him."

Peter was silent for a moment. He looked at the man with the gun and felt profound pity for him. "This all unraveled because of the woman in the waves. Two women, actually. I'm curious. Was Emma just another girlfriend? Like Marisa?"

"She was my daughter." His voice was a barely audible rasp. "She threw herself off the cliff. Took my ring with her."

This time Peter was taken aback. "Your daughter? Dear God."

"Oh, don't fret, Peter. She meant nothing to me. I just wanted my ring back."

Peter snorted. "In case you're wondering, they know the diamond was your mother's. It's laser-inscribed. Who bought it. Where and when. So they knew Emma had to have gotten it from you."

He laughed. "I should have known. My demented mother. Still haunting me from the grave decades after I killed her." He shook his head as if emerging from a dream. He took a deep breath. "I have to hand it to you, Peter. You've been a worthy opponent. You've had some good moves."

"But?"

"But I counter your feeble check with a final checkmate." He narrowed his eyes and struck like a serpent. "I'll be filing a report today with the police that my gun was stolen. Don't know when. I've been so busy at school I haven't used it in a long time. When Effling refused to let me carry it on campus, I never even bothered to look for it. Until today, when I thought I'd go to the range for a little target practice. Just to relax after all the commotion."

"You can't be serious."

"Oh, but I am. I'll bet my gun was snatched the same time the ring was. Probably some lowlife after drug money. I certainly hope the police can retrieve the diamond for me. That ring is a priceless family heirloom—my dear mother's parting gift to me."

Peter was astounded. "You can't make those pictures disappear."

The biologist nodded. "You're right. Not sure who's been trying to blackmail me with those fakes—maybe my ex-wife?—but thanks for returning them. I know you've spoken with Grace. She was mortified, but I think we can save her reputation. And I'm glad no one was hurt when those goons came to extort money from me. No one but the goons, of course."

"What about Wise? You lied to him."

"Yes. Poor Franklin. I didn't want to see such a promising student get expelled. I told him the police were after him in hopes he'd clean up his act before it was too late."

"What?" Peter's head was reeling at the fantasy Sterling was spinning. "No. No. That's not what happened at all."

Sterling dismissed his objection with a flick of his hand. "Put those pictures back in their packet for me, would you? I'll take them and be on my way. After all, that robber will be breaking in any minute." He watched Peter comply. "OK. I think we're done here. I'd like to kill you and get home to bed. I'm a bear if I don't get enough sleep."

Peter recovered from his stupor. "Just a minute. I need to show you something." He slowly unbuttoned his shirt. "I'm wearing a wire. Officers Whitehorse and Esperanza have been recording our conversation from the comfort of my garage."

Sterling roared. "They'll never get to you on time! You don't have a gun!"

"That's right. I don't. But my friend Chris? He's got lots of guns. In fact, if you look at your chest right now, see that red spot? It's his laser sight on your heart. He's in the backyard, just beyond the lighted area."

Sterling shrieked in rage as he turned toward the glass slider. That moment of distraction was all Hammer needed. The dog launched at him, clamping his jaws like a steel trap on Sterling's wrist above the gun. The man howled in pain as the weapon fell from his grasp. Losing his balance, he fell backward with the dog on top of him. He flailed and thrashed to no avail. Hammer crunched down harder, thrusting his head violently back and forth, growling in fury. Whitehorse and Esperanza came rushing in through the garage door. Chris pushed the slider aside and leaped into the fray. In a heartbeat, Chris joined Hammer on top of Sterling. He landed a massive roundhouse punch to the man's chin, knocking him unconscious.

Chris regained his feet as Peter tried to calm his dog.

"It's OK, Hammer. Good boy. You did a great job." Peter stroked the dog and persuaded him to release Sterling's arm. Then he went to fetch towels to stanch the bleeding.

While Whitehorse picked up the .45 and bagged it, Esperanza called for medics. "Better check him, Charley."

Whitehorse knelt by the body and felt for a pulse. "He'll live."

"Don't sound so disappointed," his partner quipped.

Whitehorse used the towels Peter brought to wrap the arm, then pulled out his handcuffs. "Don't want this bastard acting all crazy when he wakes up from his little nap." He turned to Peter. "That was pretty brave," he said.

"Thanks, Charley, but I may have pissed myself. I'll have to check."

Chris looked at his friend. "Pretty foolish, if you ask me. It took every ounce of restraint I have to play it your way. I wanted to nail that sucker as soon as his gun came out. I still think I should have. Violated all my trainin'. You took a helluva risk."

Peter took a deep breath. "We did it just like we planned. It went like clockwork. I had complete faith in all you guys. And faith in Sterling's narcissism. He wanted to milk his 'genius' for all it was worth. Wanted me to admire his superior intelligence. He couldn't compute anything contradicting it."

They heard the siren of the approaching ambulance. Hammer bayed in response, and Peter scratched behind his ears. "It's OK, boy. More friends coming. Want a treat?" The dog barked excitedly.

"Was that a rhetorical question?" said Chris. "Never met a dog who didn't want a treat."

"I want a treat, too. You got any of your famous Scotch with you?"

"No. But I know where we can get some."

45. Epilogue: Another Ring

The first week of May was glorious. Temperatures at the coast climbed into the low 70's, while in the Willamette Valley, they soared into the mid-80's. Whitehorse had a much-needed week's vacation, and he began it with Chloe. First, they drove to the correctional institute to visit Kaitlynn. Then it was on to Portland. They had a room at a downtown hotel booked for Saturday night and Sunday night and planned to drive home Monday afternoon.

"It's so good to get away," she cooed. "Thank you, hon."

"We've postponed our trip long enough. Dinner and dancing tonight, after hitting the jewelry stores hard this afternoon. We're on a mission."

She turned and looked at the man she loved. It was hard for her to imagine what being married to a policeman would be like. Putting up with a doctor's or lawyer's hours, only more dangerous? But it was this particular policeman she would be with, and that made all the difference.

"I'm going to love living with you, Charley. I mean that."

Without taking his eyes from the road, he said, "I'll hold you to that. I still think I'm getting the better part of this bargain."

The city with its buildings and bridges sparkled in the late morning sun like an exotic jewel. Chloe caught her breath. "It's so beautiful here. I come so rarely, it always catches me by surprise. Want to see if we can check in early? Get a light lunch and head out?"

"Sounds like a plan. I've got my walking shoes on."

Whitehorse pulled into valet parking and stopped the car. He took their bags from the trunk and got his ticket from the young man who took his keys. They wheeled their bags into a lobby that looked like a botanical garden, with its enormous potted plants and hanging vines. He approached the Asian woman at the front desk.

"Reservations for two under Whitehorse?"

"Let me take a look." Her fingers whizzed over the

keyboard. "Yes, sir. I have your reservation, but the room isn't ready as yet. Would you like to check your bags with us and perhaps get some lunch while you wait? We can lock them up back here." She tagged the bags and handed the receipts to him.

In moments, they were out the main doors and onto the sidewalk, hand in hand.

"Can't hear the ocean from here." Whitehorse smiled at Chloe. "Love your outfit, by the way." He watched how Chloe seemed to bounce down the sidewalk, the lightness in her step a perfect complement to the flowered blouse and short white skirt she wore.

"Thanks. It makes me happy. Reminds me how much I love spring." She pulled him close. "And how much I love being here with you." She kissed him playfully on the cheek.

They passed a street musician, strumming a guitar while he played the harmonica harnessed to his neck. Whitehorse tossed two dollars into the man's guitar case. "Gotta support local talent," he told his bride-to-be.

Chloe found a natural foods restaurant that appealed to her. "Eating here will make you feel virtuous," she promised her fiancé. Forty-five minutes later, they began their quest. As they entered the first jewelry store, Rheinhardt's, Whitehorse removed a scrap of paper from his shirt pocket.

A jeweler dressed in a gray suit with a red-striped tie approached them. "May I help you with something?"

He read from the list. "We're looking for an Ideal or Excellent cut diamond. Color in the G, H, or I range. Clarity VS1 or VS2. Shape will be up to her, though I'm kind of partial to the classic round."

The jeweler smiled at them. "I always appreciate people who do their homework. How many carats?"

Chloe was gawking at Whitehorse, as if aliens had swapped out the man she knew for one of their own in disguise. "Where did you get all that?" she whispered.

"At work. Chiara has been coaching me."

"I approve," she said, as she snuggled into his shoulder.

Five stores later, Chloe had made up her mind. What astounded her was that the ring was there, in her size, and she could walk out of the store with it. "This is a dream, Charley. Please don't wake me."

"I'll have to wake you for dinner, darling. We have reservations at *Le Toit du Monde* for six o'clock. Very hoity-toity, so you'll need time to make yourself even more beautiful than you already are."

She punched him in the arm. "Watch it, mister."

"I intend to, my dear. Every moment of it." He smiled and embraced her.

The End

About the Author

William J. Cook is a Connecticut native transplanted to Oregon in 1989. He is a graduate of the State University of New York at Albany, where he received a Master's Degree in Social Work. Years of study in two Catholic seminaries and a long career as a mental health therapist have shaped (or warped!) his world view. He is spending his retirement with his artist-wife Sharon, who paints in the dining room while he writes in the kitchen. He enjoys babysitting for his fifteen grandchildren and sneaking away to mid-week matinees at local movie theaters, a vice which he claims he contracted from his mother, an inveterate fan of action and sci-fi films. He is the author of the novel *Songs for the Journey Home, The Pieta in Ordinary Time and Other Stories, Catch of the Day,* a collection of short stories, and *The Driftwood Mysteries,* including the novel, *Seal of Secrets,* the short story, *Eye of Newt,* and the novel, *Woman in the Waves.*

Visit him at https://authorwilliamcook.com or at https://www.facebook.com/writerwilliamjcook/